MW00810346

THE WRETCH OF THE SUN

By Michael Cisco

Animal Money
Celebrant
The Divinity Student
The Golem
The Great Lover
Member
The Narrator
The San Veneficio Canon
Secret Hours
The Traitor
The Tyrant

THE WRETCH OF THE SUN

Michael Cisco

HIPPOCAMPUS PRESS

NEW YORK

Copyright © 2016 by Michael Cisco

Published by Hippocampus Press
P.O. Box 641, New York, NY 10156.
http://www.hippocampuspress.com
All rights reserved.
No part of this work may be reproduced in any form or by any
means without the written permission of the publisher.

Cover art by Harry O. Morris.
Cover design by Barbara Briggs Silbert.
Hippocampus Press logo designed by Anastasia Damianakos.

First Edition
1 3 5 7 9 8 6 4 2

ISBN 978-1-61498-166-4

PREFACE

The haunted house is, among other things, a manifestation of the concept of secrecy, which encompasses both concealing and revealing. A house whose ethereal visitants and ethereal occupants are never discovered, whose secrets are kept perfectly, and whose invisible contents never become visible, will not acquire a haunted reputation. Maybe the most well-known haunted houses are the ones populated by the most incompetent ghosts. Does this mean that we only know the botched jobs? The blunderers who can't keep a secret? If so, it would suggest that the really excellent haunted houses are the ones in which nothing out of the ordinary ever seems to occur. On the other hand, it might mean that a secret must be known in order to be a secret; a secret is precisely the known thing. The open secret is the thing that everyone knows without knowing that they know, and is the biggest of secrets.

To be known for haunting, a house must conceal a secret imperfectly, and it must be the secret itself that, by its very nature and not primarily through any other agency, persistently resists concealment. A haunted house draws attention to the existence of its secret and will even go so far as to provide some inquirers with what appear to be clues to the unraveling of its riddle. That riddle, however, can never be unraveled. It's just activity, enjoyment. The Gothic novel took the form of a whirl of stories within stories, explaining one story by means of another, which then stood in need of an explanatory story of its own, and so on, building a house of cards with no foundation but storytelling. In the ghost story, the tale of an encounter with an apparition is followed by the explanatory story, recollected by the decrepit former servant or extracted from a suggestively incomplete archaic document, which identifies the lovers who committed suicide or the hanged man or the abandoned child. But knowing what these ghosts once were tells us nothing about what they are now, where and how they exist, or what their experience of events is like. Why should natural laws bend to serve what appears to be at least human justice? The story is explained by means of unexplained explanations, which only open out onto deeper mysteries.

A haunted house is a house with its own story. A ghost is someone about whom stories are told, who is unable to tell his or her own story. Death can be understood as the inability to tell one's own story; whether that death is literal is another question. Ghosts exist in imagination, which is real. A story, to be a told story, needs a listener or reader. Ghosts, as I have been saying, appear to need someone to whom to appear. So we discover the story of the suicides, and we solve the riddle alongside the narrating busybody of the story, and bury the bones together in one grave; the disturbances cease. But a house once haunted will always be haunted; it isn't the disturbance but the story that haunts it.

The haunted house draws attention to the secret it keeps like a master who teases his pupils with unanswerable riddles. Or like secret police, who can't be entirely effective if they are entirely secret. These aren't questions that contain their own answers, like math problems. I do not have the answer any more than you do, because the answer isn't in the question, the answer is to leave behind the idea that a question is a door that an answer pulls finally shut. Once we've dutifully recited to the last syllable everything we know, we are chastened or even taken aback by the paltry incommensurability of what we've just said with the haunted wealth that extends within and without us in all directions. At that moment, the suggestive ambivalence of a story will have to seem truer than the abbreviation of a hollow answer.

THE WRETCH OF THE SUN

(0)

Public drunkenness, disturbance. The call comes in on the car radio halfway through the afternoon and A. and his partner respond. The streets dart by, the car lurching over the dips. B. pops out when they reach the plaza, a cold, nervous, flinching feeling inside him. They both made their man at once: dark skin, loose white shirt, standing on a bench, shouting, flourishing a handful of paper above his head. He made them, too, jumps down and tears off into the park where their car can't follow and no time to drive around to the opposite side and anyway this park opens along its length to the outskirts of the modelsuburb. C.'s partner curses and the two of them start pounding after him on foot.

"Le-het's sto-hop him be-he-fore h-e ge-hets t'the ro-hocks!" his partner says, running hard.

Now D. catches sight of two more officers on the right. Up ahead, the soles turn up one after another, so fast it doesn't seem humanly possible. His shirt is a shimmering, jagged white flame in the air.

He gets clear of the park, across the macadam road, and into the rocks. E.'s partner curses some more, half-strangled. Two men in plain clothes are getting out of a car parked on the macadam. F. has never seen them before, but they're obviously plainclothes. No driving after pamphlet boy now, not on those rocks. He's angling toward the beach. The two weird plainclothesmen are running and pointing and yelling orders.

"Stop him!"

What is this? Six officers for a vagrant?

Their man zips down and out of a depression filled with air shimmer in the heat of the day, a mercury pond seething there, and his outline goes crazy, like a reflection in a flexible mirror. The sun keeps getting brighter and brighter, salt in G.'s eyes and

11

his whole field of vision is turning into pink flash photos—the blood of his own eyes hues everything he looks at.

The weird plainclothesmen bark "Drop it!" over and over.

Which makes no sense—the guy isn't carrying anything, his hands are up in the air as if he's just kicked a goal. There's a sound like popping stitches. H. glances to the side and nearly tumbles over the rocks, the two weird plainclothesmen, who had actually said "Drop *him!*" are firing at the back of an unarmed man with grease guns they must have kept slung round their backs. His partner is clumsily dragging out his revolver, too. What is this? Up ahead the man streaks across the ground—he seems to dance in place, as though his shaking outline dodged the bullets and his arms go higher and he stops, spins.

—They shot him!
—He whirls spinning with his arms in the air!
—The others rush up, stop, shoot, rush, stop, shoot!
—Now he sees it! He's seeing it!
—She's coming down in a pillar of sun! There's thick dark hair, heavy bangs, and beneath them, the sun, where a face should be!
—Her body is a dress made of light shells!
—Her pink hands are floating down toward him!
—She's embracing the vagrant!
—She's four times his size!
—She's got him! She's carrying the vagrant off into the sky! Cradled in her arms like a toddler!
—He erupts in hysterical laughter and stutters taunts at the police "Putas! L-l-locos! Maricones!"
—Kicking out his legs fifty feet off the ground!

Bright as it was, the light gets a thousand times brighter it crashes down on him in waves like a million panes of glass smashing him in the head one after another after another and the pieces are flickering all around make a whirlpool of sparks their glints lance the brain like bullets and now white out like a snowstorm and he can't hear anything but the whistle in his ringing ears . . .

"–n't believe it. Hey!"

A blow to his shoulder, a voice from somewhere further behind him. His partner's.

He starts groggily. He is lying on his side, on the ground.

"He fell!" his partner shouts back.

Rough hands half drag him upright, and his partner is muttering under his breath.

"Fainting. What are you, a little girl? What's the matter with you? Walk."

Shoves him in the direction of their man. The ground is searing white fractured by the dark edges of the rocks. A dazzle hangs in front of his eyes wherever he looks, regular pulsations shave it down like dust settling in sheets out of the air. I. follows his partner.

A smashed dead body, face down, sprawled, cratered back glistens in the sun. The other two regular police are there, outlines quivering. J. squints at the body. It seems he can't quite lock his knees. He starts and looks all around suddenly.

"What happened? Why'd you shoot?" his partner is asking.

"I don't know. I didn't see it," one of the others says.

The other other one sighs. "I guess I'll call a van."

They keep glancing at K. and scanning away from him, eyes tight against the glare. The second one, not in any hurry, picks his way to the radio car parked on the road.

Wind blows their voices around.

"They must have fired from over there," the first one says to his partner. "Why don't we go check for casings?"

"Yes," his partner says strangely. He turns to L., looking him hard in the eye. Points to the corpse. "Search him."

M. crosses over to the man numbly. He can hear first one, then, after a moment, another set of footsteps going away behind him, voices warbling in air buffets, like a burlap rag flapping against his ear. He looks down at the shimmering body, black spattering the blinding white shirt, dark hands half in the sand exposed roots. Turn the body by the shoulder, dark face crusted with sand, features slack. The image of a cackling, hysterical face nearly burned out in the sun swims in his mind. He lets his grip loosen. The dead man slumps onto his face again. Nothing in his pockets but an empty old wallet like a burst blister. He stands looking down at the dead man, drops the wallet.

His partner's fist thuds lightly against his shoulder.

"Wake up," he mutters in disgust. "What'd you find? A wallet?"

Picks it up and goes through it, flips it back to the ground.

"Nothing," he nearly whispers. His next words are so faint that his partner misses them, drowned out by the other cop, who calls—

"Van's here."

just as he whispers—

"It's not him."

"Looks like your boy's still a little green!" one of the cops says, says with forced joviality. "Never seen a stiff before?"

The voice comes through him, from the day. As if the day wanted to know.

His partner tells the other to shut up. "Sun's got at him."

Get in a car.

"You just sit there."

N. sits by himself a few minutes. Then he whimpers, bends

forward grabbing his head, and sobs once. Panting, looking around. Sees the body bobbing on the stretcher, going away. Covers his face a moment, his breath sounds hollow in the cupped space. The sun face is looking through him, as if he were an invisible man. Gigantic, transparent, ghostly hands hold him up.

Driving in to the station. O. stares at the dashboard out of a slack face. The glowing modelsuburb veers across the windshield.

"All right," his partner brakes, jerking up the transmission bar on the steering column. Turns to him. "You had better think hard about how bad you want this job. Because I am not going out there again with a man who goes to pieces. I *don't* . . . you— *nobody* gets used to seeing men get shot, nobody. Any man who does is crazy the other way, and he's even—he's an even bigger headache. But you've got to keep hold of yourself when you *do* see it. Or you're just no use."

P. entered the station in front of his partner, his eyes open a little too wide. As he strides past the barriers and into unique-coordinated-intersystem he holds himself with exaggerated attentiveness, looking sharply at everything, greets everyone he sees and does it first.

Now they sit side by side in front of the sergeant's desk. His partner is doing all the talking. The sergeant is asking many questions right at the outset; their two voices are droning together. Q. peers at things on the walls, the foliage through the blinds, and each unique crushed paper in the wire waste basket.

"—then the other officers shot him."

"What?" R. says abruptly. "Who? Which ones?"

He sounds almost indignant. His partner looks him in the eye.

"What do you mean who? You been daydreamin'? The guy!"

"Which guy, the runner?"

15

The sergeant is watching them both.

"Of course the runner which oth–"

His partner stops and addresses himself to the sergeant.

"There was only the one guy!"

"No, no, there was the runner and there was the other one." S. looks at the sergeant now, too. "The man they shot was there already, I don't know what he was doing there but he was there already—"

"There was nobody—" His partner presses a hand sideways on the sergeant's desk, but T. doesn't stop.

"He was there already. They shot *him*, the two officers in plainclothes. They shot him. They had submachine guns. They shot the man who was there already. The one we were chasing was taken into the sky."

Why can't he stop?!

"A woman came out of the sun and she carried him into the sky with her."

They look at him.

"That man is still at large," he says.

They look at him.

"I repeat, the dead man was not the man we pursued into the rocks. He was already—he already was there. The other guy got away. The guy we were chasing."

The sergeant heaves himself ponderously out of his chair, goes to the door, bends around it, hand on the wall, and says something quickly to someone. Then he shuts the door.

U.'s partner is rubbing his hand over his forehead and eyes.

"Uh, Herman, you'd better get started on the reports," the sergeant sniffs. He drags his forefinger under his nose briefly, not looking at anything but his chair as he crosses the small office. "If you want to get home at a reasonable hour."

His partner leaves without a backward look.

The sergeant sits, hands on the arms of his chair, looking at V. in silence. W. still looks earnestly at the sergeant.

A moment later, the supervisor comes in.

"Yes, what is it?"

Sergeant flips a finger at X.

"Thought you might want to hear his statement." His eyes switch to Y. "If you still want to make it."

"Yes, sir."

The supervisor stands by the sergeant's desk, leaning back a little with his arms crossed all the way across his chest, right hand up on his shoulder, as if he's hanging it there for the time being. Z. repeats his story, describing in detail the appearance of the solar woman. By the time he's finished, the supervisor has drawn up a chair and sits, legs crossed, arms crossed, head forward toward A.

They thank him for his information and send him home.

B. lives in a subdivision on a narrow, undulating alley. It's lined on one side with little gardens behind plastered walls, gates and paths and the houses a few feet recessed; all facing the backs of houses and a few small shops opposite. He takes June seriously by the hand, sits down facing her on the loveseat, and tells her about it. She listens, her eyes big and pale in the gloom, short rapid nods at intervals. June is unusually pretty, habitually cheerful. C. narrates in an even tone, calmly, but making big gestures with his hands, rising now and then a little from his seat. When he's finished, he sits back in the chair like a statue.

"That's *amazing*," June says.

Later that night he is sitting alone drinking coffee at the kitchen table, in a little island of carrot-colored light. June is already in bed. He notices a low hum, a vibration coming from the street. He has to see what it is, because it seems as though it wants to slip into his consciousness unnoticed.

17

There's a car, idling a little up from the house. It idles there for an hour. Its windows are dark.

As he's shaving the next morning the phone rings. June answers, and a moment later appears in the doorway of the bathroom to tell him he's to expect a visitor from the department in an hour, to stay home and wait. She relays this message to him with a neutral expression and goes back to her breakfast. When he steps out of the bathroom, face cold around the jaw, she is eating and scanning the newspaper, glances up at him and smiles briefly. As he dresses, D. seethes with nerves. He puts on a tie and a shined pair of shoes, changes his tie. He goes to comb his hair, but it is combed. The bell rings and June calls asking him if he could answer it.

Woodenly he goes to the front of the house. The door reveals a tall man with a round face, short brown hair, his hairline at the crown of his head, and glasses. He's wearing a pale, light jacket, no tie, and he carries nothing in his hands.

"Hello—E., isn't it?" he says, blinking. His voice is throaty, like an oboe. He holds out a hand with nails slightly too long.

"The department sent me." He exhibits a badge in a wallet. "May I come in?"

They sit in the parlor and F. repeats his story, pausing near the beginning to introduce June, who is on her way out the door. Shopping. She hates being a bad hostess, but the ration cards expire at noon. He suspects the man to be a psychologist from the first. He doesn't have the build or manner of a detective, and the man's questions reinforce his suspicions. When he introduces himself, there is what sounds like a momentary pause before the name—pronounced "robe," last name. Is that where "doctor" usually goes? Every now and then, "_ Robe" mentions reports, higher-ups, talks about getting the details of his story straight. And more often than he should he reminds G.

that this is procedural and that the department considers his information *very* important. "_ Robe's" line doesn't blend well with the types of questions he asks. Finally he all but breaks cover and leans in with,

"Now, you understand I have to ask you this, so please don't be offended. But, you understand, I must make absolutely certain, so that there is just no doubt at all about it, as a matter of procedure. You understand. If you have any family history of ... mental instability, it's vital that we know about it because, after all, that could be used to discredit you. We have to be especially careful in how we handle information of the particular type you're giving us."

There is nothing to tell. H. sits there, earnestly.

"Well," says "_ Robe," putting his hands on his knees and leaning forward to get up. "I've been instructed to inform you you're on leave for the time being, until the next phase of the investigation is determined by you-see-eye, the supervisor, and the chief. You know the chief himself is involved, very interested in your case."

I. continues to look at him a moment, then rises.

"He should be. It's of the utmost importance. I mean, I don't think we can possibly have had much experience with this kind of thing."

"They do think, though, that it would be best for you to keep quiet about it for now. You understand. As you say, we don't know what we're dealing with here, not quite, and so ... And moreover any officer involved in a shooting is given time off right away. That's you-see-eye policy. Even if he was only a witness."

At the door, he holds out his puffy hand again.

"I'll tell the supervisor he can put his complete confidence in you. Speaking personally, I think you've handled yourself very well, quite well. And do," he says, turning as he goes, "remember to keep this cozy for a while, eh?"

J. nods and closes the door.

Two hours later, K., out of uniform, walks into the station. He enters the main room, stands on a chair, and calls the officers present to hear him.

All the way there, drumming in his mind, a voiceless voice incredulously demands of him what he thinks he's doing, whether or not he really is crazy.

"Can I have your attention please?" he calls out in a strident voice, loud and clear but with a little tremble, a little haltingly.

"I don't know what you've been told, but the man who was shot yesterday was not the perpetrator my partner and I were pursuing. The man they brought in was already there at the time we, and the suspect we were pursuing, arrived on the scene."

He sees his partner appear in the doorway across the room from him, mouth ajar.

"The suspect is still at large."

He tells them about the woman coming out of the sky with the sun for a face, and the disappearance of the man in her luminous arms. Tears well at the corners of his eyes. The words gush from his lips. No one is snickering. He speaks like a man who is about to be executed.

His partner is bustling forward, bringing the supervisor and a pair of other men.

"Also," he says, his voice cracking, accelerating, "there were two officers present who were in plainclothes. I've never seen these officers before, and they left the scene almost immediately after they shot their man—"

His partner and crew break into a jog, swinging their arms.

"Th-they were the ones who shot him, i-if he was shot then, I'm just about certain of that—and they had submachine guns.

They were not detectives. I believe they may be watching me—"

"For Pete's sake!" his partner says, standing in front of him and drowning him out.

The two other police reach up and L. steps obediently down between them.

"I think they may belong to some other organization—"

They grab him.

"Remember what I said!" he cries.

They rush him outside and leave him on the curb. His partner, who has plainly been given charge of him, paces to and fro, fuming and disappointed.

"I thought they told you to shut up about that. You know they said they'd handle it. Listen," he puts up his hands when M. tries to talk. "Just get back to your house and stay there, all right?"

He glances around.

"Look, the plain clothes guys? Those were just regular cops."

". . . What are you talking about? They had submachine guns."

"Yeah, look, those weren't submachine guns. They were pistols modified to shoot rubber bullets—look, you've done your part. You stood up in there and said what had to be said. Now you have to stand down and let us do our part. The matter is under investigation. Now you could have blown things for us in there. You got to rest because the full—"

He gropes a moment.

"—uh, force, of this kind of situation, always comes down on you later than you'd expect. After you get over the initial shock."

His partner holds his eye for a long moment, then starts to walk away, then turns back and comes up to him again.

"Maybe you should get away for a while, huh?"

His voice is low.

"You and June haven't been married that long, right? Let me

ask the super, maybe he'll give you a long leave. Clear your head, uh? You and June?"

It's the first thing he's said that he hadn't rehearsed.

N. drives home again and parks in front of his house. He sits there for a while, without getting out of the car, lost in a wafting, disembodied, dreamlike feeling. As though he'd become transparent.

He looks at his house.

June's inside, but suddenly the thought of her smile repels him and he turns away from the front gate. He walks down the street and angles toward a little park nearby. Walking its lanes with his hands in his pockets, from time to time he throws his head back to peek curiously up at the sun, which winks at him through the leaves of the trees. He'd thought of this as going off on his own to think, but he isn't doing any thinking. At most, he's just seeing images. It's like he can't think.

"Maybe I am still in shock."

Here the lane passes between two dense, tall hedges, like a gap in a wall, overhung with trees whose branches knit with vines to form a heavy canopy. Dead center in this dark passage, he suddenly hears a shoe scrape on the path behind him.

His hands turn clammy. His tongue swells. Two figures step out to meet him from behind the hedge. He stops, turns, and sees the other two behind him as they firmly grip his arms, all of them in dark, plain clothes.

He shakes, they are crowded around him like the four corners of a box. A paralyzing fear like nothing he's ever known sluices through him. Their eyes are like glass. They are so silent they don't even seem to breathe. O. struggles against a suffocating weakness, trying to make any kind of sound, and a bag of coarse fabric drops over his head and cinches around his neck. Handcuffs roughly bind his hands.

Now he struggles. Now he cries out. They are lifting him off the ground. He is smashed over the head, and goes limp, though he murmurs through his sack.

*

A barren room with two high windows, or vents, near the ceiling. Footsteps rasping on the floor, brush trash aside.

The air on his bare, wet legs is cold. He's in his undershirt and shorts. There's a gag in his mouth and his wrists are tightly bound to the arms of the dentist's chair.

Four heads appear above him. He can feel the warmth of their bodies through their uniforms as they close together, with him in the middle.

Street sounds come in with the daylight through the vents. The sound of a bus. He can smell a little diesel. The bus is revving. His fingers are like ice. The bus groans and its voice rises to a howl as it pulls forward. There's a sustained, swelling roar that gets louder and louder, and does not dwindle, as if the bus were standing still. As if it were only a recording of a bus.

He looks from one face to another, as if there were still some way to escape through them. The faces, all together, suddenly, tense. They bend over his body with tools in their hands.

(.)

In the window, there's a reflection of a black young woman in a shawl. She stands in front of an iron fence that squares off a little patch of shattered paving stones, and to her right there's a message case on a metal pole. She's been reading the notices pinned to the board inside the case, and rain drummed on its metal roof, ornamented in cut steel siltische that reminds her of the top of a cuckoo clock. Her name is Trudy Bailey.

Her eyes slide from the announcement lists. She can see her

counterpart in a transparent, washed-out image that sways in the glass.

Trudy is hunting all over for registration instructions. Although she's only done it once before, she approaches registration with the tested sturdiness and know-how of a proven veteran. None of the information you find will mean anything, but you still have to play along until you find the right person to talk to. That's how it's done. Registration is semi-accidental. She's lost some time today following posted instructions and, having returned to subject these same instructions to a more exacting scrutiny, she notices, just now, last year's date down at the bottom of the sheet.

There is no campus and no map. The college called Chthethostoa originally occupied a pair of buildings that faced each other across Agua Seca. Over time it was forced to move to other buildings in the area, mixing classrooms and offices with private homes and shops. The school owned (under assumed names) two houses that were nowhere near each other: you had to rent a bicycle or take a once-a-day bus to reach them, then walk back. There was no boundary dividing the school from the rest of the town of Cimelia Cisterna. Each class or office had streets and businesses between them, so that you couldn't feel but a very fleeting and weak sense of shelter in school when there was the usual trouble just a wall away. But there was a mood boundary all the same that couldn't be missed. Trudy could always tell when she was in the presence of the school. Something heavy would lift slightly, and something heavy would sink slightly.

Initially meant to be an academy for exceptional children, endowments that invariably managed to be both generous and insufficient at the same time made possible its eccentric growth until it warrened a whole neighborhood. Walk down Corcoran past Agua Seca, go by a lunch counter, a laundry, a ration office, a bookstore with classrooms above it and in the back, three police kiosks, a tiny pharmacy. Out of uniform rows of concrete houses, a few with signboards or message cases on every side street.

Trudy walks, holding her shawl around her. She's a twenty-six-year-old graduate student in art history, specialty textiles. She shields her incongruously heavy bust from view with her shawl, folded arms, and unflattering sweaters. Her face, never adorned with makeup, has a smoldering, stoic look, and she keeps her hair drawn severely back into a bun. Trudy's eyes are keen, the whites very white and the irises a deep brown. Those eyes can level themselves so steadily on a face that her gaze seems to press the other person back, away from her.

She recognizes Vicq d'Azyr and turns downward following its slope, a furrow five feet wide. It bends out into the little square in front of the red brick swimming school, faced by several buildings habituated by the academy. Students and professors like to gather there and exchange information informally. Chthethostoa's students couldn't afford to miss a single class, because most classes were held at different times and places from session to session and the location date and hour would only be announced at the preceding meeting. Many professors and students made it a point to be found here at certain times, just in case any absentees needed to know where or when to go and how to prepare. Word of mouth was safer. Originally just a wide section of street cut off from traffic more or less by chance, some students years ago began prying the asphalt up in the center of this place, and now some bushes, and small trees even, have emerged from the exposed earth. Trees line the shallow sidewalks, making the area a partially paved park.

As usual, there are students strolling the circle around the "planter," many of them with teachers. Some of the faculty like to teach peripatetically, as if they were merely making conversation. Celada is there—Trudy sees him first of anyone, at once—walking and speaking animatedly, in his big weightless way, to Dr. Crapelin. There's Miss Houseman crossing the square, and smooth William behind her, canopying her head with his umbrella. Professor Czochkralski has stopped and is heatedly jawing at three students in front of the dentist's office. The first one to greet Trudy is Dr. Cottataris, who smiles in passing and dangles a hand she can't raise because she has an armload of books, disappearing into the offices closest to the swimming school. The looks and gestures are furtive without any acuity of fear, and mixed with the uncertain gaiety of getting away with it for now.

Trudy glances again at Celada, uncertain whether she wants to greet him, an ambiguous heat playing over her entrails, a little embarrassment. So as not to be seen looking in his direction should his head swivel her way, she steers herself into his wake and is hailed by an old chum named Brandy who tells her where to retrieve the right forms. Last year, she had the money for school but couldn't attend full-time because she couldn't get time vouchers, even with a recommendation from her boss. She kept working at the bank and took classes part-time. This year, no recommendation, but she applied for new vouchers anyway and got them. She'll quit the bank and take up school full-time.

The school is officially recognized, but only for the purposes of providing some supplementary secondary education and vocational training chiefly for accreditation purposes; the rest of the school's business, which is the vastly greater half, is illegal education. The degree Trudy is studying for does not officially exist, but will have more actual weight with other scholars than a similar degree from one of the sanctioned colleges, which are staffed with functionaries and relatives of officials, all more loyal than learned.

Registration supposedly happens upstairs in one of the rooms facing the square, on rickety tables in front of filing cabinets. The place smells like the inside of an old tube radio. She's putting her index cards in her bag by the window, peeking out through the grime to see if he's still there. The sun has broken out; clear, red-orange light of intense color but not intense brightness rakes the square diagonally. Opposite, the baleful swimming school throbs with red. It has insect composite-eye windows of glass blocks and a throat clogged with trash and dead leaves. The space in front of the doors is enclosed by a warped metal comb. She's always liked the ominous expression of the swimming school, its sinister name. Celada has been inside; he's described to her the phosphorescent blue craters, the upright ranks of tin caskets, tiled caverns with metal stalactites and mushrooms of spotted steel, and said every sound you made went on forever in there.

A cloud throws its shade over the square very quickly and the swimming school's shadows change indigo, its red turns violet, and leaves go tumbling past it.

As she heads back toward the bus station she stops to look at the rooftops against the sky. Not having to hurry just at this moment, she wants to luxuriate a bit in her own time. This is a good vantage point, near the corner. The sky is metallic and the shadows of the buildings are purple. There's one of the protruding angles of the library, formerly a fine home and architectural something special, or that's not the library that's the Milk House, which stands on its grounds.

Trudy looks at the skyline expectantly and listens down into herself. A sexual feeling appears, adjacent to her kidneys, her microsexual way.

(The ring she wears belonged to her father, which is the only reason she wears it; it is made of plain silver, with three steel nail heads melted into the inside, so that they are always in contact with the skin of her finger. These are the heads of nails, taken from the coffin of her grandfather. Her uncle drove the nails in himself on the day of the funeral, then drew them back out again in order to fashion this ring, which is supposed to prevent seizures.)

A man steps around her without a word or a glance.

(So what do you think? Are these just 'black memories'? Is that a name a memory can have?

When she was six or seven, she lived with her parents at the building on English Street; her father was having trouble with the bank and needed to go downtown. That day, her mother had to go to work, and so her father was forced to bring her along with him because she was not to be left alone in the house.

The office at the bank was expanding, with many cubicles, and walls of glass that let in light but made it nasty. Her father was tense and on the verge of anger, which was unusual for a sleepy sort of man like him. While she loitered off to the side, her father sat across a desk from a young, slicked-back white man, and she heard her father's voice growing steadily more insistent. The clerk called another man over; his legs scissored in crisp slacks against the white light of the windows, and his hair had been sculpted a little in front to form a bit of a visor.

The three of them kept on arguing, all standing in front of the cubicle. Her father was making gestures that looked like dividing, measuring, weighing, sometimes tossing something aside. If he had been invisible, an observer might have thought the two clerks were gazing at a natural wonder off in the distance, along a line of sight that only coincidentally passed through her father's face.

Then he was crossing angrily to the exit, waving to Trudy to join him, preoccupied.

He walked . . . He slowed . . . He swayed against the doorway stayed there.

She went round to the front of him and looked up into his face. It was drooping, and there was a dead gray anti-light glowing on it. His head had died, and the rest of him still lived in suspense, waiting anxiously for some word down a line that was never supposed to go silent.

She didn't understand, and she didn't want to say anything. It all seemed shameful and dangerous. She only tugged at him as inconspicuously as she could, with a little spasm of anger at him for making this trouble for her. She knew this kind of thing happened to him, and he would be her father again by and by.)

Trudy's internal sexual system involves subtle settings-in-motion, one thing leading to another, and one of the things she likes about it is the way it starts up entirely unpredictably, instead of being humiliatingly chained to a menu of conventional triggers. This does mean, however, that once it starts she has to take advantage of it. There is something in that she likes as well.

Trudy pictures cold, glassy embers, incandescent marbles, doing a minuet on a dark, polished floor in front of her kidneys. Her face wears a look of profound boredom, but inside she's drinking. Very often a landscape would set this off, so much better! Her body relaxes all at once, as though a rigid inner scaffold had been released. There's even a virtually palpable thud at her feet, and deep inside now the system is keyed up and operating, giving way with an inner sensation like two pelts dragged hard across each other. Above her, the candy shell, and infinity beyond that.

A student named May passes—she's at the very periphery of Trudy's vision. Trudy imagines beautifully fine black lines, so slender they look gray, spiralling out from her outline toward May in a streaming shapeless diagram with distinct spaces between the lines and clear angles. They are sharper the farther they are away from Trudy. May passes right through them without interrupting them. When she was a child, Trudy had attended a grammar school separated from a vacant lot by a chain-link fence she spent a fair amount of time staring through. There was one day she really studied the fence, as it appeared in relief against uniform white haze, and suddenly and unaccountably became interested in its regularity, especially because she had for so long taken it for granted; and when she had gone with her parents to the wharf and seen a fishing net being drawn through the sky onto a spool or something, she had been fascinated by the flexible grid, the idea of sinuous angles . . . the scene solarizes black and mirror-colored, there's an ominous calm in her mind.

She can feel her dismasted body sag inside, and undulating spasms no one can see. May is walking. May turns into a tunnel of transparencies of herself. William veers toward May with long smooth strides. Students and teachers, just shadows, foam around her, drain past her.

Eventually, Trudy feels herself filling up with normal sensations again. Now she can turn and leave the square, hugging herself under her shawl. She's always been a little self-conscious about her figure and doesn't like to be looked at.

May faints.

Celada, emerging from a basement door, catches sight of Trudy and notices her expression. Fait accompli, it looks like it to him. She hadn't seen him just then, but she almost indubitably saw him earlier, and had, for any one or combination of a variety of reasons or no reason, not approached him. Pointedly.

"Well," he thinks, "what would anyone want to approach me *for?*"

He had fallen for her Brontean severity and formality and

30

tantalizing intensity, and he never understood why she had agreed to go out with him. If her desire for him—what an idea!—but if her desire for him (her hypothetical desire for him) could vanish justlikethat, then what—was it desire at all? On probation on credit, so that when it collapses it's as if it had never happened, and meanwhile his desire endures unchanged. Intensified, actually. A clear, hallucinatorily distinct icicle in the dream she is driving and he sits next to her, very close, he sits too close to her, and he can see small lines around her mouth—a disappointed, sad feeling . . . beauty must age.

When I see you, my soul begins to you (infinitive verb).

Trudy sees Celada in her mind, walking with Dr. Crapelin, waving his arms and seeming to pole his round, hovering body along on tapering legs, triangular feet, just floating along like the ghost of a rhinoceros. As he talks, his head lunges and swivels, topped with two wings of blond hair fine as gossamer that were always brindling into stray wisps, wouldn't stay combed. Not that he tried. Last year, Trudy had complained she was bored to a friend among the filing cabinets, who had suggested setting her up with him. They went out a few times; this was an experiment as far as she was concerned. He turned out to be the sort of person who says totally unpredictable things and so rapidly that they pile up into bewildering locations; he's tiring and fascinating to listen to. You can't quite tell if his manner was an affectation or if he really doesn't know how to act.

"He is wandering," he says, pointing to a student asleep over a book.

When they were together, Trudy would retire to the back of her skull and watch him as though her face were a front porch, and he says he was raised by mummies, by which he means his late father was an Egyptologist. The museum has long since been destroyed. The mummies' croon he told her about . . . once

31

in a while the mummies leave the dioramas in which they are displayed, displayed incorrectly—they creep through the museum on dried corn-husk feet, stalking their victim: a little girl. They pounce, seize the captive, painlessly pull open her chest and ribs in the roped-off reconstructed stone crypt at the back of the museum, and languidly take turns licking her palpitating heart with their papery tongues until she dies from the sheer horror of it.

In the tiled passageway at the foot of the stairs to her rooms they'd been chatting before she went up to bed. Celada was in form, and when this happened he relaxed, his face lit up. Cute, as if he'd just won the spelling bee. Trudy wasn't nervous then, but she knew to keep an eye on that confidence. She was on the first step, both hands on the end of the banister, when he leaned across the rail and kissed her, on their next-to-last date. In a flash, he'd said goodnight and disappeared out the door with a self-effacing draft she could feel evaporating the moisture on her lips.

(.)

Celada is listening to a steady high-pitched whine. Several whines. That move in and out of phase. A migraine. Imagine webs of orange fire playing gently over the belly of a black iron pot or for that matter over the skull. A steady, insistent, undeniably real pain.

Trying to get some relief in sleep, he lies on his back in the dark counting faculty.

Professor 9, a small, stationary man with big glasses, who smells like the inside of an electric razor.

Professor 88 is businesslike, speaks in flat factual statements with distinct pauses, a little like an old-fashioned television announcer. Eye to eye, with a tendency to list his reasons enumeratively, and to list a bit to his right, often with one fist on his left hip. Nearly never said "uh." But he wrings his hands, which are reminiscent of long, soggy slices of pizza.

Professor 547 (the numbers are doled out arbitrarily) has an elusive personality, and a twitchy mouth. She is so thoughtful, and prone to reverie, that she could strike you as having been drugged, or drunk with thinking. She seems always to be consulting an inner associate as she speaks, so you don't quite feel you could trust her. Not that she strikes anyone as phony, but her impressions of any given thing will most likely be so idiosyncratic, and her idea of the meaning of words so peculiar to herself, that you can't be sure you know what she means even when she says something apparently unambiguous. You can't help but suspect that what is perfectly clear to her will be unintelligible to anyone else.

Professor 5322 is an old man with glossy, honey-colored skin, who laughs and says, "You may be right!"

"Explain nothing," Crapelin said, farting silently. *His* behavior is strange. It's as though he were always doing an impression of himself.

Parodies, imitators, followers, liars—are they fakes? Or are they just flimsy, or retarded, but stunted? Just as bad whisky isn't "real whisky," nor is it therefore unreal whisky or not-whisky; it's just not very good at being whisky.

Pain like the application of a white-hot wire along the left side of the skull, and he groans and hugs himself until it subsides.

Dr. Crapelin glides out of a field of stars on one foot. Celada's teacher, discoverer of the hermetic methods of Orthonoia . . . not his real name, certainly . . . An exotic Sephardic Swiss Estonian with degrees from twenty reputable foreign and far-off colleges. He saw him for the first time on ice skates, a muffler wrapped neatly around his throat, tweed suit, vest, a cigar in the center of his mouth. Raising first one foot and then the other, nearly poking with his skates the two hands he clasped behind his back.

Swallow your sheepishness and ease your way into the back of the lecture room, a lectorium they're called. Not that there's any lack of empty seats closer to the front. Dr. Crapelin is already halfway through his lecture. He reads in a round, liltingly accented baritone without raising his head, or moving at all.

"We are condemned, it seems, to rely on the anecdotal evidence of folklore. This is, in my opinion, the very worst possible source. It is bad enough we should have to draw upon it at all, but how lamentable we are so fixedly dependent on it."

No, skip ahead to the conference the week after that, in his office.

"Don't be surprised at the emphasis I place on empirical observation. You will find this is the way."

Now I answer with something rambling and not good.

Crapelin resumes.

"You seem to believe that there is some inconsistency between the projective theory and a rigorous adherence to empirical data. But, of course, if that were true, we would have nothing but fantasy, don't you see? Nothing but hallucination as it is traditionally represented. A purely solipsistic exercise. The Versailles case is one of the more compelling, because here we have something like a clearer appreciation of the circumstances. We have slightly—I would say only slightly—better information upon which to draw."

The doctor at his desk, which blazes in the sunset like a rectangle of burning gold. . . . He has a system of his own, Orthonoia, drawing largely on texts already old enough to be old enough. He has not yet explained it, and he may not. The doctor studied with *the* so-and-so, who, while not famous, is a name to conjure with in the right circles, or some of them anyway, in part because so-and-so himself studied with such-and-such, a Diotima with a perennially recharging battery of reputation, on and on back into time an endless tantric succession of smart alecks. You get into a circle and conjure something with their names, among the very few.

Don't be fooled by the numbers, Celada tells himself, any idiot can slap up numbers all over. Anyone can pull flashy stunts with sequences. He has only these fifteen minutes already, he thinks, although he knows he'll have fourteen and then thirteen, and that he already knows he'll overshoot and get late, so let him be terse.

Watch this: a wave of a hand you don't see, and he means *you* chum, all those little black birds with pale yellow beaks beeping and scooting around in the square before the swimming school react, zip up en masse to the branches in the tree adjacent, on the opposite side of a brick wall so weathered it looks as if it's been soaked in cold tea and the white balls and stone planks topping it are crummy with soot—*watch*—the birds move and they sweep along with them like a net they're all caught in the invisible tissue or trireme of the *characterizations* and the *novelizations* of Celada's *imaginary biography*—not an autobiography though, he will insist—

Let's use the biblical "let"—Let the flock be dashed into the air, like a handful of gravel, and now Celada is a "he" who says "I'm Michael" or "I'm Brad" and so on . . . Then down we come, back down to the street, to pick seeds and crumbs from the cobblestones and forget it. But don't forget *that* you forgot.

The only the only thing that matters is that you're here with him.

He knows you're not there. You never are.

Four minutes left. Let him think.

You pass each other in the street after so long, you see each other and you know you see each other, and you glance away, and that's all. Forget it. Nothing happened between you. Nothing happened any more. But Celada is angry because it isn't fair or reasonable for something as sudden and startled as a glancing-away to mean so much.

The important thing, he thinks, is to avoid the pitfall of generalization. *For him* it is axiomatic that things will have this complexion *for him*. For *others* it may be any way, literally. There's nothing special about him, fat old Celada, which is why he must not mistake his perennial truths for binding insights with respect to passersby. Even though this makes them no less absolute for him. For *him*, the act of love is lovelessly consummated at the grossest biological register, between a contemptuous woman who takes out on her *lover* (so called) her anger and embarrassment at being moved to desire by someone, the male, not to say man, who is a senseless mechanism and applies himself as numbly to this exertion as he would to walking or bolting his food or carrying furniture. For him, the proceedings must end in dissatisfaction and surliness, once the onerous pressure of the drive is relieved. Turning away from himself, however, it is no less necessary that he understand that the act of love is, for those other than himself, a perfectly wonderful thing, with nothing wrong with it at all. If he says, "Love is a worthless illusion," and then says, "Love is real and precious," he can avoid mere contradiction by simply dividing these two propositions toward two different sets of subjects, so that the first axiom applies only to him and the latter to everyone else. He wouldn't waste his time with all this if he thought it were only a matter of point of view, but then again he doesn't really think or feel this way at all, not at all, he only thinks so, but he doesn't.

She overheard him in a bookstore. She recognized his voice gradually. Then a physics singularity happened and the universe split into hundreds of clear slides on which are projected her face in every possible expression, his face same, and each variation produces its own consistent line of expressions of face, hand, posture, tone of voice, speech, to form an infinite number of films. She seeks him out, and they stand together conversing awkwardly. She keeps her hands tucked under her shawl.

"So ..."

"How, etc.?"

Celada rises from a dark spot on the floor like Nosferatu, just a shadow made of dense velvety stuff. His hands and face glimmer on, being tenuous, wan movie projections on the stuff in the right spots, but velvet body emerges from another dimension vaster than this one, and empty and alien, *reverberating,* filled with his velvet body, and what she sees is just his life-sized hand-puppet poking up into the bookstore.

"Hello, Persona!" He flaps his hands and forearms like a trained seal. His voice is muffled, weak, and shrill. He raises his right forearm and bends his upper body toward it in an awkward bow.

Celada groans again and mashes the heels of his hands into his temples.

"Are ya happy?" His puppet bows at the waist from side to side in a horrible joyless dance. Then he shrinks to an indistinct shadow in the far corner of the store by the back door.

"Did you forget me yet?" it asks silently. "I never managed."

Opening the back door lets in salty-looking light.

"Glad, glad."

The back door closes, the wall and door go dark.

"Well, back at it."
Twenty-two minutes late. Twenty-five.

(.)

Trudy returns the next day for her medical and to fill out some more forms. Part of the subdivision is closed off by a police cordon, and as she passes the barrier, a vast, languid plume of ruby-red flame ripples up into the sky over the tops of the buildings, not far away. A big moan goes up, like a whole mob getting sick at once.

Trudy shuttles past, feeling the eyes of the police on her through the one-way golden flip-down visors. Not too fast. It's suspicious to be in a hurry. Suspicious to have no particular place to be, too.

The modelsuburb is far up from the Roseate Lamina and stands a little inland from the northeast shore. Bleached colorless by wind rain and cold, its streets are lined with drably streaked, watercolor buildings. What wooden structures there are slouch and peel, a bit like carcasses blasted by a steady wind. The streets of Cimelia Cisterna are more convivial than the insides of its buildings. Small parks and little semi-plazas are everywhere and one not infrequently encounters stretches of street that have been obstinately domestiformed by the residents, making it impassible with their canopies and furniture.

There is a proper medical office at Chthethostoa, but it is small and reserved for emergencies. The routine check-ups are carried out in one of three converted homes in the campus area. Trudy's takes place in an eerie little bungalow with cracked plaster that bubbles away from the ceiling or hangs in brittle shells, faded wallpaper, charred-looking heating vents, inexorable drafts. A pair of female medical students perform the examination efficiently. They take minimal notes. Keeping detailed records these days is not necessarily such a good idea. One never knows who might get their hands on them or what use might be made of them.

The work office is only just opening when she arrives at three, and she has to stand in a line that stretches outside into the wind.

She turns sees Celada standing nearby, posing like Mercury with one leg sticking out behind him, one arm flung up past his head, not looking in her direction but with a wry face that knows she's looking at him.

"Hello, Celada," she says with a watery smile.

"Congratulations on your triumphant return to school," he says, then drops his pose.

"There's that way he has of talking that shows he spends too much time alone," Trudy thinks. "Although I spend a lot of time alone, too. But I don't think I talk like that."

She feels sorry for Celada, because people don't often spend enough time in his company to realize that his way of putting things isn't an affectation; it's an idiosyncratic idea of wit he can't change, a part of his weird personality. His doughy face is expressive and animated, plus it kind of jiggles, and he is as changeable as a television skipping channels.

"Oh," he moans, pressing the heel of his hand to his temple, then walking over to her. "What a headache I had last night! I still don't think it's all gone. How are you?"

"I'm fine. You shouldn't drink so much if you don't like headaches."

"You're right not to assume out of hand I don't like headaches, but this was a migraine."

His habitual tone is professorial, it's one of the first of his mannerisms people make fun of. He obviously was once a precocious child, and nobody likes precocity in an adult.

"What I shouldn't do is eat the Chinese food laced with fistfuls of what-you-ma-call-um."

Trudy glances away.

I can't manage it, he thinks.

"Well, I'll see you," he says abruptly, starting to move away backwards and bowing into the motion. "Be good lucky in the job they give you."

He turns and walks quickly away, stunned at how badly he spoke. She watches him go.

Now it's Trudy's turn in the office. When she comes up to the desk, which might have been the front desk of an old rooming house, the administrator who emerges from the back office takes her cards and shouts down the hall.

"Czochkralski!"

"Hah?" a voice calls back.

". . . Czochkralski!"

"What? What?"

". . . Czochkralski!"

"*Well?!*" The voice is coming down the dingy corridor. "Look, if you call my name once more so help me I'll— Yes, what can I do for you?"

Professor Czochkralski looks over the cards handed him by the administrator.

"Just a minute," he says, going to find her assignment.

"What did you get?" her friend Merle asks her as she comes back out.

"The library," she says. "—Sanglade," she adds, since there's more than one.

( )

The boy shows his teeth in a little spasm of feeling. He wanders off from the group because he's more interested in the filmy brick and lead-colored vines of the embankment. There's a narrow, sandy path right along its base, fringed with tall grass that glows from within like neon, all spangled with rain. The grass brushes his legs as he hurries down the path until his pants are sopping from the knee down. He imagines how he'll catch them up and knows already he won't care if they notice his pants. They might dry.

He slows his pace once he knows he's out of sight, not only of the group but of anyone. He has secret freedom, private and out of doors, stops to piss into a rigidly twiggy bracken that doesn't want to enter into the permissive mood of the grass, the squirrelly wind that burps at him.

He does up his pants and follows the embankment until it becomes brown gray concrete; he runs his hand along the ragged fringe of water stain at his shoulder height—three feet eleven inches.

Now he crouches down—across the field, half screened by the grass, an agitated police car turns this way and that. The car lunges forward in one direction, halts abruptly, retreats, the wheels turn, it charges again, retreats, repeats, probing the field with its beams. He imagines a helmeted giant thrusting its head up out of a hole in the ground, peering about with blazing eyes. The car acts like a cow floundering in a bog. Finally, it spins away.

His confidence falters, a few big rain drops make his face twitch. An archway takes him through the embankment and shows him a small yard beyond, a distant wall with an open gate, an intriguing little brick booth by the gate, and the extensia of adjacent brick buildings. The archway is smelly. The boy trots into the yard.

Suddenly a loud male voice blasts at him from his right.

"Damn it!"

The boy ducks the sound like a blow, feeling his insides launch themselves toward his head, and he wavers a moment wondering if he should stop and try some talking or bolt for the gate in an admission of guilt. The gate is close enough and he's already moving quickly, so, guilty or not, he dashes through it and doesn't stop to look back until he's well up the empty street and no thudding behind him. The man is not pursuing him—he had been yelling something confused about property, but now he's shut the gate.

The boy takes in the sloping street, new to him. The only sure way back is back the way he came, but the gate is now impassible. There were other archways in the embankment, and he knows he came from a direction now to his left. A painful metallic flake low in the sky that way, so that's west. Maybe an alley parallel to this street will take him to the wall of the yard and he can press on, close to his original route; most of the alleys he sees are fenced in back and full of trash cans. So he'll keep going and find a westerly street. The group is probably further south of the place he broke away, unless they're looking for him and have gone back to find him.

The boy doesn't know this part of town and wanders with an increasing fear and terrible freedom.

"I'm lost," he thinks.

He can go anywhere.

The sun sets behind the clouds; everything turns the color of television. They don't turn the streetlights on until late, to save power. Police roam the streets in pairs, with flashlights the size of lunchboxes. The boy takes refuge in a cul-de-sac, all blue-black like oil; the police will pass the main way soon and all one has to do is ray his flash down the alley to see the boy. The boy looks at the wall, uncertainly jumps up, and finds to his surprise he can get his hands onto the top.

The other side is bushes, and he turns this way and that trying to figure out the best way to get down, then lowers himself carefully, drops the scant distance and hunkers behind the bushes waiting to see what will happen. Nothing happens and, with pride, he sneaks along the wall. No way out that way, he turns and repasses the flattened spot he made on the ground when he dropped from the wall, which he scrapes out with a bit of frontier ingenuity, then goes on sneaking in the other direction.

Another wall, but this one is a little more promising, and he begins shakily climbing it with the help of a thick vine. Feeling uncertain in the pit of his stomach, he lets himself back down and starts again within reach of a tree growing by the wall. He pulls himself up and lies lengthwise. There is a narrow space on the other side between the wall and a big windowless stone building with a slate roof, the edge of which is within arm's reach. He lets himself down, his feet crackle on the packed grit.

Around the stone building he goes. The wall bends to block his way and he turns left, coming out onto a sloping meadow with a fringe of trees like black wool. A big building up above him, hidden by trees and bushes, with an overhanging platform. The boy walks quietly in the grass, looking back helplessly at his silver footprints, along the other side of the stone building. There's the front, with a single off-center door, and a gravel space in front of it. There is a light under the door.

Not wanting to risk exposure by dashing across the gravel toward what looks like a drive, the boy looks around and notices a dark passage through the bushes a bit to his right. Investigating, he finds a path of beaten cool earth, smelling strongly of dirt and wet plants. Following the path, he is more and more aware of the looming presence of the building above him.

He emerges from the path and follows the edge of a lawn up a slope; he feels exposed and turns and sees the vast house hovering over him, its crazy, irregular outline lividly scarred here and there by a reflecting window or a white lintel. A paved walkway leads to a gate in the brick wall many yards away—is the gate open? He angles toward the walkway cautiously, glancing often back at the house, scanning the windows for a light or worse—a shadow with a head and a loud voice. Coming closer to the gate, he sees it is open, apparently latched back as well. A narrow street there on the other side.

With this escape surely waiting for him, the boy turns back to look at the house again. Gnawing his lip, he sneaks with exaggerated caution up to the porch steps, which are perfect crescents of dark stone, gleaming and sheer-edged like glass. Those won't creak if he steps on them, but he scrapes his shoes in the grass to be sure he doesn't crunch or leave prints. Now he stands tentatively at the very edge of the porch, which, generous as it is, still seems too small for the house. Large, dark, with a disproportionately small brass knob, the front door is set into an angle of the house; it doesn't face forward, as he imagines the house to be oriented toward the street. There are a number of windows, all dark, with pale curtains, the kind that are tied back to form a calligraphic shape in between them. Even tied, these still nearly cover the windows, the aperture pretty small.

The porch is all stone, he sees, like smooth concrete, or maybe they're stone slabs. Moving with cartoonish stealth he tiptoes forward, wanting to peer through a window. They are like pools of cold ink, too high, relative to the door.

The boy goes over to the door and takes the slender-stemmed knob in his hand. The knob is neither warm nor cold. He takes his hand off the knob and looks at the door, the color of which can't be made out in the shade. He runs his hand over the wood. It's smooth, the paint is glossy and leaves his hand feeling slickened.

The boy is just at the gate when in midstride he turns suddenly, as if he'd been called by name, to look back again at the house. At that moment he trips and falls backwards, landing hard on his back. He doesn't get up again.

An hour later a passerby spots him through the open gate. Soaked in dew, he is eventually conducted unconscious to the quarters of some medical students who live a block away. He's alive and unconscious, with evidence of an injury to the back of his neck. The student who found him there, who noticed him only because he'd gone to close and lock the library gate for the night, says that his head was lying beside one of the big foundation blocks of the outer wall, right by a typically sharp corner. The medical students agree the boy must have fallen, striking the sharp corner of the stone with the back of his neck. He likely has broken vertebrae, and perhaps a damaged spinal chord.

Eventually an ambulance comes and he is conducted to a hospital. The doctors confirm the students' diagnosis. The boy's neck is broken.

It soon becomes clear that his injury has entirely destroyed his senses. He cannot see, hear, or feel, and doctors believe it possible he may not be able to taste or smell either, although how this could have happened they can't say.

The boy regains consciousness roughly a day after he is admitted. When he begins to scream, it is necessary to move him to a private room, so he will not disturb the other patients. He screams all but continuously, calling for his parents, calling names. The nurses take him in their arms, but he doesn't feel them. Only fatigue interrupts his cries.

"Why doesn't anyone come?"

( )

The boy's hair had been a lustrous black when they brought him in. Shortly after he begins screaming, his eyes racing in his head, his arms darting, striking objects, fumbling at everything within reach, a doctor notices something like a halo around the face, as though the boy's head were glowing from within. On closer inspection he sees the boy's hair is growing in white at the roots. By the end of the fourth day, his hair is white as snow.

The boy's screams become more intermittent, with long stretches of sobbing.

The following week he seems to hold calm, measured conversations that often go on for hours. The nurses avoid his room, duty or no, because it is too unnerving being present while these one-sided conversations are taking place. His arms and legs move unpredictably, and on several occasions he is discovered wandering the halls, still conversing pleasantly, even intimately, with someone. He keeps tearing out his tubes. Without the physical sensation of hunger, without taste or even the ability to know whether or not there's food in his mouth, he does not and probably cannot eat.

Much of what he says is fragmentary, emerging from a murmur that becomes more constant, finally continuous.

"Why don't they change piss?"

"Un humano . . . ! . . . Humano!"

"They buried in the snow . . ."

". . . no quiero leche roja . . ."

". . . isquierda to the phonebush."

"Eso es en el cuarto del infinidad?"

There was a snatch of song, too:

"[mumble] is a burning thing, a burning thing . . ."

"Save me, what that means!"

The records aren't complete, but a little digging turns up the epilogue to his story. The nurse, despite her protestations to the contrary, seems to have neglected his restraints one night; the next morning he is not in his bed, or anywhere else they look for him. Seven hours later, a little body is brought in. Killed by a car. The nurses gasp when the face is revealed.

(The driver rounds a shoulder and swerves to avoid the sudden boy, veering in front of another driver who veers the other way, accelerating right into the boy in an attempt to pass the first car. The boy is slapped to the ground. His spine whips his head against the highway.

the sight: the house standing against the sky

the sound: a bell ringing *in frenzied triumph*)

A doctor looks at the map on the wall and shakes his head. No one traveling on foot could get to that road, the site of the accident, without climbing a steep embankment and getting over a low barrier.

"Could he have recovered use of his eyes?" a nurse asks.

"It . . ." the doctor sighs through his nose, compresses his mouth, and shakes his head uncertainly.

"I mean it was spinal damage; recent."

They're looking at the map as though it might show them breaking news—

"Huh!" one nurse says, and raises her finger. "He might have been heading home."

The finger drags left from the spot, sweeping a line along the map.

"If he lived anywhere near where they found him."

(.)

The migraine has a metal ion in its molecular composition. The word pain doesn't do justice to it. He can write only when he has a migraine; it's the only thing that can get him to concentrate. By aversion.

Go out the window for a while to let the clairvoyance in. Not that Celada believes he is really clairvoyant; he is, but he doesn't believe it. It wriggles into his skull where the hot band flexes the bone-crevices. He sees a tall, middle-aged man getting off a cart in front of the swaying fronds and the stone wall. The man wears a big, shiny, dark grey suit. The light that falls on this man is piercing yet dim, like a headache. Miss Houseman is already advancing to greet him. William, in shirtsleeves and a shiny rubber apron, shades her with the umbrella. She greets the man without extending her hand, bowing a little to one side as she invites him inside.

William draws a dead body, wrapped in a sheet of stiff material, from the back of the cart onto a gurney. The cart rattles off, and William glides the body along a gravel drive lined with green-black bushes, overhung with huge locusts and beeches. He goes through a gate in a brick wall, shutting it behind him.

It doesn't occur to Celada that he is genuinely clairvoyant; as far as he's concerned these are just daydreams. He thinks the same is true of Ukehy. Dr. Crapelin of course is real, but Celada has overlaid his image with increasingly fanciful daydreams, until he has become something like a fantasy despite his studied, prosaic stolidity. That they are only daydreams, and nothing more, Celada simply assumes. He takes it for granted that he is only seeing, not creating.

There is a streak of pale earth, like a part in a head of thick hair, exactly the width of the corpse. The body floats among black foliage down the length of the path. Inside the Milk House, which has no windows, William turns on the hanging ring of lights, illuminating wooden and metal tables, covered with tools of embalming. There are sinister, gleaming metal cabinets prostrated on little wheels, with double doors.

Removing the sheet discloses the body of what was an elderly man, with distinguished-looking hair.

Swiftly and efficiently William opens the man's shirt, then draws up the right pant leg to the knee. The exposed, transparent skin is marbled blue and gray. On a round table with a thick stone top rests a leather block, bristling with many upright rows of needles of varying lengths. William plucks up needles judiciously and swiftly, dabbing them into a leather vambrace covering his left forearm. Turning to the body he begins with care to insert the needles into the inert skin. He moves to and fro, now the leg, now the face, now the chest, now the back of the left hand, which he turns over carefully.

When this is complete, William gets around to the feet and pushes the gurney, setting the embedded needles trembling. He positions the gurney between a number of upright transformers, which together form an implied rectangular bay. Over this there is a squat, broad spool connected by cables to ominous-looking machines, large smooth bolts studding its upper circumference, and upright spinnets like skinny teeth between the broad flats. From these spinnets William draws needles on fine fishline threads. Giving each a single efficient tug provides him enough slack, and William places these leashed needles precisely in the cadaver meridians—

—the distribution of which is entirely different from that of a living body, Celada decides—

—then dons a pair of thick goggles designed to focus his odylic force, which must be extremely strong if he is to hypnotize the cadaver. William is a pro, he's done in twenty minutes. The client has meanwhile just signed his check at Miss Houseman's desk and is getting ready to take his leave. William completes the sequence of passes, now he crosses to and fro, flipping switches and turning knobs. There is a gathering drone, a grey rattle like headache, and the smell of hot insulation. The electroacupunctural procedure is called "kindling," by which the seizure threshold of dead muscles is lowered. There are large magnets, like black doorknobs, around the body, which sustain the hypnotic field. A "special kind" of electricity, stored in carbonation capsules screwed into the steel ring, charges threads attached to needles on retractor spools. As each carcass meridian comes up to its proper charge, the needles softly begin to sing. Celada can't hear the sound, but understands it is a chorus of very faint, pure notes, like high organ pipes joining one at a time into a chord. The overtones of this chord, he believes, oscillate from an octave below to an octave above the main tone. When the sweep becomes strictly consonant, William cuts the current and pushes a button; all the electrified needles retract to their spinnets.

Scooting alongside the body, William checks the temperature of the head and hands with the backs of his own, squeezing the earlobe judiciously. Celada imagines him tucking a sprig of parsley back there, but of course William does no such thing. The results are evidently satisfactory. The dead man's exposed skin has turned a liverish color. William deftly extracts most but not all of the needles, returning them to the leather vambrace. Those that remain he smartly drives all the way into the stiffening flesh, with a thimble.

He passes a hoop over the body, like a magician.

When he rolls the body back out of the magnet bay, he once again makes hypnotic passes over it. Reflected lights ripple elastically across his goggles. With a gathering gesture above the body's face, he is coaxing it to rise.

The body sits up, one leg slides off the cot, the foot slaps the floor.

Now the corpse is standing upright. William keeps up his

passes and seems to be giving mute instructions. The dead man dreamily begins arranging his clothes, does up his shirt without looking at it, settles his tie, makes himself presentable. For that matter, the liver color is fading from his face, which, while pale, now has a trace of pink in it.

William quickly needles the upright man at the back of the neck and in the spine, then directs him toward his coffin, which lies on the floor. The old man's corpse walks like an experienced, dignified old drunk, climbing into the coffin and arranging itself there. William kneels by the body and adjusts the precisely positioned acupressure clamps attached to the coffin's interior. A few final passes and the body—laid out as naturally as if it were merely asleep—is inanimate. William swings the coffin lid lightly into place, performs a final pass and the lid bolts screw themselves in. The electropuncturally embalmed body is ready for the funeral. It will keep for weeks in this condition, unrefrigerated, unmolested by knives, and without undergoing any cosmetic indignities.

(. . .)

Be grateful! Life is hard! Take what you can get!

(Never underestimate the sinister power of this way of thinking.)

Low-flying intimidaters groan round the clock. They groan and groan. Round the clock. Burning gas. Groaning overhead you can hear their snarl warp the air, dangling the spies of notre dame.

(.)

Trudy sees, there in the doorway, a field of drifting stars, motes of illuminated dust that rise and fall in air currents. Imagine that each one could be a galaxy or a universe. Some

motes twinkle, some flash, and given that, and their propensity
to veer horizontally, it's almost impossible not to think of them
as alive.

She spends the evening with friends in Cuerda Candencia.
Merle is seeing a tall, neurasthenic blond man, and he is getting
angrier and angrier as the night goes on. Evidently he feels
slighted. Celada was easy to get along with because he expected
nothing from people, least of all women. He was glad of
whatever came his way, or he gave the impression that he would
take whatever he could get. If he hadn't tried so hard to make
everyone like him, he would have been better still.

What a meager idea of me you have, he thinks, when my idea
of you stretches to the far horizon.

Or should she be easily satisfied with people, the dumb
pricks?—

Alone with her thoughts—already she has said her goodbyes
to her friends, almost without disturbing them (her thoughts),
and while not seeming more distracted than could be excused
by ordinary politeness. And now she is flung right up against the
chill, steely flame of a flinty sky, with mauve serrations, almost
like a patterned medallion. Mauve air flips over her cheekbones.
Odor of red soil, like bloody clay, a tree stands bolt upright, a
scabby column without a single shoot below four feet. Where
she is now, five streets meet. To her right, there is an iron fence
of black wands, guarding a gaunt, octagonal house whose walls
emit a faint pink radiance. The curtains are peeled back from the
narrow leaded windows upstairs and, from this angle, they
reveal nothing but a circle of yellow light on a ceiling of white
plaster. The ground floor is dark except for the window on the
far angle, facing away, where someone is writing at a desk:
spotlight on the writing hand, which is all she can make out.

The hand is pink ivory with thick green veins, now oddly

small, now oddly big, and warm with reposing health. She imagines how strange and horrible it would be if it were cut off. Her own pink-palmed hand cut off. Her hand, she imagines, severed, just lying severed there, on a table in a window. Once a part of 'me,' but not any more—never again. Now it's only an unspeakably bizarre object, discarded without use or meaning, that will rot away in time.

—Celada, reading a book after his dinner, alone in his apartment: there it is again, he thinks, glancing down at my puffy, dry, old-womanish palm, etched with parallel lines, seamed and fractured and creased. My palm turns toward me a little, like the face of a small animal, returning my gaze.

(0)

They record him and play back his screams, sometimes when they are leaving him alone, and other times they make him do a duet with himself. They explain that one of their number was impersonating him with June, that they have films of her entertaining a number of them, later that she has been arrested. They pull stunts on him straight out of comic books. They parade him in front of clean people. He is always too hot or too cold, tired, hungry, in pain. They pull out some of his teeth, they gash his face, let a dog chew one of his ears off, cut his scrotum open. They want to know why he is a liar and a traitor, *why* he wants to destroy the state, and how he plans to do it. They pile nonsensical demands on top of each other and then beat him down before he can do one thing.

On some day or other he is dragged from his closet and flung into a station wagon with no windows in the back. The door slams with a jolt he can feel through the car. Two more from up ahead. The engine fires up. His body begins to jostle with the movement of the car. His eyes are still adjusting to the light.

Sparkling sunlight branches a smell of dusty ground wet with dew.

They stop. The men get out in silence. They go behind the car. He waits.

They haul him out suddenly. He is stepping high through tall weeds into a stand of slender trees. A sudden rush of terror nearly cuts his legs from under him, and he staggers.

The men shoving him don't speak a word. He hears the rushing wind, a few bird calls as sharp and distinct as any he's ever heard.

Up ahead he sees more men in plain clothes, and three others—in their underwear—with hoods over their heads. They are standing like votaries, with shaking knees, like him, barely able to stand. The image has the persistence and clarity of a painting. They are right up to the brink of a huge trench that he can already smell.

P.'s hands are roughly tied and suddenly, with a dull flap, there's a cloth bag over his head. He fills it almost at once with hot, stinking breath in a panic and stumbles forward.

The men casually point their carbines at the backs of the captives without bothering to aim all that carefully.

They fire.

The captives are ripped apart and fall down dead. Q. turns as he falls, and lands on his side.

The captives fall into the pit at their feet. Clouds of flies scatter as they fall.

The men withdraw in silence.

The flies settle down once more. They flit down in broken spirals.

Some pain. From the fall into the pit. The stink.

Strength undiminished though. And coming back in confusion.

He's all right.

He was missed.

R. begins working his hands vigorously. One suddenly springs free and he gets up onto his knees. He claws off his hood.

He stares all around him, at the corpses, the trees.

He stares at the golden sun, which seems to hover among the trees like a dazzling glaring calmly curious blazing will-o'-the-wisp, beckoning to him. Eyes starting from his head, he lurches to his feet, climbs up out of the trench, and runs toward the sun.

(.)

If he could jump around like a maniac while staying fast asleep, this would satisfy Celada in this nervous, irritable, groggy, sparking, bachelorized state.

On the street, every now and then, he would encounter those fierce, closed faces. The faces belonging to a sullen tribe of intense, earnest, high-strung young white men. Always insulted, on short death leash of shame, and when discussing life they toss off the most extreme-sounding views with every indication of a long and easy familiarity with them, and of no real experience. And sometimes words so violent come from them that even they are abashed—those words teenage too much. They are all too obvious tokens of a visitor from a foggy, naively grim inner world.

—shame (*she's* left you): it's as though other people can see it on you in the street, like a mantle of caustic light glowing across your shoulders—

Celada is hurrying to be only a little late for his appointment with Dr. Crapelin.

Now something about Ukehy.

At first, he thought the name was "Eorla." Old English.

Crapelin once said that in politics, the philosopher's stone is despair, which is a far better weapon than terror.

"But this is just glib talk," he added right away. "There's still plenty of terror to go around."

Ukehy, the correct name, is the secret police. That is, the people keep them a secret from themselves. Just Celada's fantasy. Plainclothes police, watchers everywhere, that exciting atmosphere of informing and spying and seeing the signs and understanding them. The disappearances.

The secret police are just like ghosts, he thinks. They watch, but are unseen. They mark their victims and wait until each is alone to pounce. They are not supposed to exist, and in fact Celada mistakenly believes they are only a figment of his imagination. That his imaginings might coincide exactly with the truth never occurs to him.

In secret prisons, often disguised as clinics or three-quarters abandoned government buildings, all but the oldest female dissidents are branded on the right buttock with an image of the flag, then gloatingly lobotomized by religious doctors using speculums. They reach the brain through the nose. Sometimes as a special treat this is done in front of her parents, brothers, lovers, or children, who may also be honored guests as she is raped by bold Ukehy officers, or other prisoners, and gently stroked up and down with live wires. The women are gainfully employed in this manner until they die, keeping the jobless rolls down. It's all entirely legal; one way or the other everyone voted for this. When, from time to time, children come to pass, as a consequence of these sports, the male babies are inducted into Ukehy right away.

What does Ukehy do?

(Brief pause as Celada changes buses.)

Answer—it doesn't matter. It all lies in what they could do, and might. And when. Whenever. And why. Whyever. Through

56

the magic of secrecy, all knots are undone.

One difficulty is this: every now and then, the children of the affluent and influential imbibe a radical idea or two—some even come up with them on their own—and naturally these have to be handled more carefully than hoi polloi. They bring a sense of entitlement to the wrong side of the equation. The isolatoes present little difficulty; they tend to assume they are the only people in history to have had that particular idea and certainly they are not unjustified in believing themselves to be something of a rara avis in terris for thinking it. So they neutralize themselves with snobbish martyrdom. For the more social there is a self-contained and discrete simulation centered principally around schools and colleges in which they may exhaust themselves in harmless gestures and altruistic volunteer work.

But for all this to function, certain barriers have to stay up and camouflaged and people kept apart, and more vigorous measures taken where someone endeavors to sap or undermine the force fields. Ukehy exists for this . . . Just a fantasy. Do they work for the domestic spying administration or the shattered remnant of the military, or are they a private organization for hire? The question isn't interesting, any more than it is all that interesting to think about heaven or hell, wherever ghosts go when they give up haunting the living.

The haunted house and the country rotten with spies. But they aren't really the same. The haunted house . . . at least the one Celada is thinking of . . . is the shrine where life triumphs over death, perfection actually manifesting itself. The country is haunted by death, spectral hangmen. The ghosts of Sanglade are frightening because they are too perfect to see without going insane or being injured somehow by intensity of adoration. Ukehy is frightening because they will torture and kill you; they are elementals of sordidness and cruelty.

(O)

The sun is sinking into the earth!

It's disappeared!

S. is watching it sink from a basement window, eyes level with its vanishing edge. Breathing through his mouth, wanting but not daring to lift and rest his hands on the sill. But they still drip blood . . . and they might be seen from outside.

The approach is of nothing but starless darkness, the real night they've merely been rehearsing for up to now.

"I'm alive!" he thinks. He shakes with fear.

For him, the silence is fraught with cries.

( )

The boy walks to the horizon, and the horizon grows no larger. He reaches the horizon and the mountains are no higher than his knees. The boy kneels on the mountains and bends forward over them, tilting his head back; his breath frosts the sky in front of him. Looking sideways, he can see more clearly that the sky has a surface, like the surface of the ocean.

The boy jabs his fingers into the cool gelatin of the sky and scoops a little of it out. The faceted gouge his fingers make in the sky gradually seals itself. A few stars had been there, and they gradually reappear too, winking back to life like novelty candles. The boy examines the indigo piece of sky quivering in his hand. There are stars in it. He squeezes the piece of sky, and it bulges without seeming to want to come apart. It draws no warmth at all from his hand, cool as a gob of peppermint jelly. The boy smears the stars around in his hand, opens and closes his fingers. Long luminous strings of star trail from his fingertips.

A wind sweeps lightly down over the concave surface— behind him a bell is wildly ringing—he starts, without turning or shifting his eyes from his hand—the abandoned bell clamors in triumphant frenzy of Sanglade: a high, regular, glory-drunk note banging from the house.

The boy is crying, perhaps from the mere intensity of the sound. His tears drip into his palm, catching the light of stars still smeared all over his fingers. Sighing, the boy droops and presses his hand to his eyes. His hand is empty when he takes it away again. Leaning nearly double, the boy holds his hand cupped beneath his face as though he were going to vomit into it; his body undulates a little and he excretes his eyes into his palm with a small plop.

(( ))

Out on the field, boys pile up on top of each other again and again. The laughing boy sound is a bubbling, robust lace of glee, and if a grown man made that sound they'd put him away. The sound is regular and lulls him with the prospect of a happiness foreign to him. Suddenly the sound stops, when one of them possibly is injured and all crowd around—no, all right, and like a tap it flows again delirium of that giddy noise. He seeks it out, because it helps him to sleep. They play on the field, and T. snatches nods in a shadowy gray lean-to attached to the brick kiosk of the public lavatory, barnacled onto one wall. In the corner, he swells and shrinks as he breathes, his ear turned toward the sound of their play.

From a nearby bench, Celada watches the boys for a moment.

Before true multicellular life forms evolved, there were in-between creatures in the ocean called colony beings or something like that, consisting of globs of individual single-celled creatures reminiscent of these boys. They rush together and come apart as though inner elasticity set the pulsation.

Back to the daydream at hand: Dr. Crappatuchio—was that

the name? A clinical psychiatrist. He is less a general expert in something than an accomplished dilettante who gives off a dust devil of small and medium-sized ideas. He says you should wait at least four hours after waking to eat any meat, that exposure to continuous booming low vibrations (from construction or traffic, zum beispiel) causes cancer, and one should not wear cushioning in the shoe. There comes a moment in any intellectual pursuit at which enthusiasm, or at least interest, while it is still present in the mind or body, begins to flag. One must learn to detect the approach of that moment and cease work before it comes, with the idea that residual impetus will then grow into a fresh wave.

He is a strict materialist and empiricist whose favorite subject is the ghost. The ghost of the malefactor . . . someone who has committed deeds so unspeakably monstrous that she acquires a near-miraculous aura, the incredulity that greets the reports of her deeds slides metonymically onto the perpetrator herself, turning her into a chimera. One imagines the malice that overflows all moral constraints, so why not the physical constraint of the grave as well? . . . The face of the villain becomes a symbol for the possibility of unthinkable acts. The face materializes over the door every time a child scoots from the safety of the threshold . . . yes, they detected and caught me, but I *was*, I was possible . . . a possibility was realized in an actual person who wore this face and was called by this name . . . there are *others* like me, I'm a *type* . . . those others have not all been detected and checked—and there is always a chance that one of me will get my hands on your sweet little thing . . .

The warning phantom is converted to the point of view of my victims and the loving ones who avenged them. I am a self-despising specter tormented forever by the thought of my irredeemable and vile acts. Don't be like me. It may seem like fun and games now ... it won't always seem like fun and games ...

Other apparitions menace us not with their malice but with their anguish. These are like the specters of warning, but they are people who have suffered horribly in life, who have sounded the depths of despair and gone so far into it that it seems nothing can end or ameliorate it. They seem to have fallen short of—or exceeded—the power even of heaven to console them ... So inconsolable are they that even death is powerless to end their despair. These are phantoms of pure misery; the pain of their lives overwhelmed their unnoticed deaths. The worst has already happened to them, and what ends can't be the worst.

Celada doodles in the condensation that has fogged the bus window.

The notion that ghosts are convulsed with hatred of the living seems a little facile. Are we to believe that the ghost of the innocent child or the sweet old lady shall instantly become vicious and idiotic? To survive the grave only for the sake of lame pranks—it's too stupid not to believe! Perhaps they are jealous, perhaps they are stricken with a preta-like hunger that can't be assuaged without a body—

No, people who turn into malignant ghosts hated others well before they died. That is the recipe. Most ghosts assault people not deliberately, but with a kind of forced voyeurism where the victim is merely confronted with the spectacle of suffering and despair, such that the attack is sympathetic, preying on the victim's own sensibilities.

Now Celada is back in his apartment, looking down at his legs stretching away under the sheets, despondently thinking nothing ever changes. Half-drowsing, he hears a phrase. "Modera omnes" realizing as he hears it that the first word is actually spelled "fidela." What is that, 'modified all' or 'ever faithful'?

He can't stop thinking; his mind babbles on and on, staying awake. His imagination is just good enough to keep him interested despite his desperate yearning for sleep.

There are ghosts in this town, he thinks. There have to be. He wonders if he might be one of them. A fog of words around the head, which simply moves on when the head is dead. It seems obvious. What anguish destroyed him?

Girls—grins—the web. Gazes and teeth. Talk. To show interest to fend off interest. They don't look his way because they intuit at once he's just impossible, like a goblin. His surface grows cold and his depths grow hot, and a heavy iron wheel clamps down, everything heaves to a stop. He can't talk to them. He feels it with despair—because some uncounted measure of time spent in pain, walking the streets totally defeated, lying at the bottom of a night like a dark pit, that time congeals in him all at once to form a dense solid, like ablative foam—(he's exaggerating)—

But something in that time, when he was humiliated, really does reach out and pinch him off. Like rabies, it makes him act in a way that propagates itself. Ponderous and slow, like the Commendatore, living bronze, sternly animated by something dark and remote and imaginary. Desiring a woman, Trudy, going after her, is like wanting to jump from a high place—no, it isn't it's just a matter of going back to the spot where he had been left.

He does it sometimes: he opens his mouth. (That was part of the mummification procedure—the opening of the mouth.) Venturing to speak is a flash of intense steely contrasts. The moments are cropped. They splutter around him. Time switches into staccato. Celada tells himself it is absurd; these things happen every day. And if he is transfixed with fear, it's because he has mistaken this even everyday sort of thing for something redeeming. Will you save my life? It all tumbles together into a lump and is done. He tells himself lamely he has a duty to open his mouth. He is the last Celada.

He used to fall into worshipful love. The kind that's plighted. He wants to be proof against them now, like Grendel, and unmovable by smiles because he already has his—but what a smile! A glacier creaking out from beneath eyes of charred glass; a worn, numb smile that just rests on his face like a bit of food.

He's turning into an avatar of the futility god Muirv, who has the waterlogged face of a monster with no mandible. The soft mouth is a cold morass of toothed mucus, smelling like old ice from the back of the freezer. Muirv croons disjointed syllables in the night like a distant boat horn. No cult either, just a vein.

(O)

Silently, her arms sweep in from space, through the air like two winds, just above the ground. Her leaves, her hands, curve in toward each other unseen across the earth like galactic calipers, until the index fingers connect in a point of intense heat within the chamber of the carbine that had aimed at his back. The bullet evaporates at the instant the trigger is pulled. The hammer strikes the base of the cartridge, detonating the powder. The gun jerks and flashes, but there is no bullet to fire. When the gun goes off, U., in his terror, jumps at the sound of the shot and falls forward. As he lies sideways in the pit below, it is not obvious in the smoke that he is uninjured.

Basement of a ruined, solitary farm house of adobe, dirt floor. The doorway slants to one side, its hinges dangle from a screw. He rolls onto his side, waking in spasms, scraping the dirt floor with his knuckles. Now he rolls further forward into an awkward position, nearly resting on his doubled right arm and kneading his rubbery face with his left hand.

Flash: the woman. The sun with a wig on. He starts with a

brief cry and his breath comes short, his eyes swell. The fingers, the vaporized bullet.

"She saved me!" he thinks.

His breastbone trembles and he giggles, lets his face sink nearly to the ground, inhale dust.

He pops up from his resting position suddenly, trips forward a few steps on legs whose knees won't lock, then flops back down on his knees again.

"Where is she?"

He stares at the blue earth in front of the doorless doorway. His mind sits on top of his body peering around like a man up a mast. Last he saw of her, she was sinking into the earth. He claws the ground in front of him, panting, getting dirt on his face and sagging lower lip, driving it up beneath his nails.

Then he freezes.

The hole is about big enough to put his head into, and at the deepest, maybe four inches down, lies a tiny ingot of light. With a shout of surprise and joy, he flails at the ground, throwing dirt in all directions, blood leaps out of rents in the skin and cracked nails but the light very slowly, perceptibly, observably, and steadily grows brighter as he unearths the buried sun—

"Come out! Come out!" he cries.

The light dims. He clutches the edge of the hole staring, streaming face slack with fear like a melting candle. Is it going? Don't go! It comes back.

He roars! He's on his feet and gambolling around the floor with his eyes riveted to the hole, laughing like a maniac.

Then he glances out the door. She is rising, gigantically, from the earth. Awe spreads over his miserable face. He settles down onto his knees and thrusts greedy hands into the little basin of gold light. Bathing his hands, the sun shines on his blood, lighting up all his veins and arteries. He flings himself down on his back thrusting his face into the stream and opens his eyes wide like a parched man trying to drink a whole river—immerse himself in sun and drown his brains in light—

(*)

Trudy keeps her eye on the minatory shadows of the swimming school. This is her first day of work this semester.

Celada is waiting for a class to begin in a room overlooking the square, his head on his forearms on the desk while the magazine subscription department that rents the room in the off hours takes its leave. He is too lost in visions of the one he loves ... which was it again, was it Trudy? Standing majestically at the head of a flight of white musical stairs, her hair swept up and the skin of her face, her throat, the wings of her collarbone, exposed by a scoop-fronted gown sparkle with gold dust making a living idol out of her. The fantasy is static; Celada can only be the rapturous eye of the camera, or supplicant, paralyzed down on the stage, basking transfixed in the theatrics that resolve out of the air around her.

William is down in the corner of the garden, fiddling carefully with his embalming chemicals. Trudy watches his efficient movements for a moment. He's been at the school a long time, and might have run it before Miss Houseman. While he continues to teach, since her arrival he's been working the embalming line and become more or less her personal valet. As Trudy pauses to look, she catches a glimpse of Miss Houseman standing in the upstairs window, gazing down at him proudly.

"He is my creature."

Dr. Cottataris hails Trudy, and they chat briefly. She is a younger professor with a great abundance of red pre-Raphaelite hair and a stunning smile that looks equivocal and surprising in her drawn, severe face.

The thing is, Celada has the idea that he has to mortify himself by making these doomed gestures to women; he's too aware of being reckless. He keeps advancing the difficulties in order to crash uselessly into them and try to impress you with all that suffering and effort.

Up ahead now, the brick wall, the gate and the black shrubs inside it. That must be the place.

Something stops her, just within the gates.

Sanglade is a Vliance house, built around the turn of the century. Houses are supposed to look like heads, or skulls, that's the convention. This one is a cubist skull, one eye somewhere in there staring forward, while the other wrenched around to the side. It's a gigantic candelabra bedecked with iron flames, which manages to be at once massive and graceful. Platforms protrude asymmetrically on either side, one on what looks like the second floor and the one on the right, higher still. There is an oblate arch half-buried under the eaves. The roof has gables like serrations that fold the slating into acute triangles, and portholes pulled in like turtle heads within them. The overall effect is pagoda-like.

The foundation is huge, and settled on the prominence of a slope; the house looms over as she draws near, even as it seems to recline luxuriously, like an imperious mistress. The base is surrounded in front by a yew hedge and trellised rose bushes, dotted with a few pink blossoms going rusty and beaten half apart by rain.

The porch is made of slabs fitted as neat as Inca masonry. Trudy eyes the front steps, whose edges gleam like razors even in the shadow of the house. Brass knob and knocker glow with sullen fire against the silken black lacquer of the front door; the elegance of the design distracts her from its enormous size. The knobs and knockers have graceful, swirling arts-and-crafts decorations.

By the time she crosses the threshold, her eyes are already swimming with pleasure of just seeing. The foyer is octagonal, spacious, and tall, with broad floorboards, an old Anatolian rug of throbbing crimson, black cabinets like cubes of glass. The windows are leaded with an irregular, very linear design, and misted. A huge gem hangs from the middle of the ceiling. Wooden groining against a white ceiling; wood panels below, glistening, tiny white tiles above.

There's a fragrance of aromatic wood, and under that, a fresh, clean, bright smell she can't identify. If cold had a smell, that would be it.

Turn to the right under an arch with ponderous, roped-back curtains and ascend steps like scimitars, crescent-shaped and sharp. Trudy has never visited this library, which is mainly law and some medical (a largely haphazard choice). The plan of the main floor is nearly completely open; one can see windows on all sides. Before her there is one of a number of staircases, wide without appearing to be wide, with tall sides like archaic church pews, a muscular angularity about the way it doubles back on itself. The landing is deep, and lit with amber radiance from a high skylight way up a shaft. The staircase seems to stand crisply at attention; its many joints and angles are perfect.

This floor is partitioned with movable screens covered in a fabric that, though gray, somehow still manages to look sumptuously deep. On the left, a spacious area of rugs, a vast leather sofa, armchairs, and many lamps set here and there in a way that immediately suggests reading or chatting at night. She can see the archipelago of lights that would form as people brought lamps to where they needed them in the dark, people sitting together on the floor in rugs and blankets and leaning on hassocks, and reflected in polished brass. The brick kiln fireplace is not set into the wall, but perches on a dais of stone. It looks to Trudy like the head of an idol with four gaping mouths. To her right is a very large and beautiful desk attended by many bookshelves.

"This is all original stuff," she thinks, scrutinizing the furniture. "The school couldn't possibly afford to buy all this."

She crosses the floor hearing only a single, quiet pop. The house is so quiet she feels too self-conscious to announce herself. Breaking the silence would make a bad first impression on the house. She walks past the staircase, her eyes vaguely on the distant windows, where clots of green sway.

As she moves around a colossal upright beam, she sees Dr. Camatsura, head of the preservation society, seated in a globe of yellow light at a little table. Her dry, papery hand rests on an open book, and a pen hovers over an index card. Trudy clears her throat, and Dr. Camatsura looks up with a slightly embarrassed, innocently discomposed expression.

"Hello, Miss Bailey," she says in an undertone. She sounds as though she had overlooked Trudy and someone else had reminded her to say hello. But then she gets up and begins explaining at once what Trudy will have to do, not even bothering to check Trudy's work card.

Trudy will work for the most part in a "parlor," which is the term they've come up with to designate the screened-off zones. This one is set into one of the many corners of the outer wall, with a pair of doors at right angles to each other in one corner. There is a desk, card catalogs, shelves, many single-paned windows overlooking the veranda, and, outside, a tapestry of virtually black trees that never stop groping the air.

When she's alone again, Trudy crouches and strokes the pile of the rug. Her eyes skip across the surface and plunge at will into the pattern, a garden of sinuous vines radiating in and out of one another; it must be a thousand knots to the square inch. The pile must be silk. Standing at her high table, with a caramel stool next to it, she gazes around herself with a feeling of happiness that grows and grows.

"It's beautiful!" she thinks. "Everything's perfect. Incredibly beautiful!"

Even the sturdy card catalog is well-made. The long drawer slides out smoothly; from it pours the fudgy smell of card catalogs, the blander one of varnish, and a more exotic, peppery odor of the wood itself. Maybe it's camphor or cinnamon tree or something like that.

Now she's starting to feel a little dazzled by all this severe beauty. She's getting a sense of the basic principles of the designers' aesthetic selections; sharp angularity, solid strength, uncompromising durability, and augustness. A surprising amount of metal and stone; thick sleeves of brass encase the beams in the ceiling of the sitting area, and brass fittings are everywhere. The mantelpieces, the bases of columns and other parts of the structure, are stone. All Trudy has to do is turn her head, and her eyes take in a blur of brass fires, reflected light in polished stone, and the colder glints of crystal ornaments.

"The whole thing's mineral, like a magic cave," she thinks.

Even the wood looks like precious stone, and, like stone or metal, the furniture has edges as keen as knives, as the facets on a diamond. And all this was made possible by wealth and privilege. They would have paid her in what was pocket change to them, to walk across town and back every day dust mop and get her ass squeezed.

Trying hard to concentrate on her work, she starts marking entries in the logs and filling out index cards. Even the fountain pen they've given her is fancy, with a certain heft. She feels the spaciousness of the house yawning around her, and the safe feeling of the heavy upper stories resting on top of her. The air is saturated with thick, delectable quiet. Her pleasure in this is intense and almost disembodied, like being excited in sleep. Sitting on her high chair, she does notice the air around her head is faintly stuffy, if not close or musty. Just warm. This contrasts with the chill, although that's too hard a word for something so faint, she feels seeping into her triceps, her calves, and the prominences of her back. That's common to old houses. The sensation is more like evaporating alcohol than a cold current of air; it doesn't seem to have a source.

With a start she hears footsteps and voices: Dr. Camatsura greeting Professor Isochronal. The sound seems to come from immediately next to her, but, judging from its volume, they must be conversing on the far side of the house. The sound, muted by wood and rugs, becomes a brown warble that doesn't distract her. Instead she distracts herself, head on her fist, with a fantasy about the faculty turning into animals.

Quitting time takes her by surprise. Turning around once on the way to Dr. Camatsura's desk she spots, in an alcove, a small Asian idol of a meditating ascetic, in purple-brown metal. Each rib stands out sharply on the withered body. Later, she will be struck by something undefinably similar in the look of the house from a distance, as though it were a huge, angular, meditating figure.

"How do you like it?" Dr. Camatsura asks her, her face rippling strangely as though there were many expressions there, rebounding against each other like billiard balls.

Glancing around her, Trudy says, "It's beautiful! I don't think I've ever been in a more beautiful house."

Dr. Camatsura smiles irregularly. "Yes, I think so too."

"What do you know about it? Vliance designed it, didn't he?"

Dr. Camatsura nods, dipping her head forward and up as though she were scooping a hat off a hatrack. "Yes, about one hundred and twenty years ago, now."

"Do you know anything about who lived here?"

Dr. Camatsura looks up diagonally. "Well, not a great deal, not off the top of my head. I know the man's name was Houseman"—she drops her head pronouncing the name as though it had a weight of its own—"and that he didn't live here much. His wife was famous for something, though, and she was here for some time. The house was donated to the school many years ago."

"Is Miss Houseman related?"

"I don't know . . . Perhaps."

Trudy looks around a moment in silence.

"Does the name mean something?" she asks after a moment, half curious, and half uneasily extending the conversation simply because she can't, for the moment, figure out how to end it.

"I suspect it does," Dr. Camatsura says with a slightly abashed, loose-lipped smile. "I'm afraid I don't know it . . ."

An expectant expression settles over her face. This pause lasts a little too long, in the silence of the house.

"There was a student who researched the history of the house. Perhaps you might ask him."

"Celada—?"

The name pops out of Trudy's mouth.

"Ye-es, I believe that was his name." She smiles warmly. "How did you know?"

"It seemed like the sort of thing he'd do, to do research on . . ." Trudy waves vaguely around her.

She hates to leave—stops at the gate looking back at the house dissolving into night, and comes away with the special darkness of the house at her back.

(.)

The name shouts in her head out of nowhere—a calligraph spelling it out in a single ribbon of gold. Then for a joke she visualizes the name in white fancy lettering swooping by her head and settling back on a black field in front of her like a movie title all sequined with bright rhinestone flashes.

Trudy left a note in Celada's pigeon box and arranged to meet him by the swimming school.

"I never did see your apartment."

Ballooning up in the dusk, sounding jaunty. His voice is oddly flattened out of doors.

"No one will!" she exclaims. She tosses a paper handkerchief into an ash can, on her way the two steps she says, "Let's walk. Tell me what you know about Sanglade."

She holds herself in her shawl, rolling along. He gesticulates high in the air, his voice rising and falling, looks like he goes on tiptoe.

It was built on a storied site. Hundreds of years ago, evidently, a spirit duplicator, or whatever you call them—a native dignitary with supernatural endowments—tracked an enormous buck through the woods and killed it with his arrow right there. Supernaturally indelible bloodstains on the rocks mark the spot where the animal died. Most likely there already was a spring, but it's more mythopoeic to think that the spring erupted from the rocks as the blood fell on the stone.

When the colonists came to Quadrigemina, and the woods were thinned and so on, it seems there was a lodge or pavilion built for those who wanted to come and take the waters. By the time Felix Houseman bought the land, whatever had stood there was not worth bothering with. The records make no mention of the spring, which must have run dry or changed its place by then.

Houseman was a world traveler who was looking to build a retreat, a place to entertain business partners, something like that. He'd made his fortune in mining. He didn't actually own any mines himself; like his father, he'd been a mining engineer, and an inventive one. He started a company to manufacture some of these inventions, but left the business responsibilities to his associates. By all accounts he was fascinated by gems and precious metals, but especially precious stone. When he chose to build his house here, he was spending most of his time in the so-called Far East. In honor of the stories told about the place, when he'd learned them, he decided to name the house Hartsblood. This was reputed to be drawn from the native name for the spring, which was—by coincidence—the identical pun on 'hart.' In a letter to a friend he'd joked he couldn't very well call it 'Houseman House.' The name change was his wife's idea.

At the time the place was built, Houseman was middle-aged and supposed by all to be a confirmed bachelor. Then he'd met and unexpectedly married a soprano named Clare Bruce on the Continent somewhere, and she came to take up residence in the house. When she first toured the place inside and out, she said she thought it was delightful but too masculine . . . "and that *name* . . ."

Happily it occurred to her that "blood" in French is "sang," so the glade of the blood of the hart became *Sanglade,* much to everyone's relief.

The house was designed by Vliance personally, one of only six houses whose blueprints had been drafted entirely in his own hand. It was to embody the exotic influences he'd imbibed during his own travels, with special emphasis on elegant efficiency, variation in levels, and, most importantly of all, the horizontal openness of floor plan, at least on the first level. Architectural experts concur that it was the opportunity to work extensively with rare stone and metal elements, reflecting his patron's geological propinquities, that drew Vliance to the project.

The workers likewise appear to have taken to the job with real gusto.

"Let me see," Celada pauses. The bobbing of those two long locks of hair, and the obscurity of his dark clothing against the dark background, make it seem as if his severed head were flying along on membranous wings against the purple sky.

The chimneys ran through the interior of the house to radiate heat, and, for much the same reason, the kitchen was situated in the basement. However, before the finishing touches had been put on the house, the kitchen flooded. In dry weather. They couldn't keep it clear of water, no matter what they tried or how hard they pumped, and suddenly everyone thought again of the spring. Perhaps they had broken it open somehow; certainly the water was very pure. Anyway, they couldn't find the source of the spring without tearing up the foundations. The kitchen never did get fully drained, and a new kitchen was set up in the Milk House.

"It's gone now." Celada turns to her a face covered in shadowy furrows. "But there used to be a horizontal dumbwaiter on a cable connecting the two buildings, so that food could be transferred to the house quickly in an insulated box. To spare the servants a slog through the rain or trudge in the snow. And so the food wouldn't arrive unpalatably cold."

Trudy smiles with closed lips.

"Do you think it's haunted?" her smile asks.

"If it isn't, no place is. Wait a moment please, I have to get my cello."

He ducks into a narrow brick building. A little cascade of firelight-colored glow in front makes an island in blue evening shade. A moment later Celada emerges, thanking some invisible person and rolling his shrouded cello on a rubber wheel. He's so large it looks no bigger than a guitar in his hand.

"Thing is," he says, "while there are ghosts in the house, it's as if the house were a spirit itself. Artificial intelligence. Edifice intelligence. The other ghosts are like its guests or disciples. Did you investigate the white room in the basement?"

She shakes her head.

"It's like an empty picture gallery down there. The flooded kitchen is adjacent to it. With the spring I suppose adjacent to that."

"Did anything happen in there?"

He shrugs happily and they walk a little further together in silence.

"No murders," he flashed.

"What was Houseman like?"

"I'd love to tell you," he says with a hasty glance at his watch, "but I do have to get to practice."

He points across his body at a building without a single lit window in it.

"Let's meet again, shall we? Just drop me a note!" He turns to go with a wave, and she watches him go with an expression of disgust that's near affectionate.

(O)

The show arrives, proclaimed wide and far. A conquistador puppet emerging from a sort of ambulatory hutch supposed to represent his gallant charger loudly soliloquizes in a muffled voice that's only occasionally intelligible:

"Our fine program . . .

". . . licensee owned . . .

". . . tell directors . . .

".... a star halloos ...

"... bar none!"

"... la sensación del titeres dar a luz para ..."

Big green paper Martians flap their tattered feelers at him.

"... el miserable del sol ..."

"... el misser a blay dell soll ..."

"... all go away, fast gone away ... oligoi phasgonoi!"

In the market place they set up their little show. C'est le tel chaud, put on a little show, puta la tela son ... their banner exhibits an elevated train running through a dismal little dell, with a solitary figure saluting it from the mouth of a salt mine (with posted sign).

The whole thing is in code, one supposes. Or to be more precise, it is in as many codes as could be managed.

V. runs the show, with the help of a puppeteer named Juan, and a shambling, overweight stage manager who goes by Gigante. He hired them in Leikin subdivision and put the materials, such as they are, together there.

The show begins; to the sound of a barrel organ and flutes, out comes a review of creatures no two alike, the puppets flimsy bodies ... alive and seeming to suffer—the stage the vessel of an exchange. The first part of the show involves full-sized marionettes interacting with W. in the story of the Headless Horseman. X. himself portrays the goblin, in a shredded cape with many layers and a ragged tricorn hat atop a fencer's mask, through which one can occasionally catch a glimpse of wildly exaggerated expressions covered with luminous paint. The hero is "Ixtabad Brane," an elongated puppet with pop eyes.

The action is confused and storyless, the performers, real and otherwise, act their parts with great verve, but the piece is a muddle from its haphazard beginning to its virtually imperceptible end. It's like an oppressive obscurity dimly glimpsed in sleep, and the poetry is bizarre and unsuccessful, intimating too much and saying too little.

The next act follows right away, even before the panting Y. has been able to quit the stage. There's a miniature squawk box up in the corner of curtains through which comes expository information most of which is too staticky for comprehension, something about processed milk and a speech or talk to be broadcast from the prison. Different voices say in succession: die musik hat schon wieder anfangen the music has already recommenced la musique a recommencé déjà la musica ya recomenzar. The next play is even worse.

A completely nondescript puppet, made of gray sacking with button eyes and a straight line mouth, is oysterizing particles of sunlight to make heliopearls.

A truly badly made puppet, like a wall-eyed owl with a pipe in its beak emerging from a baked potato, enters stage left and asks him, a short rough code warbled through a vocoder, "Have you b-been kneeling?"

The grey puppet looks dreamily into the distance, ". . . that makes me think . . ."

"Think what?" the owl asks solicitously, without moving at all, beak included. Maybe the operator took out his hand and fled. No one would blame him.

". . . I see my soul inside me, a whispering planet. But," he turns to the owl, his voice gentle, "I haven't been praying, if that's what you mean."

The owl chuckles, moving a little, unless it was lightly shaken by someone bumping the stage as they leave. "Heh-heh-heh."

"Like blacksmith's iron, we are shaped by blows," the gray puppet adds a moment later, hanging its head.

Image of a hammer descending slowly through a thick, clinging mist and a banner that reads 'confusion of ideas.' It

77

appears as a shadow projected behind them on the wall with barred windows.

The owl zigzags back and forth across some of the stage,

> "Awash in sea water,
> feet touch down.
> Planetary orienbation."

Then he rises up in place and an arc of water sprays toward his interlocutor from somewhere (the owl thing has no anatomy suitable for spraying it), who zips out of its range. The owl dries up, turns to the audience, and yodels "He's impissible!" and waits, even looking this way and that, for laughs that don't happen.

"B-but then I'm not really *good folks*," he adds waggishly.

A live piglet floats into view and a voice says, "I am the pig who kept his promises."

The owl, now sagging over the edge of the stage, mumbles something no one can catch.

The nondescript turns to the piglet and says, "Using a book as a drum, having studiously found your page, instead of reading it."

"Dirty pool," the owl says. "Even in my embty rebespectaclebility, I always did the assignments!"

Twilight . . . sunlight changes by increments to moonlight. On a bare stage, a puppet bird lies beside a pond, long neck stretched out on mud, crying out repeatedly as it dies. Then it just lies there in silence for many minutes.

A bumpkin marionette in a straw hat and overalls, with stubble browned onto his cheeks and white smears for eyes, bobs out from the wings, a long wheat glued to its lower jaw. After looking at the inert bird, he turns slowly to the audience and says, his voice breaking,

"God killed a crane."

The moon changes everything, as it rises. The scene shifts and another nondescript puppet, very large, is talking to the owl about swords. A steady evacuation of the theater is well underway.

"... but who can say why an instrument of destruction like that should have such magic power in it, why it should gather all colors to it?"

Deftly the nondescript draws her sword and addresses it.

"You have preserved me against enemies who seek my life, and buckled on, you shield me from shame ... and I am able to hold my head aloft like a courageous man, not hold it down low like a slave."

She remains there motionless for some time. The audience continues to leave.

"The sword is bread," she calls. "La espada es pan."

The moon says, "One."

"Hielo Apostolico," she whispers at her sword.

"Sisters of life," the awestruck owl says through a kazoo.

The piglet is illuminated in the back of the stage with a spinning colored light. "There were tears in my guns," he murmurs. "All the while."

It seems the sword-carrying nondescript is preparing to take revenge for some crime committed by the piglet or his party.

"Tears count," says the piglet.

"At the time, it was just grass for cows," the owl says with a flap of whatever its limb is supposed to be. It's so uncouthly put together.

"No!" the nondescript cries, turning, apparently, to the owl. "They are trespassers on earth, anywhere on the earth."

"The airline now bermits only a single carrion," the owl says, laughing. Its mirth goes on and on, the puppet wobbling crazily.

Against this storm of hilarity, the piglet says, with what is supposed to be a tormented, sleeptalking tone, the effect of which is largely undermined by the necessity of shouting over the owl's laughter, "... what is that? White faces? Buried in the snow?"

"B-buried in th'infinity room!" the owl wheezes.

The sword bearer answers the piglet calmly, owl notwithstanding, saying, "Death always says the same thing: *count on me.* But the ghost is the sun, what is—what it does by night *is* night *for it.*"

The owl is gasping and sighing, whacking the edge of the stage.

"My love," the sword nondescript goes on, "have you forgotten the fractured coupling that joins us? His deep sleep is a non-presence because he is not in the present—but in ... infinity!"

The first nondescript steps out from behind the second and advances to the apron as the lights sink and he is picked out by a follow spot. As she fades from view, the sword-bearing puppet says quietly, "He stands up and obscures the sun like a sugar blade."

Tears drip onto his face from above. He recites, in a gentle voice.

"Oh puppeter,
putting me right down there
in the weeping stone
of the airless catacombs,
Do I now meet the dawning of
the sunrise of our separation, pierced light
beneath the austere bones.
The gale of the house, it blows in the columned room,
pulping and tenderizing that face—
Oh,
The flower is fierce it wants to bite the air ..."

A faceless puppet in a distinctively plain, ordinary-looking outfit comes on stage. It advances on the nondescript puppet, who retreats in terror. With every step the plain-looking puppet takes, there is a cymbal crash offstage.

"You can't . . . !" the nondescript cries.

Black out.

It *still* isn't finished.

Z. appears, still wearing his costume although he has removed the hat and mask and wiped much of the paint off his face. He sets up a stool and, throwing a guitar around his neck, launches into an interminable song with an earnest political message, set to the monotonous accompaniment of two chords.

The song is terrible. The tent is long empty. When he's done, he simply goes backstage in silence.

"You're embarrassing yourself with that song. It's the worst. It'd kill the show even if the rest of it were the best thing ever. You've got to cut it."

"*No!*" B. screams, as if he were seeing his torturers returning.

He has to watch as audiences of his fellow citizens walk out again and again on the story of his arrest and torture, useless warning that you will recognize too late. He has to absorb the indifference of an audience that callously expects to be entertained, and struggle to present them with what they are by preference unaware that they know, by means of arts he can only manage with humiliating ineptitude, so incommensurate is his paltry talent to his desperate earnestness. He's a bad artist and he knows it. He stares, his face crumpling, eyes fixed. Frozen, he trembles as tears trickle down his cheeks. Staring at the other puppeteer, and trembling.

(.)

Celada's migraine speaks.

At the window. A band of pilgrims fills the streets. The streets bulge with pilgrims. The city is in the desert. Desert grit blows over it. The buildings are tawny—the sky mad blue.

The pilgrims adorn themselves in an unheard-of way, and familiar things are lost among the strange stuff they have on. They walk strangely. Their speech is a wailing that is strident without being mournful; the whites of their eyes startle. They raise an arm and shake bangles down from the width of their hands. Their shrine is invisible behind the densely crowded trees. Glisten slides over them like clear oil in the sun. Glass pilgrims, filled with colored gases that don't mix, divided into internal compartments and electrified by the sun. They wave their arms, playing with the glisten on them. Huge gobs of mercury they might be keeping as pets, slide to and fro on walking talking carpenter's levels.

Wailing voices lighten the air, adding a pale, clear light, the kind preceding a fall of snow. Their polished metal shrine has glass vanes or sails, and a coterie of bronze figures seem carved out of the gloom in the shade of the boughs of the trees; thoughtful, black, naked men with arms crossed or folded behind their backs, half-dematerialized into the dark, and fashioned for the eye by dim streaks of glisten. The pilgrims have brought offerings of glisten to recharge the shrine. They have a shining metal vessel vital missal sanguine blade a song a lay a steely brittle vessel brittle brittle tested mettle a saw blade prattle brass steely vital metal pedal medal modal idyll idle stop, stop. *Stop.*

Migraine. Each grain of hurt pile up. Don't rhyme. Don't alliterate. Don't assonate, or the other with the consonant, eternal consonation, to sound-with, soundwithing.

Lie down.

He still sees the window. Don't rhyme, don't set words off. Put them down one at a time, with care.

The black figures.

The pilgrims, their offering, the shrine.

There is a metal device, a container, ornamented container, they carry on . . . a plinth.

They are surrounded by men in long coats, with hats pulled down nearly covering their eyes.

Or are they men in generic down jackets, blue jeans, and baseball caps? But there they are, shooting from behind cars and out of windows, into the crowd. Screams erupt from the middle. The container carried by the pilgrims is damaged by gunfire. Pilgrims running in all directions—complete confusion. A few lie crumpled by the side of the road. The colored gases inside them turn drab, curdle, and blubber from transparent, elastic wounds, to form milky puddles in the street. A truck driven by beefy men in plain clothes pulls into the scene. On it there is a huge spinning gray egg that churns inside like an upset stomach, like his head so hot on top and empty and open on the sides. Drive in a spike for relief.

There's sunlight beaming down in octagons out of a white sky, and two orange lovers, spirits out of an old nudie movie, strolling in the exuberantly lush meadow. Her bangs toss in the wind. Silent music swells around them (sick feeling now) . . . the man wears a white shirt and blue jeans, has a moustache. She's wearing a sort of peasant print dress. They're kissing now, in a filmy close-up saturated with orange sunlight and a brown haze.

She's looking at him, at *him*, directly. The whites of her eyes blaze out of all that brown air. She talk-sings to him in a vocoder voice, her teeth blazing too sharp, too white and too clear in her dun face, and now the man has turned his face to Celada and speaks to Celada as well, his eyes and teeth fashioned from lunar glow like hers. Suddenly they're naked, she on all fours in front of the man. His head obscures the sun, solarizing the sky around it. Their brown and orange colors dim and their eyes and teeth fluoresce, both sing-talking in harmony to Celada with vocoder voices, fucking and smiling complacently, and glowering at him with paralyzing malice, making garbled threats. Celada's skin bristles in waves. He trembles.

He groans and raises his hands to his head without touching it, wanting to squeeze the skull until it bursts and imagining a relief so great he'd moan with bliss even with blood and brains oozing from splintered bone . . . knowing miserably that there will be no relief, just a begrudging, long-drawn ebbing out.

Ah, this complaining is a mundane task.

Warn him about what, or why threaten him?

The chairman of Ukehy. Who is he? He might be a massive man, like an idol ensconced behind his desk, brutal and crafty, with smoldering, beady eyes and skin like lead paste, or he could be an erect, spare, efficient man who stands at the window and peers out into the street. The sort of man who keeps a pair of small dogs and attends to their many needs on a minutely detailed schedule.

The family is jarred awake by a crash in the hall. The treasured heirloom clock or the Ming vase or the Fabergé egg lies shattered at the base of the stairs. Who did it? Poltergeist. The whole nation crumbled under a plague of poltergeists. Poltergeists can't be jailed, because they aren't citizens, have no bodies. They can't be deported either, because they aren't immigrants. They have no country of origin. Borders are nothing to them, not even the gauziest of veils to be brushed aside. Ruins everywhere, and nobody living, nobody with a name, can be found responsible, even as palaces spring up within fortifications like fenced-in garden plots. The rubble dwellers became silent onlookers, and then ghosts. Some knew and some did not know that they were no longer anything but images in a nightmare that also didn't belong to them.

Ukehy must have a chairman. Anyone? Perhaps the chair is enough. There is nothing so reassuring and quaint as a villainous leader. There is some leader or other, but he only coordinates what must happen. He did not invent Ukehy; Ukehy invented itself when the conditions were favorable. An evolution of death, mocking parody of the evolution of life.

(.)

She feels a thrill in her hair as she comes back into Sanglade, which is larger than she remembers and has an cool invisible shimmer just below the ceiling and down its sharp cutting angles. She came early, using her key. No sign of Dr. Camatsura. She's alone inside. I'm in possession, she thinks. The key is my token.

She stands in the open space toward the front of the house, breathing in its stillness. Following her eyes, she moves over to the staircase and gazes up its length. Now she climbs the stairs, which do not creak. She feels as though she's creaking inside. Not wanting to make much noise—although the sounds she does make seem to fall away into a more powerful, special silence—she ascends slowly. Actually she is relishing the savor of the house.

"Felix Houseman," she says to herself. "Clare Bruce Wilcox Houseman soprano, mining company, Vliance."

Dead wasps. Their houses, their music. Does it all deny her or is she supposed to deny it all, when there's no denial anywhere? Nothing but enchanted acceptance.

She comes up into the second floor. The air is soft up here. Soft rugs, spicy varnish smell, and none of the earwax smell of old houses. The stairs continue steeply up to a remote skylight.

The landing is a broad hallway. The ceiling is plaster with dark wooden beams gridding it, ornamented at the groins. The doors are reddish wood, black molding all around them with tiny square niches at the upper corners. From across the hall she can see there are tiny, light-colored things, designs maybe, or perhaps miniatures, set back in these deep niches, which are about three inches square. She'd have to climb a chair to see them clearly.

"How crazy," she thinks, "and great of them, to install decorations no one could see. Or see easily anyway."

She crosses to the glass-paned double doors. Through them, she sees daylight on the far side of a spacious, dark room. The doors are locked. While they aren't heavy, they don't rattle when she tries the white china doorknobs. Her key doesn't fit them. Without touching the door, she peers through the panes; the floor of the room beyond seems surprisingly bare, and there are many thick pillars standing in the room. They don't really harmonize with the structure of the house, which has its own unusual consistency. They seem more like objects on display.

To her left, the hall runs to the balcony, and to her right, it bends away out of sight. She goes to the right, because she wants to investigate a small skylight directly over this corner. The glass is frosted, so the corner is filled with snowlight that seems not to come from anywhere. A circular table is set into the corner, with a lamp on it, webbed lace, a pair of portraits in hinged oval frames. A narrow, tubular vase of dried blue flowers.

Gingerly, she picks up the portraits, feeling certain she is looking at Felix Houseman and Clare Bruce. The woman stands by a pedestal with an urn on it, wearing a white dress swathed over with gauzy scarves, one hand on her abdomen and the other resting by its tips on the pedestal. The backdrop is a gray blur involving vines and flowers. She is gazing past the photographer with an expression of dignified transportation, a solidly-put-together woman, with hair of no distinct color, complicatedly arranged. A blunt nose, her mouth is nicely shaped but charged with force. Trudy imagines it opening up, a little black spot in the picture and letting out a tone that would break the glass. Her eyes are small and seem, maybe it's the contrast of the picture, queer and pale.

Houseman's photo shows him sitting by a table in a wicker chair with a big haloing back. The light falls on the table before him and on the floor behind him, illuminating him indirectly from below, isolating him from the background, so that his image seems to hover in between. He's wearing a light suit with a vest, looking very relaxed, a cheroot between his fingers, legs crossed. The other hand seems to have been permitted to droop into his lap, holding a lump of stone. His face is a high oval, with hair maybe light brown, thick and fine, carefully parted. He has a catlike chin, and a frowsy moustache over his mouth. The nose is sharp, the brows are straight, and the eyes cool and narrow. Where Clare presents a kind of stolid dreaminess, he manages to appear shrewd and wry and neutral.

She's running out of time, and wonders if Dr. Camatsura has come yet. Giving herself permission to investigate just one more room, she goes around the bend in the hall and picks the middle door on the right. There are none on the left, just a wall with high transom windows in dark moldings, the wall itself covered with a web of coarse, purple-gray satin.

Trudy opens the door and pauses in the doorway. The room is deep and not too wide, lit also by skylights. A vast carpet, covered over in identical small medallions the size of a child's hand, fills the floor. The wallpaper is covered in a single repeated Chinoiserie figure, so that the whole room is like a grid of dots. Then kneel to look at the medallions—an Anatolian boteh pattern, scarlet with yellow flakes, and a blue-black outline, set into a dark burgundy field. From this lower point of view, the repetitions buzz out into a flattened, vibrating infinity, that takes in both walls and floor. Trudy finds she likes the feeling of dynamic extension it creates in her, as though the patterns were drawing her out, like taffy, through her eyes.

The door snaps downstairs. Footsteps on the hard floor.

"I'll visit the 'infinity room' again later."

Trudy shuts the door and hurries down to greet Dr. Camatsura. Going to her own table, she works steadily in the quiet.

After lunch, the flickering light in the room undulates. The leaves are unusually agitated. There must be a real wind kicking up. With a start, Trudy realizes they're birds, not leaves. A flock of birds is streaking past the window toward the ground in a long jet of living darts. On and on. And someone's in the doorway. She turns her head to look.

The impression was perfectly distinct. She had done more than merely notice something. Trudy stares at the empty doorway with an image both vague and vivid in her mind, wondering if there is a dim swatch of daylight reflecting from the wood at about the right height? She turns her head to and fro, keeping her eyes on the spot, and there does seem to be an indentation in the gloom suggesting a corseted waist, but nothing like a face. It occurs to her that glass doors throw off reflections which, as they are opened and shut, will travel along walls and ceilings. Are there any glass doors in line with that doorway?

The image, though, involved the folding of hands at waist level, and eyes. She, or it, receded into what they call the fabric of the house. Trudy imagines a transparent model of Sanglade, sleeved in a trembling forcefield, like water pouring in thin sheets down every surface and at certain times folding out to emit an approximation of a person. They circulate inside the envelope, which must be a spacious mansion from their point of view.

Trudy finds reference to the construction of Sanglade in an architectural anthology. Vliance didn't have much to say about it, but then he was never particularly open with the public.

> Some delay in transporting rarer materials to site, but less than feared. The weather excellent; the land cleared rapidly. We the object of considerable interest to committee of white hounds, who welcomed with snouting and wigging of pink ears. Foreman presented shovel and I broke ground at H. on third day April.
>
> Men threw into work with gusto. With haste but with care. Lanterns brought and pushed on into night, finishing around ten. Entire foundation excavated and concreted basement: fourteen hours.
>
> This typical at H. Entire period construction, omitting only finishing interior, twenty days. Rate of work diminished after that, at my insistence. No qualms re: handiwork. Frankly wanted to linger.
>
> For me, H. was by far most rewarding project.

Elsewhere she runs across a note complaining to the prefect about "vagrants" loitering in the vicinity of the house at all hours, and persistent trespassing. Attached records show that the intruders and loiterers, when accosted by police, invariably turned out to be men who had helped to build Sanglade. They kept coming back to admire it, or, as some said, simply to be close to it. They would return in the middle of the night, some still in pyjamas. They would come and stare at the house until someone moved them along.

(.)

There is a length of Agua Seca that is virtually ceilinged by projecting rooftops, dusty and shady, where Celada likes to stroll, haphazardly expatiating on his favorite subjects with Dr. Crapelin.

Celada: "While I admit that religion is rather silly—but show me what there is that's of human origin that's not marked by silliness? How is capitalism, for example, not completely silly? If silliness were a criticism with any real weight at all, the world would already be far more rational . . . Anti-space, anti-time, are as logical as anti-matter and the retrotemporal particles—or another space and time—so how can time end?"

"You like to start at the end," Dr. Crapelin says smiling, hands behind his back, looking down at the ground. He places his emphasis heavily and deliberately.

"Well, but doesn't what you think, or perceive, or . . . doesn't that have to do with the end you're looking from?"

Dr. Crapelin dodges a boy on a tricycle, sidestepping into a blast of daylight that half washes him out.

"Problems of subjective and objective are in part a consequence of the assumption that the subject, or soul, is *in* the body, bottled up in the skull, or the heart, for example."

He lights a cigar, and the smoke fumes around him like threads of daylight, making his outline even less distinct.

"If we grant, instead, that we are linguistic elementals or processes—and I mean 'process' as in a kind of a growth, a protuberance, or excrescence, or a shoot—and if also we grant that language is neither inner nor outer, but sticking out, maybe half in and half out . . . or a third and two-thirds, what does it matter? What matters is that the language is lying across the line, on one side of which is inner and on the other side of which is outer—you see I mean the 'inner human being' and the 'outer human being.' If that is the case, then who we are couldn't be inside us or outside us."

Dr. Crapelin stops and turns toward Celada. The daylight streams over him and he looks like overexposed, colorless film.

"Alternately," he says, putting his left hand into the inside right pocket of his jacket and resting it there, "we can speak of expressions, in which what is deep emerges or protrudes from the surface, or of situations that produce selves, perhaps by fusing, cophasing, or interlocking with a protuberant language process."

"Like a neurotransmitter?"

"Like anything, like rice and beans. In any case, we could account thereby for possession, speaking in tongues, prophetic or mediumistic clairvoyance, and for ghosts, demons and the like. These things can all be said to be real . . . I emphasize *said* . . . without entailing the concomitant notion of supernatural dimensions in defiance of what knowledge of physics, etc., that we now possess. The stories we all know, involving ghosts and other spectral events, are not 'just stories.' They are structures or structuring instances, situations. Of course, they are also 'just' stories, as stories of *justice*. They are not exactly psycho-logical"

—a word he would always pronounce in a particular and suggestive way . . . A cloud drifts across the sun, and, in its increasing shade, Dr. Crapelin gradually materializes again—

"or folkloric in origin, as they are not effects of such causes but belong themselves to the echelon of causes. They are—they are—it is not necessary to read them that way. They can be far less accidental, nor archetypes, nor in fact representations of any kind whatever, although they—the situations—of course may be represented. They arise, a fortiori, precisely at those points at which someone has trouble drawing a clear distinction between being and representation."

"What I mean," Celada says, always just on the brink of getting lost, which is, for him, often a pleasant sensation, "is that we are accustomed to think of language as the instrument of consciousness, whereas it may be that language and consciousness are one and the same. As some people say ghosts are energy fields dissociated from bodies, but the ghost is not energy, not some thing with the name energy, while it is 'energy'—the word, the name itself. Does that make sense?"

"You find yourself wondering then if energy is energy, or quote-unquote 'energy' *is* energy. Are the ghosts transcendent?"

"Yes," Celada says with conviction. "They triumph over death. Like artists."

"Even the ghostly Ukehy?"

"They are death," Celada says after a moment.

A society of police spies and businessmen, he thinks. Existing only for itself. But then again, all good things exist only for themselves, don't they? You don't explain the value of a painting or a novel by referring to something else, the real value, you must value them in themselves. But do those people, whose decisions affect us so totally, and who are so difficult to affect, have any values we can share? So do you get up on the winners by defying them to the death like Amiri Baraka and run the risk that you are only inflating yourself by pretending to wrestle with a giant that takes no more notice of you than it does the fly in the corner, or do you reflect their smugness back at them by insisting the hardships they inflict on everyone else is really hardening up a generation of losers to fly at their throats?

They will bring ruin on themselves. That's the universal anesthetic. What if they don't? Or if they bring ruin on everyone else too? What if a few destroy themselves or are sacrificed, and the rest are always able to buy more time?

Walking again in silence, they come to a place where the houses pull back a little on one side to make room for a tree. A flock of birds sing cacophonously from the branches, a sound like glittering foam.

Celada says: "I also wanted to ask you about . . . what could be called the chronically overlooked question of time, and whether time, as an indispensable dimension of experience, or aspect of consciousness if you prefer, is so demonstrably uniform that one can say with certainty that no one could, for example, observe events across more radical intervals than the ones we're ordinarily better acquainted with.

"Of course—" he adds hastily, thinking he spots a bit of impatience or distaste on his mentor's face, "this is only a possibility, and one for which there is more or less no evidence."

Dr. Crapelin, his voice emerging from the tintinnabulation of the calling birds, asks, "What, and where, would 'evidence' be, in this instance? Unlike yours, my hypothesis is not scientistic, nor is it an expression of principle, or even probability. It is a fantasy, but my earlier hypothesis is *not.*"

"What's the difference between a fantasy and a hypothesis?"

But suddenly Dr. Crapelin turns and disappears into one of the doorways, which here open directly onto the street, with unseemly haste, as though he'd caught sight of an enemy, someone absolutely to be avoided.

Celada, not unused to Dr. Crapelin's abrupt departures, walks to the corner and passes a ring of students. In passing he catches

"How's life treating you?"

"I live like . . ."

That's all he hears.

How would I answer that question? he wonders. Celada gropes for words that would mean at once a patient in a mental hospital and a prisoner, and some other thing—an idiot, a man stuck waiting somewhere or for himself to do something else.

She's already there, by the fountain on Espada Nieve, clear in a thick dark outline daubed on the air, watching the water vibrating seriously, as though it offended her. They greet each other murmuring, still a bit dazed and drifting in their own thoughts.

"What do you know about Houseman?" she asks.

Her tone is a little funny.

"Not much, but that was typical. Nobody seems to have spent much time with him all at once, or gotten to know him well."

"Did he die in the house?"

Celada glances at her.

"No," he says. "He was not much of a mountaineer, but every other year or so he would climb something somewhere. He died on a mountain, in a fall. In the Far East."

"How old was he?"

"Forty-five."

He says it as though he found the number surprising.

"Is he buried around here, or over there?"

"They never got him. He fell into an inaccessible place. If he was above the permafrost line and not too exposed . . ."

He widens his eyes at her.

"If you're interested in him," he goes on easily, "you might look him up in Driscoll's manuscript—you know that? That manuscript?"

She shakes her head.

"It's a book about the family that was never finished—the book I mean. The manuscript is part of the collection."

"At the house?"

"It should be."

"I'll look it up."

"Not much of it left, I'm afraid."

"Driscoll's it's called?"

[The manuscript is short and fragmentary, typed on two dozen sheets of onionskin paper, with a few neat emendations and interpolations in faded fountain pen.

Trudy will find this:

. . . Felix Houseman was a man who never was all there. Judicious, his spontaneities originated deep within him. He was private without being at all secretive; the analogy to buried treasure in his case made itself. Widely traveled and traveling, hence unable to develop any sedentary hobbies, he had none of the substantive traits that normally go into making up what is, rather fatuously, understood to be a man's character, so like handles, so like available labels. No one, Clare Bruce, perhaps, being an exception in this as in so many other ways, seemed to be able to address him in his native language, to converse with him *viva voce.*

Marriage made, seemingly, no difference in his life. He continued to travel as before, seldom saw Clare, who accepted his near perennial absence without any too demonstrative dismay. One imagined he'd warned her. The servants observed the voluminous correspondence that passed between them, with letters from Houseman coming nearly every day. It was invariably remarked that the house was ever electrified by his return, and a Miss R——, once a maid beneath Sanglade's eaves, commented she thought he'd tended to stay away as long as he could, and that he habitually wore the aspect of someone who'd been not unhappily embarrassed to be caught falling back again into some harmless vice, on these sojourns at the house. He would grow downright "bashful" at the joy his presence brought out in his wife, although this perhaps was, in truth, regret. But, and all those in any way connected or familiar with the menage commented on this, Houseman was, without fail, positively deferential to his wife, and plainly loved her without reservation, albeit in his own way.

. . . It seems the both of them had such force of character that their presence in the house was immediately apparent

95

even from a distance. If reports are to be credited, one would know if either of them were at home with merely a look in the direction of Sanglade, and seemingly by way of no sign apart perhaps from an imaginary sort of "hum."]

"Where was Clare Bruce buried?" Trudy asks, sitting down on the fountain's edge.

"I never could find that out . . . I suspect she may have wanted it that way—burial in secret, or something . . . After she died, Sanglade—"

Trudy nearly flinches. She wishes he wouldn't say the name aloud.

"—passed to her uncle, who maintained it for several years without getting around to visiting it, and finally sold it as part of a larger liquidation. I guess he had to get his hands on money in a hurry. So it passed, with all the furniture and everything, into the hands of his business partner—wonderfully named Enceladus Fletcher—who bestowed it entire, along with some adjoining properties, on the preservation society a few years after that."

The preservation society was whipped up by the school and staffed with professors when it became clear that the house was going to become available.

"Did she die in the house?"

"Mrs. Houseman? Well, yes, she did die in the house . . ."

Celada looks down at his feet, evidently uncomfortable with the topic.

"Did you know, she actually wore out two pianos?" he asks abruptly.

"Wore them out?" Trudy asks, generously taking his cue to change the subject.

"Was she still performing in public? Or did the wonderful Felix stop her?"

"I don't know. I don't think so, but then she may have stopped on her own. I know that she fell out of favor . . . I wish I could remember more."

He rubs his head.

"After about fifteen years she was rediscovered, I do remember that. And she performed a few times more before she died."

[The manuscript comes in a box with a number of other relics, including a small photo album labeled "Felix Houseman." The label might be in his handwriting. The album is filled to overflowing with photographs of fires, mostly campfires, and nearly all either shot or cropped to exclude everything but the fire. Here and there, a bit of a foot or a pot or something of the sort could be seen, the back of a fireplace. These colorless, wispy, slightly time-lapsed fires are like crystallized vapors, the photographs have an understated beauty that only cumulatively affects her, and in proportion as she adjusts to the eccentricity of the idea.

Also in Driscoll:

After her husband's death, Clare Houseman no longer gave music lessons to the local girls. She did not abandon music, and passers-by often remarked her singing to the empty house. In her latter days, there was a revival of interest in the long-lost chanteuse, and she was invited to perform at the Calliope Society festival. Her voice was by then only a remnant of what it had been, but even this was, by all accounts, astonishingly powerful. Armand Pressburger noted "one detected the singer she had formerly been, still alive inside her voice."]

"She wasn't that old, though, was she?"
"In her early fifties."

"Was it disease?"

He shrugs.

"Something sudden. They found her on the long staircase."

The steps flash in Trudy's mind.

"At the bottom?"

"That's right."

"Do you think she fell?"

"No, no question of a fall," he says with assurance. "She was found seated."

He turns from her and scans the crowds, his face screwed up against the brilliancy of the sun. She's wondering if he's protective of the story, as if he doesn't want to share his special thing.

"One interesting thing was," he abruptly begins again, without turning to face her, "that she was holding an empty vial in her hand. There was something dark, like ink, they said, in the vial, but they tested it and found it was just water."

"Dark as ink?"

"Yes. It was the doctor who realized it was water from the spring."

"In the basement?" Trudy snaps out of something with that question.

"You've never tried it?" he asks her, smiling ironically.

They have been walking, and stand now in front of the gate. Trudy looks up at the house. Celada looks at Trudy.

William greets them briefly, gliding toward the Milk House.

"I thought maybe this might interest you as well," Celada says, pulling from his satchel a scrap of typewriting. He seems oddly hesitant to give it to her, but then he becomes resolved. "I copied it from one of Cobet's books a long time ago. *The House of Triumph* I think it was. It mentions the house."

He doesn't say Sanglade this time, just "the house." Did he

see her flinch before? She wonders if, instead, he too is self-conscious about naming the house in its presence.

(..)

The typed pages, hairline thin letters, she reads at her table, in Sanglade. Up at the top stands the title: *The Chapter House at Pell.* Then this excerpt:

> We approached the house through the meadow, and my heart sank as we drew near. The place had a dire and an imprisoning air about it.
>
> I had seen pictures of the house, taken from divers angles, and found they didn't agree. It was hard to understand, studying first one, and then another, that they were all photographs of the same building. From the meadow, it appeared to be a plain, unadorned box. It was narrow, dingy, and low, resisting the meadow and the trees. Viewed from the road, it was a looming, angular, drawn-up looking place, that put me in mind of the prow of a docked ship. Overlooking it from the belfry of the church, the disposition of the trees seemed to break it up into a collection of smaller houses. It called to mind, with persistency, the somewhat ungainly image of someone unpacking witches' hats, pausing now and then to perch one of them atop the lids of the hatboxes. When, however, I had an opportunity to study it, I found the floor plan surprisingly simple. The chapter house was a rectangle, with a gap at the northeast corner, a disproportionately small atrium, and an extension that ran along one side.
>
> But no matter what aspect it might wear, and no matter from what angle I might draw near to it, the house never failed to impose the same dismal impression upon me. It was soiled by layer upon layer of bad feelings, which, when taken together, lodged in one like a mood of final defeat. Looking at it, the full burden of the phrase 'ill-fated' struck me, sensibly. I imagined it would dirty me somehow to go inside, where I might breathe invisible particles of something mummified, long dead, and wretched. Emotionally, the chapter house was a cesspool—an old one and a full one. When I first saw it, the sky only just managed to illuminate the blanched dullness of the stone and

wood. The sun seemed robbed of its power to summon color from any object associated with the chapter house. Even my green jacket seemed to grow drab as I ventured inside the walls.

No greater contrast could be imagined than that created by a comparison of Pell with Sanglade. It was dazzling. The only similarity between the two houses was perhaps in that the outline of the facade was elusive. The effect in Sanglade's case, however, was playful, rather than sulky. One's eye liked to roam around there. But Sanglade's perfections could be almost cowing, like the presence of an uncannily beautiful child. One fears for that child, or fears one will love it too much.

Trudy flips the papers, although their transparency shows her there is nothing written on their reverse sides. Is that all? Or is he stringing her along . . . ?

Notes notes notes, and diaries. Celada has read every book ever published entitled *Diary of a Madman*, and nearly all of them were disappointments. The 'real' ones are never crazy enough, and the invented ones always try to tell some other story instead of sticking to impressions. The impressions are all that matter; they are the particular adjustments that make it possible to adopt the mad point of view.

An epidemic of the writing of *mad diaries.* You read one, go insane, start writing a mad diary of your own, someone else reads that, goes crazy, starts writing, and so on.

Celada knows Trudy keeps a diary, and entertains a scenario in which both her diary and his are found by a third party, years from now.

Yes, someone (claiming to be) connected to Chthethostoa says, persons of those names and descriptions were in attendance then, but there is only written evidence of their existence. No photos, no recordings, no movies. No physical remains.

Shots of the discoverer of the diaries going in and out of buildings, walking the streets alone, sitting thoughtfully by a window. She mulls over the possibilities:

a) Face value, Celada wrote the diary attributed to Celada, and Trudy wrote the diary attributed to Trudy.

b) Trudy wrote her own diary in earnest (or as a personal fantasy) and wrote Celada's diary as a work of fiction. Her Celada might correspond closely to the actual Celada, or might resemble him only very superficially, perhaps in name only.

c) Vice-versa. Celada wrote both texts, and Trudy is the voiceless one.

d) Each wrote the other's. Either in coordination, as an exercise or something, or spontaneously, and without the other's knowledge. Or perhaps one undertook the other's diary, the other found out, and replied in kind (with or without alerting the other).

e) They collaborated in writing both diaries. Both wrote both.

f) An unknown third party wrote one, and either Trudy or Celada, or both, wrote the other as a reply, or coincidentally. and (hopefully finally)

g) An unknown third party wrote both diaries, either attributing them to their putative authors or simply using their names and descriptions. Unless, perhaps, this nameless third party had invented both Trudy and Celada as he or she would have invented any fictional characters, without being aware of the actual existence of these people, and the whole thing is a frantically unlikely coincidence.

How often, he wonders, do imagined things turn out to be real somewhere? Are there real Ukehy somewhere, for example?

There is a reputedly haunted house at Pell, and the photographs of it are pretty well described in that passage. Will she try to find *The House of Triumph?* Or did she know whose work that scrap of writing really was the moment he handed it to her?

(O)
and sunrise and
sunrise and
sunrise and
sunrise and sunrise, each superimposed on the other. The only fact of the day is the moment, peeled down to its bare skeleton, that the first point on the sun's circumference punctures the horizon and hits him like a laser. The sun rises bald and naked, like a newborn, but about half or three-quarters of the way up all at once he can see its lustrous brunette fringe, the wafting locks of silky hair, the outstretched arms, and the billowing white dress.

He buys a newspaper at the stand on one side of the square, folds it under his arm and crosses back to the tents, a corncob pipe in the corner of his mouth. He can never entirely manage to clean away all his stage makeup. A few smears are always left. Above him the sun floats in the sky, like she's face down in the water, and he's on the bottom looking up. He is always in her sight, at her feet. He glances up at her and smiles formlessly around his pipe, in a brief and private instant of blissful collusion.

Into his squat behind the tent: no door, one room, concrete floor, one big square window in the cinderblock wall, no glass, no curtain. One square table in front of the window and one chair in front of that, facing the window, where he makes the puppets for the show. He's making one now. It has a distinctively plain, everyday sort of outfit on. He sits in the glare of the sun, daubing paint on the lumpy, bland and smiling face, even though no one is liable to see its expression from the audience. The brush starts to shake, and he has to proceed very slowly to avoid blotting the features too much. Slower and slower. He is breathing through his mouth. He inhales some smoke and coughs. He puts the pipe aside. He glances up to the sun, still floating there, for reassurance.

A recent performance of El Miserable del Sol began with a few very simple, childlike song-and-dance numbers brutally interrupted by these puppets, who beat and tortured the others for an hour of nothing but screams and sobbing and moans, with snapping twigs to represent the breaking of bones for example, and would have gone on longer if the theater hadn't already been fifty-five minutes empty.

A woman enters the room; she runs the grocery on the square and sells him most of his food. She feels an uncertain combination of pity and desire for him and has brought him a mesh bag with three oranges. They talk amiably, she standing by the table, he sitting. The oranges nestle incongruously among the glue, wire, and twine. He is friendly and even flirtatious in a gruff sort of way. She fondly likens him to a bear in his cave and lays her hand on his shoulder.

Very calmly he puts the puppet he's working on down. He glances at her hand on his shoulder, hearing her continuing to talk pleasantly to him without following what she says because there's another . . .

With a slight turn of his head, he glances out the window at the sun, which is now immediately outside the building. It's so close that her hair is brushing the outer wall, and her transparent hands are sliding into the room just starting to rumble.

He's been walking directly toward her for a long time, eyes riveted on the sun rolling along the horizon, virtually horizontally, arms outstretched as always. Snow pours into his face from over her shoulders. The fluttering snow augments her light, the flakes are transformed into chill embers, and as the billows strengthen, pushing hard against him and getting thicker all the time, that gush of snow admits more and more of her heatless illumination which propels the snow—

The woman from the grocery is beginning to notice how still and abstracted he is. This is, she realizes, because he's choking. He staggers to his feet and claws at his throat. She calls for help and grabs at his hands without any clear idea of what to do. Sweat bursts from all his pores and his clothes are immediately soaked with it. He feels limp, although there's a kind of wild pulsation she can sense inside him, in his bones maybe. His knees won't lock.

The wind splits the edge of his right hand, held up to screen his eyes, and blood oozes out, flattens into a paste matted with snow and spatters and thickens on his face. It's a relief, as if his hand had been intolerably swollen. The blast scours the tissue from his bones. With a sigh, he folds into a drift of sharpened snow his skeleton clean and cold. Snowflakes bristle inside his long bones scrubbing the marrow out with a harsh tingling sensation. With an unbearable relief, his ligaments finally give way and the bones tumble apart in sections and pieces. The mandible comes loose from the skull with a gulping sound and lopes down the snowbank like a broken hoop. All the while, her arms arching over the ground are curving in toward him again, where the heap of him lies the foremost part of a comet with a long tail of red debris streaked back in the white.

The woman from the grocery has him leaning, his head and shoulders against the wall in a white square of sunlight. His face has a weird epileptic dignity, though sweat trickles from his scalp.

El Gigante takes the puppet head from C.'s table and flourishes it at the crowd outside like a ventriloquist dummy.

"El Miserable del Sollll . . . The finest in *entertainment!*"

(.)

An intimidater hovers over an intersection a few blocks away. Trudy glances up at it with hatred. What's it watching? Is it watching anything? They fly them low, whoever they are, just because they can, to show us how little we mean to them. It's great, they can step on a whole neighborhood at once, rattling windows and waking up babies. A prowl car oozes by with warbles and chirps, goosing pedestrians with the sound. Preceded by a spoiled-brat bawl, the police van slithers up behind it. You see them hanging around everywhere now, just parking with their headlights splashed across a sidewalk, the front of a house. They shine their lights right into the windows, blind everyone who goes by.

Celada used to complain about the construction in his neighborhood.

"My whole neighborhood is blasting with this carcinogenic noise," he would moan, rubbing his forehead. "I can feel the vibrations in my bed when I try to sleep. It's like contact poison."

Celada referred to these instruments of urban torture collectively as *disruptors*, and then Trudy had suggested disrupt*ers*, since the "-ors" ending sounds a bit too grand. He'd agreed, laughing heartily. He had a funny laugh, a little like a clown's. Shortly thereafter she'd coined the word "intimidater." She couldn't talk with anyone else about that kind of thing. No one else she knew liked to play with words much.

Walking home one evening along the outskirts of the park, suddenly a van with tinted windows zips up alongside her. It keeps pace with her while she's walking, the entire length of the park. The stillness of the houses and the emptiness of the unused sidewalks becomes ominous. When she turns into a side street, the van disappears with a whoosh.

A few weeks later, a black-and-white had darted in on her as

she was walking along the same route, in keeping with both rule
one, use of vehicles to intimidate pedestrians, and rule two,
employment of surprise. A light plays over her and a voice
squawks from behind the radiator grill, demanding to know
what she is doing.

"Going home," she replied matter-of-factly. Trudy could
stand completely still.

"buck What were you doing here tonight?"

"Walking."

". . . buck The reason I stopped you was because you were
making what you call furtive movements you were moving
furtively."

Apparently Trudy is supposed to answer this somehow.

"I was going home," she says simply.

"buck You know the park closes at sunset."

This is a lie. People can be seen doing things in the park at all
hours. There are no posted opening or closing times. In the
silence that follows this lie, Trudy imagines a greasy look slide
up and down her person. She holds her hands relaxed, and
plainly empty, at her waist.

"Oh, it does? I didn't know."

"buck Yeah. So do me a favor and walk outside the fence,
understand?"

"Just right around here?" she asks flatly, pointing to a gap in
the fence a few feet away.

". . . buck Yeah, right around there."

The street is empty when she emerges from the gap. Looking
around she watches the car crawl up under a railway trestle and
beam a spotlight into its groin. The car eats bats, and huge rats
bloated with garbage.

"That's just police," Celada had said later, with a flip of his
hand. "Not Ukehy."

"What's oo-kay-hee?"

"Oh, didn't you know? They're the 'they' everyone talks about. They're *them*, behind what-have-you."

"You mean like spies?"

"Secret police. *Open* secret police," he says, holding up a finger. "Everyone knows about them, subconsciously. In fact no one has to be told about them, because you know they exist. Immanently. I don't mean by intuition, but because they're like . . . what's . . . drawn in the spaces between things. Like a negative image."

"Implied?"

"Exactly."

The implication is conveyed by a professional sneer and a look of supercilious rejection that wants to rediscover itself in other faces preparatory to gang-up. It's a look from over the wall of the impregnable fortress of their hostile ordinariness, and majorness, and she would look them back squarely and say, if not quite aloud, not quite silently, either, and with equal parts weariness and anger:

"Yes. All right. Pretty scary. I'm a nigger. I'm stupid. I'm dirty. I'm ugly. To *you*.

"What are you? What do you do that's so worthwhile? Because from my point of view I can't see what's so amazingly worthwhile about you. I *am* afraid of you. Yes, you've done that. But then I'm not the one who's hiding. That's you. Why do you hide from me? What makes you think you can?

"Nigger . . . stupid ugly and dirty crazy, bad . . . the oldest and the most boring of words. You'll sit back there behind your ramparts and your walls and your secrecy lapping at those words forever like a stale old salt lick, chewing and chewing that same gravelly as the whole world falls to pieces and all the lights go out for the last time. And do *you* ever get sick of it? Don't you ever get tired of that nasty taste in your mouths and get the urge to ask innocent questions? Or is it lotus flower, turning your brains to mush while you love it more and more?"

Trudy crosses Plaza de Invierno and takes a wobbling side street that curves out of sight, lined with crooked houses that jut across the pavement or hang back, creating cavernous gaps. This is one of many abandoned areas in the modelsuburb. Most of these houses are untenanted even by squatters, there being fewer people in Cimelia Cisterna than there used to be. There used to be much more money, if not much more variety. Then the crash, and, some things changed. People couldn't afford cars after that, and the modelsuburb was built around cars—without them, every journey suddenly became significantly longer. Everyone who stayed had to move in closer together, or use the handful of overcrowded buses that still run.

The sound of hissing weeds. Then the air shudders, and suddenly there's an intimidater's metallic gargling in the sky. Plenty of fuel for them. Trudy ducks into the shell of an entryway and climbs a few steps toward the elevated front door, using the stone rims of the steps rather than trust to the fibrous gray wood. The gargle flaps gracelessly by and the building trembles, the sound jolting and fading awkwardly. Trudy is invisible to it, sheltered beneath the roof of the deep porch. When the intimidater is gone, she descends carefully and checks the street in both directions for prowl cars.

Now her route follows a guttered alley between a brick building and a plank fence. Her face in the black windows. Turning the corner, she walks up a short cement ramp to a sliding barn door, which is a little ajar, looks around, then waves her hand in front of the door. A voice greets her quietly inside, and she goes in. Standing just within and to one side of the door, she is taking a parcel from her bag and giving it to someone with a ragged sweater sleeve. She gets back a packet of tape cassettes, which she shoves well down in her bag and drags other stuff over before she snaps the snaps.

Celada jerked the crumbs off his plate into the sink set plate down heavily on the dresser turned back to retrieve his coffee with a loud sniff. Dunked the rest of the coffee from the bottle on the little gas ring into his mug added a spoon of sugar from a jar and stirred it around making a noise like a streetcar going by. Clang clang clang.

He clears his throat in the empty apartment. He has an open book crushed in his armpit, carrying it into the other room.

A sentence like this one, with respect to a house supposed to be haunted: "The ghost was reputed to shoot from the alcove, cross the master bedroom in a flash, and thrust its cold, thin arms under the covers at the sleeper."

This is the type of absolutely incomprehensible statement that characterizes the haunted house in the literature. It seems bizarre to take something like that, which could only be described as an entirely unique experience, and turn it into an example of typical goings on. The gap there between the particular and the general is so enormous that it creates a charge, a charged particle . . .

. . . a negatively charged particle: let's call it an *isolaton*. Pronounced ICE-oh-l'ton.

(Celada never does anything because he's too busy trying to solve the problem why he never does anything, as if he's going to forge ahead finally by means of collateral construction.)

Like the gluon, the isolaton is its own anti-particle.

Go to the window.

a bird singing in the empty street

note note

high low

109

if the sound were visible it would look like a Chinese
character

God mutters something through this bird right
now

He must, it's telling him, synthesize the isolaton . . .
accelerate the isolaton, raising its energy level, to see what will
happen. Will it change? The machine would involve let's say a
book—its age might be a factor—about haunted houses, set into
a metal frame and exposed to . . . a field, he'll figure out which
kind later.

The book is exposed to a field, and this, à la Faraday, should
cause the isolaton generated by the disparity between general
and particular in the book to accelerate out of the book and to be
captured in a vat of glue or something.

Some days he staggers home hamstrung, feeling useless,
prematurely old, hyperbolically rejected . . . That humiliation
rises from memory again as he lies in bed. Don't think it, he tells
himself, and don't not think about it. Just roll on it, like a clear
rubber ball on a water, until it's worn itself down. It's physical,
like nausea. You just ride it out. Never open it.

The book won't open, it sits across from the reader.

The reader says: "Tell me a story, book."

The book says: "No." (Wiggling sassily in its seat.)

"Why not?"

"I don't want to. I don't feel like it."

"I'll come back later, then, when you're more in the mood."

"No, read me now!" the book says, with a perverse glint in its
something.

"Read what?"

. . . written in blood, everywhere he sees the word flash at
him

COWARD . . . COWARD . . .

Celada can do anything he wants to, and he does practically nothing. And yet he is always busy, as though he had a demanding job in another dimension. It's because countless things happen in his imagination. He's always astonished when people ask him how things have been going or what's been up, because nothing's been up, and yet so much has been going on in his imagination.

There is something else, which may have been a real tour de force of his imagination, or not imaginary at all. One of his many little projects had been the exploration of Sanglade, last year, shortly after the fizzling out of his romance with Trudy.

Now entirely unused for any purpose, the conservatory is a separate structure attached to the outside of Sanglade. It consists of a metal frame, painted white, and many panes of frosted glass of a murky gray color. As ivy has overgrown it, the conservatory has become a sinister heap of dark flakes that shiver in the sun. Sepulchral old trees and a trellised, ivy-fleeced wall shade it. In the little enclosure before the door, there is a paved space where one can find a frayed wooden table, stacks of red pots, rusted clippers and weeding tools, an orange spade with a disintegrating handle, leaf litter.

The door opened reluctantly, seizing the floor more than once. Celada left it drawn back, because the carpet of ivy on the glass roof, obscured nearly all the nickelly sunlight of that day.

The air was rusty in there. The light threw a faint shadow on the bricks, on the gray, concrete floor, scratched with rust where steel tables had once stood in ranks. A broad sideboard ran at his right, sacks of potters' earth stacked under it, strewn with pots and planters trailing wilted rags of long-dead plants.

His feet rasped against the floor. The only other sound was the regular interrogative call of a bird somewhere in the vicinity. To his left, the sullen gleam of a steel table, slotted and indented for irrigation. A faucet above it. Celada glanced at the rear wall, imagining it opening directly into the house by means of a grand staircase, and people descending in ball gowns and archaic finery. He imagined rows of orchids, and, incongruously, a butterfly collection in a wooden case down in the water too—why not? The steel was bare, with a crust of dried green scum along the edge.

A silhouette stood between him and the door. It was so close that, when he turned, he was nearly looking down at it.

The silhouette had been a woman's. Nearly at his eye level, the bun in her hair was frizzy. The egg-shape of the head, the ears against it, the taper of the side of the face—but nothing of the eyes or features. The slender neck and the shoulders, the hands apparently at the sides, a dress.

He swung wildly away, around it, and reeled out the door backwards, tripped and fell without feeling the jolt, then scuttled until the enclosure stopped him, all the while shouting with fear. He imagined the silhouette advancing to the threshold to look at him, and he might have seen that. He rolled sideways and lunged to his feet, dashed onto the lawn, staring around himself at the sunlight and the trees, the familiar surroundings.

He hasn't been back since, although the thought of the shadow no longer really scares him. Embarrassment, as much as fear, keeps him from going back.

No. He is really afraid. Not exactly of the figure, but of the stealth, the silence, the suddenness, with which it had appeared, and which seemed likely still to be invisibly there. And worst of all he had looked like a coward—been a coward!—in full view of the house.

((..))

One of the puppeteers, a slender cigarette dangler in a knit vest and a doily cap, a scurf of beard around his chops, sips from his beer bottle daintily. He can't keep ordinary jobs because he can't be bothered to keep track of other people's business for them. He stalks past D.'s squat on long asparagus legs and stops a moment.

Glancing in the door, he sees E. sitting on a canvas folding chair looking at someone standing across from him in the thin shadow at the corner of the room.

"I thought I saw a boy in here with you."

F. looks at him steadily, his face blank. "Perhaps he's still around here somewhere," he says without emphasis.

"You didn't see him?"

"I'm not sure." G. pivots and picks up a hand mirror from the table.

"Light blond hair, nearly white—maybe ten or eleven? Dark skin though."

H. shrugs and puts on his makeup. In the mirror his eyes have a sinister, half-asleep look.

Trudy had trouble sleeping last night. When she knows she's alone, she drops down onto a sofa in one of the parlors set aside for students. It's time for her to be going home, and she waves to each of the people she met at the conference, who are all together in a clearing; she looks at each face in turn, mentally saying goodbye one by one. After a while, the road becomes a remembered route through buildings; she climbs in a window to find a pit at her feet. She knows she came this way before, on her way to the conference, but she doesn't remember how she did it. She doesn't remember the conference. There's another window separated from this one by a buttress with an alcove in it—she could swing out over the pit, put her foot in the alcove, transfer herself into it, and then swing out to the next window, but instead she retreats outside and almost immediately finds a much easier, and far less dangerous, way to go.

Indigo of dusk. The boy is dark, with fluorescent white hair. He has eyes of inky black jelly, dotted with soft points of clean, intense, very far-away light. He's shyly half talking to her in a hoarse voice. Sanglade is the half subject. Behind him there's a field of faintly glowing wheat, lined with a murky scrim of trees, and wind in the trees and the incessantly repeated song of a cuckoo. He half says something involving a month late in the year, one of the—embers, and half specifies year and an issue. This is half couched in the form of a favor he's half asking of her, timidly. She can tell he isn't used to speaking with girls. The boy, who from time to time undulates as though he were projected on a slack and rippling screen, makes a gesture, rounding his arm up past his face and pointing down at an angle, showing how he would point to the drawer the newspaper he wants her to see is in, if he were able to be there with her when she finds it for him. He doesn't know the numbers of the drawers and ranks of cabinets and so on, but he wants to be as helpful as possible. In doing what he can to show her where to look, he is giving her an idea of how high off the ground the drawer is, so she knows at what level to set her eyes as she looks for it. The curtain rises, exposing another, velvet, curtain, with an enormous image of the star printed on it. The boy approaches her. She stands before the stage, and he on it, so they are nearly the same height. The boy plucks the shawl from Trudy's shoulders and lays it aside, out of her reach. He is unbuttoning her blouse when Trudy wakes up repeating the name with the idea that it is either important or funny, she can't be sure until she's fully awake.

She does remember the year. The newspaper had at least four words in its name and there's only one paper like that in the collection. YOUTH STARVES IN SPLENDOR.

A man of twenty-six, name withheld, amanuensis of Harold

M. Wilcox (Clare Houseman's uncle), had been charged with the task of collating and organizing the paper estate. The young man was seen less and less, and then vanished. An associate, asked by Wilcox to check up on the young man, found the house shut up. There had been no order to close Sanglade. Wilcox instructed his associate to enter the house. A living skeleton was discovered near the top of the long staircase, and carried out on a stretcher, deliriously protesting he must remain inside. Evidently he had clung to the banisters fiercely despite his debilitated condition, and had to be restrained. The house was thoroughly examined and nothing was out of order; the papers with which the young man had been charged were perfectly arranged. There was ample food in the Milk House. He simply hadn't been eating.

Looking carefully, Trudy finds another article extending the story slightly, in a later issue; the young man, still unnamed, had been diagnosed with paranoid psychosis and institutionalized. At the bottom of this article there is a faint date and page number written in erased pencil. There are still a few crumbs of eraser in the roughed-up paper. The handwriting is Celada's.

At that date and page number she finds: MENTAL PATIENT STARVES SELF IN HISTORIC HOME. The young man's name had been Herman; he'd been discharged from the State Neuropathological Hospital after nearly a year, and had evidently gone back to Sanglade the moment he'd been let loose. He'd entered the house secretly, and somehow managed to hide himself away, eluding all detection by the housekeeping staff until his wasted body was found on the second floor, in what the article called the Gramophone Room. He'd starved to death. A gentle fingernail underline ran beneath the next part of the story, which said that Mr. Herman had been found with an empty glass vial in his hand. Traces of fluid were extracted from the vial, tested, and found to be water.

"The house is intelligent," she thinks. "It's a mind. A living mind."

Crapelin is called away for a moment, and Celada is now sitting in his office alone, on the supplicant side of the desk. We sit and talk, he thinks, and periodically one or both of us is astonished to find himself in harmony with the ridiculous person sitting opposite him.

Why show people anything? Why tell people facts?

The ghost returns from the grave most often because it has something important to say, but even with the miracle of resurrection it's still all but impossible to *say* anything important, or to say the importance, and the message can only be set out in garbles, in the House of the Seven Garbles—and a mum pointing, jabbing the finger and staring with wild or sullen portentousness in the face.

"What?" one asks helplessly, as one would a baby. "Look at what?"

Point. Point. Stare. Point. Stare.

It urgently needs to speak, came back from the grave to speak, and now that you're listening, it's mumbling and pointing at nothing and staring at you.

If somehow you do accidentally say the right thing, the spirit melts away, evidently satisfied. But have you understood? And why care? Why not ignore the spirit, the way one ignores every unfortunate living thing?

-;-

A spot where many narrow streets converge, their distant ends like soft, marshmallowy blobs of light. The whole scene is dim and rich, cloudy and gray.

The streets are completely still, everything is momentarily abandoned, and Trudy is standing on the spot looking at tell me who you are—

"Why should I?" Trudy says back.

Won't you tell me who you are?

With a coy sort of turn of the waist, same level, malevolent look.

Yeah Trudy, go on let loose.

Her look gets a wary shade.

"You can't find me, and you want me to come to you."

I do.

"I don't know that I want to."

Please try.

A few fractional expressions sprinkle across her face, around the mouth and nose, light and dark at once like gleaming water seen from an acute angle.

"You're going to make me more beautiful?"

And powerful.

"Powerful," she says smiling her close-mouthed smile. "Hm."

Tell the audience about how you discovered the Brontës, cold rain, the beauty of gloomy days and simmering reserve.

"You tell them," she says, still smiling.

You think I do it better?

"I find it amusing, watching you try."

Do you love Celada?

Something happens around her smile, which changes it without it changing. It looks the same, but some of the ease has gone out of it, and the warmth retreats into her eyes.

"No."

Really?

She's getting ready to end this seance. She can break it off in mid

((.O.))

He is still piebald with streaks of makeup, the window shows him. Rubbing his jaw thoughtfully he steps toward the tents, feeling easy just at the moment. El Gigante shambles by with a nod, carrying a length of rope and the stoic, put-upon look that characterizes all stage hands everywhere.

A trembling, faint nausea or nervousness inside, and a feeling of weakness, washes over him. He remembers rope, voices, and the fingers . . .

The sun is gathering in her arms and getting ready to duck below the horizon.

Not yet!

With a plummeting feeling of being abandoned, he starts running toward the sun as fast as he can, zigzagging through the streets trying to keep sight of it. She lowers her head and sinks down as though she were contently succumbing to death.

He runs crazily.

Don't leave me!

The next moment the light seems to fold up and run out of the sky, forming as it sluices down the silhouette of a vast house that confronts him as he lunges around a corner, nearly colliding with a couple and their little girl, who stares at him. Sourly. He runs across the street to the brick wall surrounding the house and follows it to a small metal door with open fanlight above it, grabs the latch and flings the door wide.

The wall had blocked for a moment his view of the sky, and now the sun is utterly gone.

Where did she go?

To the rest of the world.

But where is she?

He recognizes the house now. Or seems to, it's as though he'd read about it in a story. Except he never read stories. Perhaps it was in a newspaper.

The police had been summoned to attend to a little girl

who'd gotten lost and wandered onto the grounds of the house, that's it.

She'd attracted the attention of some people with her screams, fastened herself onto a column on the veranda, screamed and wept, terrified of the house but clinging to it with all her might. They'd had to pry her arms loose, and she'd been carried away struggling so hard they could barely keep hold of her. He never did find out what had happened to her. Everyone assumed she'd just gone crazy somehow. It had been this house.

Now he has it! It's *her* house! It's *where she goes at night*. He looks up, and *there she is* gazing down at him from the high balcony!

The sun leans out with her shoulders lifted, hands on the rail, her hair swinging a little, her face an eclipse with a wan crescent around the chin and cheek on one side.

He trembles. His knees shake, and he sinks jerkily to the ground. This is where she goes—that was why the girl was worked up. It's charged with all the withheld force of the sun when it doesn't shine, and has nothing to play with.

. . . Celada rubs his hands. They tingle. He's standing on a corner overlooking Sanglade, which emerges from one side of a narrow slot between two gaunt buildings, as though it were— but it wouldn't be like the house to peer around a corner. I hate thinking stupidly. I don't know how to stop. Is there anything wrong with my circulation? Aren't my hands a little blue? Or is that the light?

Sanglade and the Milk House are like the heads of two strangers who commute side by side. From the lower right-hand corner of this picture a man walks into the frame toward Celada, oddly out of proportion as he comes up a little incline. He seems elongated. His white shirt, which is loose, shines in contrast with his darker skin and his wrists stick out a mile. He might be drunk, or perhaps only very tired. His head wobbles a little, and walks without swinging his arms.

As he comes near, he takes a look at Celada. His face is haggard, but not old.

Celada is frightened by the man's look. It isn't the look of drunkenness or fatigue, but the slackened look of emotional distemper that comes after the sort of rare experience that dilates you like a balloon until you stretch and develop runs with the strain. He looks like an empty balloon, Celada babbles to himself in fright, because the man has stopped and is obviously getting ready to say something insane to him. A deflated balloon, he thinks, or a flat locust seed pod, the kind that look like leather straps or hardened gobbets of melted rubber. The man is not drunk. He looks crazy. There are white marks on his face, as though he'd rubbed the sweat that soaks it with chalky hands.

"She's inside," he says, like a partner. "Have you come to see her?"

Celada mumbles, not knowing what he says.

"You can tell me," he says coming closer.

Celada doesn't dare withdraw.

"How long have you known?"

His breath spatters against Celada's face.

Coward—the word sizzles in his mind like hot fat.

The man is panting a little now, and his eyes are livid, dotted with tiny scabs.

A shocking smile tugs one side of his mouth. "I'm not Ukehy, if that's what you think."

The word Celada had invented thrown back at him by a stranger. And plainly in its intended sense.

"Ukehy!"

He's looking toward the house, now his head swivels back to

Celada, and his tugged lip ripples exposing his upper front teeth. He nods.

Cimelia Cisterna is quiet.

"Uh-huh," he says quietly. "They can never know about this place, you know that. Not that"—his eyes swivel back to the house, it seems to draw them—"*she* could come to any harm, but they shouldn't disturb her rest."

He looks back at Celada, expecting to see some sign of understanding.

"It would be profanation," he says, matter-of-factly.

Celada nods his head with a jerk, so the flesh of his face shivers.

The man looks around levelly.

"You should come to the show sometime, if you haven't," he drawls. Celada catches a little something in the throat and gags lightly. A darting silver ache in the breath.

Coughing, suddenly, he backs away from the man, and it occurs to him he can escape from behind this cough, like a squid in a cloud of ink. Celada throws himself into it, and the stranger watches him a moment.

"Right," he says decisively.

Celada coughs on with abandon, leaning against the wall, watching the stranger walk up the way. The man turns his head back, his stride quick and light.

"We've set up in Patio Esbabelado."

Further away.

"Every day."

Step. Step.

"Two shows."

Step. Step.

"Three and seven."

Step. Step. Step. Turn corner.

A mew from the doorway grabs Trudy's attention. Dr. Camatsura is standing there with her habitual look of objectless surprise on her face, holding in her two hands a thick old record in a cracked paper sleeve. She takes two steps into the room.

"I hope I didn't startle you," she says.

Trudy shakes her head untruthfully.

"Well," Dr. Camatsura goes on after a moment. Her mouth moves a little too much when she speaks, as though she'd just been eating peanut butter. "I thought this might interest you."

She offers the record without advancing, so Trudy quickly steps up to receive it.

"I ran across it in the basement, where some of the other collections keep . . . what they haven't enough room . . . to store in their own buildings."

The label is indigo with matte silver letters, and VIVA VOCE arching over the smaller print. The V's are jagged, calm little lightning bolts. Directly beneath the spindle hole, in the midst of a clear space that makes it the real center of the label, Clare BRUCE is written in gothic capitals. Beneath it is a tapering paragraph of foreign words in sets of quotation marks, her program.

"It's a recording of Clare Bruce," Dr. Camatsura says.

"Thank you!" Trudy says, delighted.

"You can play it," Dr. Camatsura smiles, pointing vaguely straight up with a loose arm, "on the wind-up turntable upstairs. I'm sure it still works."

She nods her head and smiles with almost intrusive pleasure.

"Where is it?" Trudy asks.

"In the upstairs parlor, toward the east."

Celada finds the side door to the grounds of Sanglade ajar, and a few fresh footprints in the gravelly clay before it. He steps through and shuts the door with care before abruptly looking up at the house. It's unclear whether or not he's trying to impart menace to its appearance. Is there anything really frightening about it, or is fear the wrong word? But he looks at the house with jabs of anticipation and excitement, and not so much with aversion.

("We don't know anything," he'd said to Dr. Crapelin, "about life after death. And this given centuries of attention. But we do know that people hallucinate. Grant hallucination. Nothing changes. Why hallucinate? Why just then and there? Why see *that*, and not something absurd and obvious like a pink elephant? If it were all in my mind, how did it get there? Was it placed there?"

Dr. Crapelin replied: "Kant said that miracles were unnecessary, because you would still have to submit anything you saw to a rational test, to insure you weren't seeing things, and such a test would require you to determine what God would say to you anyway. But Schreber stood Kant on his head when he said that any hallucination would have to be subjected to a similar rational test in order to ascertain whether or not it had been placed in the mind deliberately as an act of communication from a supernatural source, so you see, square one turns out to be the only square. It's the horizon.")

In the shadow of the house, a faint, trembling, yet soaring voice sifts over him, coming from high up in the house, a song and a voice he's never heard before.

Trudy keeps her eyes riveted to the whirling record, watching VIVA VOCE spin, while the thin, rich, faded, remote song sternly rises, seeming to go too fast. She can hear the voice's reflections in the room in which the recording was made, which, although she knows it wasn't, she seems unable to believe wasn't this room, with its infinite patterning. And where someone named Mr. Herman crawled, and stretched out his emaciated form, and died.

The voice soars to a long throbbing note, and Trudy's throat closes.

What does Clare Houseman look like now? A few palings in the gloom of a half-crushed coffin. The skeleton of the one who sang this, and whose song now soars like a denial erupting from the empty space where her throat melted.

Where is she? Is she there? Is she here in this grave, or anywhere?

Trudy feels a bubble has landed on the small of her back and burst there: a feeling of the emptiness gaping behind her.

A resourceful singer. The voice, alternately wailing and steely, flits up and down a wide range. Why is it so affecting, to think of Clare Houseman singing by herself, even this abruptly beautifully, abruptly, this intensely, because the intensity cancels the intervening time, bringing Trudy Bailey right up to the other side of an instant of Clare Houseman, whose name has already grown to monumental size.

Celada can only hear the topmost, wafting layer of the sound, and this is nearly inaudible to him, not more than fifty feet from where Trudy stands. The sound, for him, is intermittent, so that only the sharpest, most pointed notes reach him. He's paralyzed. The singing is virtually inside him and imaginary, but he knows he hears it with his physical ear, thrillingly distinct though faint. *She's there.*

(.)

Trudy waves to Dr. Cottataris and receives a distracted, half-hearted wave in return. Dr. Cottataris moves away, fumbling with an address book and a newspaper. Trudy is unsure whether or not she's been slighted, which would not be like Dr.

Cottataris. A moment later she suspects she has the answer—the distinguished African professor, Dr. Cicoya, is, arms folded, eyes hardened, in conversation with a tall rumple-faced man in a waterproof coat. The coat is pressed and very straight, and at odds a bit with the haphazard look of the man's face and hair.

Miss Houseman suddenly emerges from one of the buildings. She strides over to Dr. Cicoya and lifts her arm, guiding him, without touching him, away from the detective.

"Hey, ma'am—ma'am, do me a favor and wait please, I wasn't quite done with this gentleman."

The man points with his pen, remaining planted where he is. He doesn't talk like a man who's asking a favor.

"Sir, come back please," he says.

Dr. Cicoya is giving his full attention to Miss Houseman. They cease conferring, and he departs with his customary gravity. Miss Houseman silently approaches the man in the raincoat.

He leans in and begins remonstrating but she has already turned aside and left him there, briskly vanishing from sight down a side street. The man drops his arms slowly. Movement catches Trudy's eye—someone on a rooftop above the side street, and a hasty intimation of motion in an alleyway. Trudy trots around the block thinking to catch up with her on the other side.

When she next catches sight of Miss Houseman, she is not so far down the side street than expected. A shape lunges out of a deep doorway, grabbing clumsily for Miss Houseman as she passes. Trudy can't see past him, but Miss Houseman somehow evades the beefy young man with the close-cropped blond hair.

Miss Houseman glares at him, full in the eye, with coltish excitement around her nose and mouth; her lips part in a smile that makes her look a little crazy.

"William," she calls.

Like magic, William steps out from the alley that opens

behind her. In two steps he's behind the man and with the barest movement of his back and shoulders somehow he has him on the ground, a foot in his armpit and bending back his forearm. William didn't even use his left hand.

The man on the ground is gasping with shock and dismay. He fell hard, and now he can't seem to move.

Miss Houseman takes two steps forward, her eyes riveted on the prone man, and now there's a light of rapturous excitement in her face.

"Hurt him, William!" she says, avidly.

William alters the angle of the man's arm and bears down on it. The man's exclamations of distress now change to grunts, then to cries. A thrilling sickliness, vivid and wicked and icy goes through Trudy as she watches. Miss Houseman bends forward, bringing her face closer to the man's.

"Am I frightened?" she asks in a buttery voice.

Her eyes are silver. She flicks them up to William, who had slackened his grip while she spoke. His grip tightens again and the man bellows, driving his knees into the ground. Trudy is suddenly trembling violently

—I'm going—

—I'm going—

A block and a half later she dashes herself sideways onto a bench and doubles over her knees shivering, teeth chattering, bulbs of ice water crashing in her brain. Her vision solarizes. The spinning coins by her kidneys turn at once to cannonballs, twirling one inside another: don't let them knock together!

(.)

Celada slumps woozily into a chair by the window in headache mist, a lead wheel coagulating around his ears. Almost every day now. More days than not. He's getting serious about them.

See and hear: the cold, level tone, and the dim form, colorless and austere, like a shadow thrown across the sumptuous leather chair.

The eorla sets down a pre-Columbian statue of Mictlantecuhtli and completes his transformation into the man in the chair, the cold correcter.

"Daniel," he says faintly.

He lets a full minute pass before he speaks again.

"Daniel," he repeats emphatically.

Only now does he let it be understood he's expecting a response.

"Yes, sir?"

"I would have thought that you might have known better by now how *very much* I dislike having to repeat myself."

"Well sir, I—"

"I find I am repeating myself rather too often with you, Daniel. I'm starting to get the idea that you lack respect for the maxims of this house . . ."

"Oh, no, sir—" Daniel says in the protracted pause. The eorla, with exact timing, says ". . . and . . ." at just the same moment. Daniel catches himself, so as not to speak over the eorla. The eorla looks up at him, white rims beneath his trapezoidal eyes, mouth pursing in displeasure. He clears his throat, which doesn't need clearing.

"—hm/m . . . and, by extension, that you lack respect for me."

"No sir," Daniel says when he dares.

"Perhaps in that case you are merely becoming forgetful. Do you find your capacities exceeded by your duties, Daniel?"

"No sir."

"Is your time insufficiently ample?"

. . . or . . .

"You were born into a . . . Jewish family, I believe, Joseph?"

"Yes, sir."

"And are all Jewish boys as lazy and indisciplined as you are?"

The voice is old and light. This deliberately crude question is intended to test Joseph's self-control.

"I don't know sir," he says quickly, after swiftly discarding a number of other possibilities, all equally deferential, but too elaborate. Joseph has learned that the best answer, under such conditions, is the quick, medium-stupid answer.

The eorla doesn't move, only blinking.

"We are *Protestants* here, Joseph. That means we learn to discipline ourselves. That means we do not have quaint little bearded men telling us what to think. We must take our own council in the inviolate solitude of our own hearts, Joseph, by means of the strictest, most pitiless self-observation of which we are capable."

He raises a finger limply in the vicinity of his lapel. He will lay it on as thick as he can. Double it, quadruple it, stifle every last breath out of him, crush him.

"The systematic and unsentimental cultivation of the self while alone, and the detection and extirpation—ruthless excision—of error . . . My decision to admit you to Ukehy, Joseph . . . was *that* an error, I wonder?"

Weighed . . . the glaring dark of reason, impersonal and abstract like a light that does not radiate . . . excised . . .

Celada sees the stranger in the silent movie of his migraine.

Ukehy is just a made-up word for the glue or the space between the buildings, listening and watching in all the gaps where it hovers like witchcraft. It's nothing more than an imaginary static, paralyzing radioactivity that can jerk to life in an instant and vaporize a human being, suffocate a whole town.

But he'd invented it. Witch police, who could be anybody or nobody. Witches aren't fake people, they're unpeople. You never catch one, never see one. They are only what might be there. This person might be a witch only for a moment.

A stunned, numb old woman, who's no more a witch than she is a doorstop, is trundled into the court. The trial is witchcraft and the secret police, judges, executioners, are the witches. Witchcraft slobbers down each and every street in town: a viscous, caustic flow of cold sludge, cameras, police, stamps . . . Fly through the air on thundering brooms, blades cackling as they churn by—witch aviation involved churns, laundry bats, pestles, rocking chairs, sawhorses, big kettles, hammers, golf bags, vacuum cleaners, cappuccino machines, bowling balls, toilet plungers, leaf blowers, baby carriages, statues of jockeys from the fronts of houses of a certain age, console TV sets, jacuzzis, insurance policies, political speeches, superficial digests of Eastern spirituality, huge blocks of wasted time and of waiting. Giant black-and-white scarab-beetle witches glide along the streets, hooting and screeching like owls.

He sees the dim courtrooms, air filled with brown film. The shadowy judges like sketched figures on a backdrop. Miscellaneous activity going on to the sides and behind. The atmosphere of doom couldn't be more perfect. Nothing is ever decided here. This is a smokehouse where a ready-made decision is cured in grime, and heat, and terror, and foulness, and despair.

Did he really say "Ukehy"? Really? Maybe he'd been overheard, telling Trudy about them—his fantasy?

Are they witches? The ones who always might be spying? It isn't necessary to watch everyone, you only need to make them believe they could be watched at any time. It isn't necessary to arrest everyone. You only need to arrest the occasional

129

example—without a word, without a sign, without warning. Whoever it is simply disappears, and no one knows anything about it. The one who's gone is erased from memory. Did it happen? That's all that it takes to get control.

He hadn't dared bring up the word to Dr. Crapelin when he saw him earlier.

Instead, he asked again about ghosts.

"Your preferred topic."

Making sure that the coast is clear, as sure as one can be, anyway, Celada edges sideways through the bent lace of the grill barring the side entrance to the swimming school, only to find the lecture has already begun. Dr. Crapelin is sitting comfortably, his legs crossed, in the high lifeguard's seat. A miniature samovar bubbles on the wide armrest, from which an elastic tuft of steam spouts toward the ragged ceiling. His voice shimmers in space above the lined blue troughs of the empty pools.

"With regard to the question of the existence of ghosts . . . Questions of an ontological character generally take yes or no for an answer, with special provision for 'I don't know.'

"Ghosts exist.

"Ghosts do not exist.

"Ghosts may exist.

"One wonders if there *are* any *real* differences between these answers.

"One *doesn't* wonder if there is any real difference between these answers.

"One doesn't *know* whether there is any real difference between these answers.

"But, in surveying them, one may notice some opportunity. An inchoate thought, in which would be re-rendered all three answers as the different moments of a single answer, such that all three are true, and none are false—provided they are not affirmed simultaneously. Whether or not that re-rendering amounts to anything other than a piece of sophistry, however deftly brought off, would remain to be seen. In any case, we're still only playing with the idea, although we keep our eyes peeled for the first indication that there may be something more to the question than play . . .

"Ghosts don't exist. If we adopt this as an axiom, the other possibilities are removed from consideration. Certainly, there is no physical evidence of the existence of ghosts. Meaning and beauty are incalculably important to us, and yet neither of them is physically detectable as such. A machine may detect vocal sounds, but those sounds cannot have meaning, strictly speaking, for it. We say these things are abstractions, and yet we can't define them as abstractions either. They are both as certain to us as our breathing, all the same. Adverbs name conditions or manners of action, but while we will recognize what it is to do something 'cautiously' or 'slowly,' can we physically detect and identify the content of these adverbs? Can a machine distinguish what is to do something slowly, if it cannot know intention? Cautiously? How would it know?"

Dr. Crapelin picks at the nubs of fabric at his knees.

"Kant's transcendental aesthetic does not amount to saying that space and time are all in our heads. To say so, is already a spatial designation."

A reasonable fanning out of the fingers in the air.

"Kant argued that space and time are forms that spontaneously develop in the infant mind as the sine qua non of all experience. One might argue that a mystic state often involves much simultaneous experience, but then we might say this is the transference of an arrangement in time to an arrangement in space, like the translation of a syllogism or narrative into a diagram or a painting. Even though one might see the thing entire and at once, it seems still to be necessary to focus attention successively on different parts of the diagram or image, first this, then that, in order to apprehend it fully."

Celada sits on the ruin of a bleacher, wanting to lean back but not feeling informal enough to, knits his hands in his lap and tries to follow the promiscuous arc of reasoning going on in the swimming school. Around him the other listeners are silent and still as dummies, but a faint rustle hums around them.

"A more significant observation, however, is that Kant's philosophy leans heavily on the distinction between subject and object. The subject is clearly sequential, more so than spatial. However, if this boundary is elasticized . . ."

Dr. Crapelin shrugs slightly.

"Ghosts exist, don't exist, might exist. These answers are *all* still entirely too crude."

His tone shifts from that of a lecturer, re-presenting ready thoughts, to that of extemporaneous reasoning.

"Ghosts don't exist—as objects. We have noted that this need not mean they don't exist at all. Ghosts exist uncertainly. This is not equivalent to saying 'I don't know.' I stipulate positively that ghosts do literally exist.

"Ghosts are not figurative. Figuration is ghostly."

Uplifted finger. Where would thinking be without gestures like this?

"The ghost story often simply stipulates that ghosts are real. Some do so in earnest, others only provisionally, for the sake of a good story. Some purport to be true accounts, others make no claims, but most will go so far as to say they present a plausible encounter with a ghost.

"Or, instead of trying to win the reader over, if only for an instant, to the idea that ghosts are real, they show the reader instead that reality is ghostly. This is promising, but here one begins to feel that one is drawing near to an eddy where all tension goes slack, and which is haunted by complaisant sighs, because here one can relax in the assurance that the writer is not going to trouble us after all by trying to posit the actual existence of ghosts. It's one thing to toy with ideas and tell stories, it's another thing to make claims in earnest about unseen things in this world. But,"

He leans forward in the chair, over his crossed legs, looking directly at Celada,

". . . figuration *is* ghostly. Literally ghostly. How can we account for the mysterious power of figures? Symbols?"

He settles back.

"Think of despotism.

"Let me say that everything that I have so far designated as being not possible is of the same order of impossibility. A distinction here between personal and impersonal impossibility should not be made; even less so between subjective and objective. This is the case in part because my ideas having to do with ghosts have also to do with exactly the spots where these distinctions can no longer be made. Or moments. Ghosts might be, and here I speculate very hastily, thought of as climatic conditions like mist, which obscures or erases—and here it's hard to see the difference—the landmarks by means of which object and subject, or persons and what aren't persons, are discriminated."

Dr. Crapelin vanishes.

(O)

Always clean, I. wakes in a stairway . . . far away, the gleaming little square of linoleum floor and the open doorway, the double flash of passing legs and their image in the floor ,,, on

Calle Cavalcanti, escalarde mo tutinga presca combolizando des puedes como eso zachrimos podestes est pluma, bon clave de condecina jorca, de cola, el banco del Sud frontas bas pieces, escujabadar como trigande „, just a murmuring drape on the stairs . . . a taste like a bad raisin in his mouth.

On Calle Cavalcanti, en el banco del Sol „, LA Sol, Sola „, y no sabe yo eso no saber, no sabre, no espada, no espejo viejo, no spade, no sapien, uniform no sapien = uninformed „, from Mediterraneanao, know sapientar, basta miserable „,

„, que serable „,

Look up to her, with love. Calm love swells every nerve and vessel. Her arms wide to embrace him in the world, crashing down power in gently breaking circles. Esmashing. Power races all around him teeming with phantoms of heat and light. A spade is leaning against the corner of Calle Cavalcanti and Espejo Viejo, not far from where he entered the street. He reaches out his hand to take it, and his fingers only crush into his palm. Someone has removed the spade. He can see a few crumbs of the dust it left at the white seam where the building is welded to the grid.

He walks without eating or looking, his head back, listening for her without success. She keeps shattering panes of light over his head. Each intangible fracture tears away a minute quantity of its mass, which is a ghost occupying matter like Espiririr Exacto no Sancto Santo. A trail of his head behind him.

His throat hurts.

He's half blind with visual bruises, and what he can see is pink. He shuts his eyes and opens them again. The house is above him, on the other side of the wall. And there's the same spade leaning against the wall surrounding the house. He reaches out his hand to take it, slowly, and his fingers clamp like a vice on the thick wooden handle. He lifts and draws it slowly back toward himself, blade down, solemnly.

He follows her pointing fingers down the streets, she at his back lighting his way without hurting his eyes this time. Perhaps she has to learn how roughly she can handle him. He can't take much, not since . . .

Her transparent, bladelike hands, and slender fingers, slant from on high to the ground in long beams.

Headstones all around in Calle Calavera. Somber black marbles like filled Gothic arches in cool shade of funereal trees. So still all he can hear is his own panting. No wind. No suburban street.

Chough of the spade into the ground. The soil is like hard cheese. Nothing there—no wonder, there's no headstone. It's not a grave. He puts the spade down. Spectral cemeteries swim in his eyes.

He picks up rocks and discards them. Then he peels his pocket from his thigh and fumbles in it, presently withdrawing from it a stout coin. He spins around in place and throws it "mas casin casado." It flashes once as it turns in the air. Opens his eyes as he throws it to see where it goes, and digs up the grave on which it lands. The coin he retrieves first, and places in the breast pocket of his shirt. The casket is made of flimsy wood he cuts open with the spade. A papier mâché hand rests on the buttoned front of the jacket. The head is shrunken and tea-colored, but there is no real putrefaction, because the body associated once upon a time with the name inscribed in stone here is itself not here, but mashed into a pulp of corpses in a sealed pit in a nameless, forsaken spot.

Waving his hands in mesmeric passes over the dummy.

"Get up and walk."

It follows him home, carrying its own casket. He puts it in the puppet show. Her advice is always good.

(.)

The two of them together on the veranda.

"Don't you want me to?"

"No, I don't," she says shaking her blond hair.

"Are you lying?" he asks right away.

Someone might have come around a corner and have seen them kissing there.

They fold and knead together. On the inside, there is a dark place his mind's eye conceives of as an organ, looking like a stone cut in half exposing the softly varied, creamy bands of minerals, grays and browns, radiating from a small hollow center with a thick outline of paler gray. A hardboiled stone egg, all made of implacably contracting tissue, which emits a warm molasses preparing to fossilize itself. Then together they shake, tremble, his thoughts snap into a single brilliant point, then billow out again and retire. Paralyzed woman in his arms. Her face takes a while to make sense. Then, in the morning, again, when he comes up behind her as she stands at the bathroom sink, and she turns around for shattering need stark and absolute.

These are only stories. Like manure, easy to spread. Spread it out like a warm quilt to get lost in. Lap the head in soft dark, unmoor, and drift . . . filled with glowing weakness. Then it contracts, because it must, with a bitter taste and a jostled discomposure in body, but nothing serious. The story cracks. Its glamor stays with Celada like the memory of fairy gold in what does last, which is the getting lost.

When he was a boy, and later in life, a few times . . .

He never saw their value until now. Those were the moments when the word pressed itself on him—"Lost!" It's virtually onomotopoeia, like a groan of shock and thwarted hope, carried through dead trees on the wind, ending with a truncated hiss. Landmarks come in strings, but suddenly everything is a landmark, and nothing is. Teasing turning vicious by degrees, and fear starting to grow, imagining having to sleep hidden in a store and to eat trash.

Sanglade knows exactly where it is, at all times, and Celada doesn't believe for a moment that its ghosts aren't anything but artfully and maliciously lost in its world. It is itself a place, so it can't get lost.

Yesterday he met Trudy in the street, and she told him about the record. When they part again, and because it doesn't erase the moment he heard the ghost, no matter how it happened to be or not to be there, he finds it doesn't make any real difference. The house is dirtied by a precious name and by an alert invisible presence that teases him for floundering and doing things by halves. It mocks him for keeping his life stored away unused inside him. That's a fugitive, other Celada, that this Celada knows nothing about, capering, snickering, and dematerializing behind the louring facade of an exotic old arts-and-crafts house. The danger is that, of the two of them, this Celada here, in the street, will turn out to be the one who is a flimsy shred of make-believe, and that *other* will turn out to be the real one, dreaming a mediocre, incoherent dream of itself.

"Reality keeps scooping me," he thinks.

It's not that his stories come true, but that it keeps turning out that they might as well have been true, when he made them up.

"My stories aren't true," he goes on, as the words of a boring lecture pass unheeded over his head. "They aren't descriptions of something that happened because I invent them, but I draw on what I see. Ergo, the bits and pieces of a narrative that I may absorb from what I see might spontaneously parallel or anticipate what does really happen.

"Happenings are one thing, but how did I guess the name of the secret police was *Ukehy?* It's not even a word."

"Blah blah blah," the lecturer says.

"The best stories always lose their readers sooner or later," Celada thinks, slouching down in his seat, doodling the outline of a familiar house in his spiral notebook. "The story ends, but the reading keeps going. Bon mots for the wind to drink. And piss into the ocean."

COWARD, he writes at the top of the page.

"Basta. It's time to do something."

(.)

Trudy pictures a crumbling skull, an orangutan in a suit and a tie. She rubs her temples, imagining the skull crumbling under her fingers. No headache, but she's been having trouble sleeping, her thoughts are tangled and painful.

Resignedly, and in no haste, she walks to Sanglade. At the gate, she pauses to take it in, and perhaps to divine its mood. She has misgivings; she is tired, her head feels as though fingernails had been gouging at it, and the shrill beauty of the house is more than ever more than she wants to have to handle. The porch swoops up anyway and closes over her, like a lid.

The air inside, and its silence, fall on her like unwanted balm, making her feel more weary. To defend herself, or at least to feel less canceled, she makes as much noise as possible going to her seat, walking off the carpets and letting her heels down firmly.

Sitting at her table, she rapidly completes her work and sits reading for a while, waiting for Dr. Camatsura to bring her another stack of papers to sort.

She is completely engrossed in her reading one moment, and the next, staring out the window in confusion. People are going by on the paths outside, through the deadly ornamental garden she hasn't yet dared to visit. Which is white with snow, in and out of the orange pools of the rust lights in the midnight dark.

The room seems larger around her. A sensation too weak for her to be sure of has broken her concentration.

The air resting on her shoulders is cool, even though the room is warm enough. She rises from her seat and crosses to the mantelpiece; perhaps the draft comes from there, an open flue or something. The mantelpiece is made of cold marble, with a strange-feeling grain; she takes the slab in her hands, and finds it is very faintly humming. It rumbles with the hum of a powerful song she can't hear.

Trudy takes her hands away with an outraged expression, as though she'd just touched something repulsive. She goes to the bathroom, rubbing her fingertips together, and washes her hands. Then, she returns to her chair. The water from the taps has made her skin tingle unpleasantly. There is no snow on the ground outside. It's daylight. No stream of people go by in the cemetery-like ornamental garden she hasn't yet dared to visit.

It begins to seem as if the air were filled with tiny wrinkles, minute closings like closing eyelids. The dim colors in the room's muted, clarifying light deepen, turn vivid, as though rain had just washed them.

Floating in the middle of the room, her feet resting on the bar of the chair and not on the floor because she doesn't want that rumble getting on her feet, she has to struggle against these dreamlike feelings, and drag her eyes along the print. Her vision, like a heavy ball bearing, keeps rolling off the page. She thinks of the door standing open behind her, and wonders if Dr. Camatsura might come soon, or if she should go to her to get something to do. Or leave, if there is nothing to do. Yes, leave.

The letters are too distinct to read; they crowd each other, vying for her exclusive attention. A. V. R!

"This is stupid," she keeps thinking. "Why don't I get out of here?"

Gradually, the letters shrink. From time to time, a written word echoes voicelessly in her mind. She gropes for the sense of what is being said with a feeling like falling asleep. Wasn't there something off to her right? She glances at an open door that she closed behind her when she came in, and the darkness on its other side. Some clown has put a dressmaker's dummy there in the doorway for a prank, with the light from the room slanting down on it. She can just make out, below the silhouetted head, the weird gray dress. A gauze skirt falls down to the floor, and the shadow of the head is just barely visible in outline against the dark. The skirt is drawn, slowly, out of the light and grows more substantial, until the transparency is solid, the gray is dark blue, and she can see its fringe.

Now it has withdrawn completely into the darkness, and there is nothing there any more.

Trudy jumps up. The disembodied, living feeling in the air is gone. The doorway is just a lightless opening with the door swung out toward her, and she knows there is nothing there in the dark *any more.*

(.)

Celada can't find Dr. Crapelin. Hunting in one of the libraries and happening across Dr. Isochronal in his karel, Celada asks him has he seen Dr. Crapelin and Czechoslovakia says "No," without turning from his work.

He thinks he glimpses Dr. Crapelin in a high window, but the figure he sees is stepping into the embrace of a pair of bare arms and this does not seem entirely to fit the bill. Dr. Crapelin has a wife somewhere, she might even be teaching at Chthethostoa. She might be a psychiatrist.

Thinking to search in one last place and then give it up, Celada investigates the offices attached to the building adjacent to the swimming school. The place has a deserted feeling. Bats swoop in the air. Celada glances left, at an empty doorway, then right, at the unattended front desk, and, when he glances left again, William is standing in the empty doorway with his thumbs in his vest pockets, looking very erect and composed.

"I'm looking for Dr. Crapelin."

William smiles without parting his lips.

"He's not here. I don't believe he teaches today."

William's steady, smiling look is hypnotic. He casually takes his thumb out of his vest pocket and beckons once.

"Come with me. I have something here that you might be interested to see."

Celada obeys him uncertainly.

From a leather portfolio top of a card index cabinet he extracts three exactly folded, immaculately white sheets. Celada takes them, his thumb bending and smudging them. He freezes; they're pages from *The House of Triumph*.

He looks up at William.

"Why are you showing me this?"

William shrugs his shoulders. The rest of him doesn't move.

"A thing or two to do with Sanglade, I'd say . . ."

". . . I hadn't mentioned Sanglade."

"Come with me," William says again, and he goes out through a second door. Celada follows him down a hallway into an alley dividing the building they had been in from the dingy blue clapboards of its neighbor. William bounds lightly up the few stairs to a high door and throws it open, extending his snowy arm into the shadow and watching Celada climb up to him.

They are both plunged into felty darkness. The air is surprisingly fresh for indoors. It seems fresher than the air outside. As Celada's eyes become accustomed to the gloom, he sees thick carpets Trudy would love to examine. William crosses in front of Celada, smiling back at him with a hint of teeth, and opens a yellow door framed by funereally heavy crimson draperies.

The parlor is dim, all plushly black cushioned and rugged and draped and embroidered with moonlight roses.

Miss Houseman sits in the deep divan by the cold hearth, looking at Celada. Her head is thrust forward by a cushion in the back of the divan, so she all but peers through her eyebrows at him.

"Well," she says jocosely. "You're Celada, aren't you?"

"Yes."

She grins.

"Sit down, won't you? I'm getting a crick in my neck. The young will grow so tall these days."

The pages and now this. Watch yourself, fat boy, Celada tells himself.

William is gone. Celada sits in a chair opposite Miss Houseman, with the low table between them. At his back, an archway opens onto a more spacious and lighter room with white plaster walls and a black floor. He doesn't quite like having all that empty openness behind him.

The chair, however, is amazingly comfortable. He feels his growing nervousness puddle in his midsection.

"How are your studies?" she asks without moving.

"They're going quite well, actually, if I do say so myself. I've been working with Dr. Crapelin rather closely, as you may know."

She nods once.

"I'm assisting him in his *Orthonoia*, which is meant to be built up over time in small touches."

Celada makes a gesture in the air suggestive of a small touch, like dabbing a single stroke onto a painting.

142

"He compares the work to the development of the technology of baking bread; a highly sophisticated art, involving a simple biological agent, a formula with no superfluities, producing something that seems as natural as fruit."

Miss Houseman is wearing a dark jacket over a white blouse. She has on a dark skirt. She is a compact woman, with small, leaf-shaped hands. Her skin is honey-colored, and somber freckles cross the bridge of her nose. Her hair is only slightly darker than her skin and forms generous curls close to her head. Her lips pout a little, giving her a habitually judicious expression. One of her arms rests along the back of the divan, which lifts her shoulder a little too high, the other hand rests palm down on the seat beside her.

"I'd heard something of the sort, very interesting," she says. She has a deep, womanly voice, but speaks rather bluffly. Celada is unsure whether or not sarcasm is involved.

"William," she calls, sounding stern but smiling a little. Her mouth opens on dark.

A stir of air behind him tells Celada William has appeared in the archway. He glances back at him, who is looking past him to Miss Houseman and nodding at something she does that Celada doesn't see, because he's looking at William. Celada looks back at Miss Houseman who says:

"Won't you?" and she thrusts her right hand at him like a dagger.

William offers him a small tulip glass with a purple cordial in it. Celada says "Oh!"

Taking it, with great surprise.

William pours another from a heavy rectangular decanter, strides over to Miss Houseman and presents the glass to her. She takes it from him, wrapping her lower lip differently around her grinning teeth. William claps the decanter down on a silver tray

143

on the table and glides from the room. Celada indecorously sniffs at his cordial, and Miss Houseman is smiling at him over it.

"It's made from berries," she says wittily, taking a tiny sip.

The glass is doll furniture in his hamhock fist; the stuff smells like grape jam on a hot, cinnamony pastry. It is syrupy and saccharine, with a strength that grows like gingery heat in the stomach.

...and later...

What did they talk about?

There's nothing but *zoom* in the top of his head. Yes boing boing she talkeda bout Sangl ade now he's hiccuppi ng. Disjointed sentences whirl in his head like marbles spinning down a funnel that points up and ejects them into space—aah phooey. It's too much trouble! He pictures himself walking down the street flailing at the air above his head grabbing for his thoughts, as they escape from a skull like a bubble machine. That would tire his arms out fast. And gain him nothing but cold gooey hands anyway.

He sees four flat hands appear one after another, overlapping, all pointing to a starburst of orange and brown light that reads *"to go insane."* They are tan, with thick black outlines and red pinstriped sleeves that fade into nothing at the elbows: a flickering pinwheel of arms in the center of a building, spinning so rapidly it can barely be perceived to be spinning. The arms fly apart and soar overhead in a row. Birds in formation become buzzing kidneys chattering teeth. Every since he was a boy he'd been especially vulnerable to music and susceptible to music in particular plucking dinging thuddihng gonging ticking would get inside him like long-nailed fingers exquisitely *plinking* his nerves and driving him crazy so he would want to throw himself on the floor or ricochet around the roomb. The effect, the crazy musicians grin and stare and

144

contract into their square decanters with their nametags on them and keep playing, their bodies and heads perfectly still, while their arms and legs blur and bells pop out all over their heads. They shoot flowered needles into his eyes and tap nails into his skull so he blinks with each tap like a patient patiently ubsmitting to a ourtine mecidal procejure . . . the drone is a glassy stare and a serene smile in a golden mask, a golden beak, crystal darts intangibly smash into his face and bax of hans. He moans like a cow coming back from the dead.

Four red hands on four tan squares of cardboard, evidently torn from boxes, point the way with lurid paint to El Miserable del Sol! Niños gratis!

A small tent, open on one side and carpeted with cross-legged children.

Celada watches the puppets with a pang of nostalgia, and something else . . .

Sorrow and anger. Why show this perfect gentleness to children who, when they become adults, will only be treated with contempt by other adults? He imagines limp puppets scattered to and fro. The puppeteers have vanished. Ukehy's markless mark on the scene.

The puppets should observe silence in front of the children, and be motionless, looking at them, and at each other.

Celada walks carefully into the main tent, following droll music. He pays obliviously and finds a seat right at the back corner, making his way to it with small swimming motions of his hands. He sits down with relief, feeling his consciousness wobble around his head.

There's someone in a golden toreador outfit decorated with yellowy tinsel, charading away with a big grin for the benefit of a shapely female mime in a balcony. She is smiling and waving at her admirer with girlish happiness. Celada isn't sure . . .

145

His attention wandered for a while. But now she's gone—yes, a pair of hands, in black leather gloves, reached through the drapery behind her and dragged her into the dark. The toreador now lies collapsed in a heap at the very back of the stage, and a janitor is lackadaisically sweeping him up with a wide broom. The music starts up clamorously, hurting Celada's ears and mind with its noise and franticness, but his body is as slack as a sandbag. He knows he can't tear himself away.

What follows is a story that proves hard to follow. No one has a name. Everyone is designated by relational terms along lines that keep displacing. This person is that person's cousin, and she's married to him but he's fooling around with that one and the other one as well, who's the daughter of this family friend, and so on. It's impossible to keep them all straight. The story is ordinary and relevantly irrelevant, but pervaded with an *encroaching, sickening fear* of something that the actors all seem diligently trying not to notice. Celada remembers blood pouring out the bottom of a wardrobe and running in long ribbons down the side of the stage. With a start, he finds he is also smelling it. Isn't that taking realism a bit far? One of the women is obliged to carry on a mundane conversation while trying to ignore the lewd and increasingly importunate caresses of a leering, masked figure with close-cropped blond hair, who finally drags her from sight. Does Celada hear muffled cries of despair and pain during the icy, halting, moments that follow, as the other characters persist in their tremulous small talk? If he can't quite tell, it is because people in the audience keep leaving, often with loud jeers, hoots, racket and scuffling of feet and rattling of chairs. One man stands up, permitting his chair to fall over onto its side, and pushes his way right out through a gap in the tent wall.

There's another flash of brass band, cavorting dancers including one in a tricorn, fencing mask and flowing cape who

146

cackles horribly and whips the other dancers. A puppet strapped into a chair, and black velvet hands emerge from the dark all around it, flourishing glinting metal instruments. The puppet is trembling, whimpering, its terror goes on and on, and the hands go on and on flourishing their tools, disappearing and reappearing.

A feeling comes over Celada and he knows he's hit the wall. He bolts from the tent quickly, finding the air in it too thick, filled with stage smoke that smells like cosmetics. And then there's a butcher shop smell, too.

The fresh air revives him a little. His nausea dwindles again. He realizes he's in no condition to do anything but return immediately home. Once in bed, he dreams. He knows he's dreaming. How desperately he yearns for simple, ordinary, untroubled sleep!

On trial. Who knows why? He's on the stand, answering a question that seems irrelevant to him, having to do with when he saw someone else.

"I don't know, about five fifteen—look, would somebody mind jostling my lawyer? He seems to have dozed off."

He looks from face to face.

"Anybody?' he asks.

No one dares to do it. No one dares to do anything.

Celada climbs out of the witness box. The room is silent. He walks around past the bailiff, looking him in the face. The eyes aren't glazed or fixed. They blink, but he doesn't seem to see Celada. Or perhaps it doesn't matter.

He takes his coat from the back of the chair next to his dozing lawyer and walks out. The modelsuburb isn't there.

Half the buildings are in ruins, and there are no clearly marked streets. People and vehicles flow everywhere. Huge mountains of naked stone tower overhead. There's a poker

147

competition underway here, with the feel of an academic conference about it. A short man in an ill-fitting suit and large glasses has prevailed on him to take his place in the game. They're walking over there now, together. This man is very excited, and wants to participate not so much for the money but simply because this is a legendary tournament.

"It is the prestige of the thing," he says.

They enter an enormous ruined building, like a blasted stadium, and travel down to the subterranean playing area strapped into special chairs on steeply sloped conveyor belts. The belts angle down into the earth like escalators. Celada is strapped in and immediately begins to sink. His client is two rows over and behind him, still talking. The opposite wall of the shaft scrolls by perhaps four feet in front of him; it's bare golden stucco with sparkles on it, bronze ornamental buttons approach to within a foot of his face as the funnel narrows. The pace is alarmingly rapid and Celada grasps at the buttons as they go by to slow himself, following the example of others near him. This tactic doesn't seem to work, but when he stops grabbing at the buttons he descends even faster. The course down is curved; the seat pivots to remain perpendicular. His associate, behind and just above him, is telling him something about the professor who supervises the game.

"He was one of the only intellectuals to wear a pinafore tie in the seventies."

The dealer presides over several green tables at once, with a blackboard behind him, covered in math. And audience watches intently.

"Your glasses will be taken from you. You will not need them, and there are many women who in the street find them . . . unattractive."

This last word is pronounced with smirking malice, and the

audience titters. Celada will remember that remark; the dealer is taking advantage of his position, and what is he? A functionary, like a croupier. Then he recalls the little man telling him about the majesty of the dealers, how they held the game together and employed mirrors so that could really see all of what was going on.

"So he doesn't bet, then."

"Of course he bets, and usually wins. But remember he has no other income, and could win nothing, or even lose. Unlike you, he does not have the right to leave, and believe me they gouge him here. He has to play incessantly just to make ends meet, so to speak."

Celada looks at the dealer. "I still don't forgive him."

"You will play in these reading glasses."

"Can I keep my old glasses in my pocket?"

"No you may not."

The reading glasses have rectangular lenses layered with hexagons of orange blue and green that create a map. There are squares of fluorescent orange where the cards will be laid. This is not poker. A woman begins discussing the professor, who sits nearby, loudly with others in the audience, commenting on his play.

"Why did I agree to this so thoughtlessly?" Celada asks himself.

The little man, his "patron," comes down to join him. Looking around, he seems to be having second thoughts, wondering if, after all, he shouldn't be the one down there playing.

The game is accompanied by soft medieval music, provided by a costumed ensemble.

Celada is seized with fear that his patron's debt will become his.

"If I lack confidence in my ability to win at poker, here's a game I utterly do not understand. Still, if I can stay alive for the first few turns there may be a chance for me all the same. I have always had a knack for games. There are always options I overlook at first."

Everyone is smaller than he is. Suddenly he catches the player next to him cheating, grabs his wrist with a palmed ace in it.

"That's part of my hand!" he protests.

"You've already got five cards in your hand."

Perhaps he doesn't, or Celada is somehow wrong, or he's dropped one—

"Well then where is it?"

The little man is leaning down scraping the floor with the tips of his fingers, "—it's somewhere down there . . ."

The man he spoke to in the street, who performed his play tonight, is strapped to a chair that stands on its own in the middle of a concrete room. There he is. He is surrounded by Ukehy, Celada sees this at once and starts tugging frantically at the dream while the Ukehy men methodically lay out their tools on a steel tray, take them up one by one, unhurriedly pass them from hand to hand over the body wracked with agony, a whole body made unwhole, cruelly marring it—

Celada wakes up leaping from his bed and runs this way and that in his apartment, runs to the window, to look outside as if he could go on running through his gaze out into what he sees, muttering "Oh no, oh no, oh no!"

(.)

Celada is up to something no one understands, and which is only made more confusing by his explanations. It involves building and setting up equipment in the swimming school for the purpose of isolating the *isolaton*. You create an ever more perfect vacuum, until something makes itself, a particle I guess. The vacuum is supposed to be "the greatest possible difference between the particular and the general" he says.

"It'd be a neat trick if you could make something physical out of an abstract relationship," Trudy says.

"There's nothing abstract about it! Vacuum is everywhere and that's no abstract concept, even though you can't touch it. This will be a very special vacuum, enclosed in my machine. It will be as separate from the greater circumambient vacuum of space as anything manmade. The more separate it is, the stricter the divide, and the greater the strain on the cosmic fabric. The strain squeezes the isolaton out!"

"Suppose it tears," she says smiling.

"Wow! What if it did!" he says smiling back.

"Could be bad," she says.

"Yes, it would be! I just have no idea what that would mean!"

Celada boldly dismantles the fencing and opens the swimming school by taking the doors off their hinges. He sets up equipment, most of which he's made himself. His ground-breaking experiment will be performed using neatly assembled machines in boxes of raw wood. The vacuum will be created in a metal thing that looks like a marine mine, a ball of thick steel all decked out in rivets and bolts with heads the size of her fist. This will in fact be immersed in water; Celada refills one of the pools with a hose.

Rather late in the day, somebody comes through with mysterious grant money, and Celada oversees a delivery of surplus gizmos, including a generator the size of a small car, massive cracked solar panels, and these mastodon magnets. They're like enormous black metal coasters in whose presence Trudy feels a little ill. There's something awesome in their weird, motionless force.

A small computer, the size of a glass egg, will run the experiment. Celada emerges from the locker room in goggles, a lead dentist's apron, waders, and long rubber gloves.

Trudy checks him out and laughs.

Look at him breaking out the mad scientist gimmicks! Someone always does in Cisco's books. You'd think he'd get tired of it. Oh yes, she thinks. I think. You think I don't think, just like you think? You think you're not made of sentences, just like me? And nobody's reading *you* right now? Because you don't believe in ghosts, or secret police? I'm talking to you, *reader*, who or whatever you are. Don't you know some little voice or other, somewhere in the world, talked you into it?

Sparks, and double-exposed translucent explosions batter the television screen from the inside. Tinny, stentorian music buzzes from the cheap-ass speaker. In the old horror movie, the lab assistant turns in panic to Dr. X.

"It's out of control!" he cries.

"Yeah," Dr. X says, calmly. This was obviously part of his plan.

(.)

Sanglade defies the brilliance of the morning, and its glamour is all the stronger; its polished, torvidly perfect surfaces blaze with light which seams each straight upright edge with searing fire, implements of torture, and the diffracted glow of these surfaces floods the shaded interior in a muted and dreamlike effulgence that doesn't seem to have a source.

Trudy sees darting everywhere. This is the process, and it takes nothing at all to get it going. Less than nothing. Suppressing a start, she turns with false calm toward the haunted doorway when she hears a soft, womanly sound there, and Dr. Camatsura is asking her if she would please retrieve the such-and-such papers from the file store, in the basement, where she has never yet been.

Trudy goes to the rear of the house as directed. Subdued

light shines through many windows overlooking the high back veranda. The world outside is buried in milky steam.

The white doors to the basement are oily. Taking one knob in each hand she pulls them open. There's a pushbutton light switch just inside the doorway; the upper button is out. It's stiff, so she has to press it firmly with her thumb before the lights come on with a loud snap.

The stairway is all white plaster and chalk-white stone steps. It smells faintly of fresh paint. The doors seem to gape behind her too widely. Small fixtures disperse their glow against the pale walls and provide clear, even illumination. Trudy climbs down slowly. There is no rail.

The basement is white, and completely bare, filled with diffuse, transparent light. There are a few filing cabinets. The silence is complete. It isn't as if the walls baffled sounds coming from outside. Sanglade's basement is just still, like a cave.

Trudy goes toward one of the partition walls, which are covered in fine-grained plaster like the skin of a peach, without a single crack, without a single blemish, without a single irregularity, without a single imperfection. There is a shallow niche in the wall by the door, with not a speck of dust in it. Nowhere does she see a trace of mildew, of webs, of dirt, or dust, or mold.

The next room is the same. Gray metal office boxes, a little more than a cubic foot each, sit on the floor in exact ranks and files, five boxes deep, with narrow aisles every two ranks. This room has the same paint smell and another, fainter odor of old paper. Everything is impeccably organized, and Trudy finds the files in no time. She approves of the order of these boxes, but they also put her in mind of the high regularity of the patterns in the infinity room, and she thinks of Mr. Herman, crawling floors above her head, slowly failing, slowly dying, lost in a rapture of regular, eternal sameness.

Something catches her eye as she returns to the stairs and she stops, but she does not turn her head to look. Don't get trapped. Don't fall for it. She recognizes her fear, and it gathers strength.

She turns her head.

A small vial of black liquid stands in the niche by the door, very black against the white. The plaster is smudged, as if the hand that placed the vial there had been a dirty hand that, having set the vial down, had slid off the niche's edge.

"It's for me," Trudy thinks. Something in the house placed it there for her, with a grubby hand.

Trudy doesn't take the vial, and she doesn't leave. She sets the folders down on the fifth step of the stairs. She then goes into the other half of the basement. The same smell, the same flawless plaster, the same shadowless, even refrigerator light, the same neutrality, the same silence. There's something about the basement that's exactly like the presence of a corpse. It's as though one were lying in the middle of the floor of the other room, out of sight.

There's no glamor in death, but I don't blame people for trying, for trying to dress up death or life with gaudy hallucinations to justify the ways of death to man.

There's no such thing as ghosts. That's what they always say. I've just gotten myself stuck somehow in a silly story not worth telling, what is thought about death doesn't matter and it's better to observe death like observing a meaningless holiday. Why think.

One moment there, the next moment not, not gone because there's nothing left to go, but the pile of trash starting to smell (tough-minded) . . . that silly voice again, asking me stupid questions just to bug me—*body* is just a word, too—body is nature so what dies. A wrinkle death smooths flat *we* know: *we* died it.

Wrinkles come back. Different ones—how different? Is the consciousnessnessnessess-ess-entially *different—*

Celada!

—from someone else's? or *isn't* it water? . . . pourable clarities, in distinct vessels, like an ice cube tray (that combs the water into perishable cubes returning to water inside or out, water in a dinosaur, a cloud, the sea, the blood of kings and slaves, later to be a river, a writer, a robin red breast, a bead of sweat . . . or do you imagine you really are a little different?) I must be and when I was a girl—the man I saw death in the mall (only a picture)

shut up: he was lying in the middle of the aisle, flat on his back, his face was grey and the medics just squatted beside him looking around at the shoppers; they knew they couldn't do anything for him, he was already not . . . And funerals, when I saw deflated faces with lips that were shut too firmly, and stiff, gaping nostrils, in coffins my crumpled relatives looking like stubbed-out cigarette ends, walking with my father in bright, blazing bright daylight outside and canopies of incandescent green, and then suddenly inside, under the hood of the chapel, and sour church smell, there was death, or a dead body.

There's a passageway. It's gloomy, and seems to sink back into a dirty obscurity, but she notices another light switch right away and flips it. Now she can see the end. There's an incongruously small door made of wooden planks painted white, held together with black iron brackets. It has a latch instead of a knob, and would be better suited to a garden wall or a tool shed. The plastering around the door is sloppy, and seems to have been applied in haste.

"I'll bet this wasn't original," she thinks. For one thing, the

155

sill is raised more than a foot off the floor. "You'd have to step high over it every time."

Cool air leaks from the other side. She takes the latch in her hand and pulls the door open.

She's looking into a spacious kitchen, with high windows admitting sunlight, and paved with large slabs of marble that tremble beneath about four inches of clear water. The entire kitchen is inundated from wall to wall. The water vibrates silently.

Trudy is surprised; the air pouring in on her, far from being dank, is if anything too fresh, virtually caustic. It almost stings her eyes, but it doesn't have a chemical smell: it is just pitilessly clean. The water forms low, wrinkled mounds over the seams between the slabs, apparently welling up in silence from below. The room is silent. There is no sound of dripping or lapping or bubbling.

Plainly, the kitchen's original door had to be removed and the sill raised in order to contain the water. Trudy leans in. There are handsome cupboards on the walls and along the floor, with varnished wood and windows of bevelled crystal that gleam like congealed water, showing the bare shelves within.

Trudy looks down at the water trembling on the other side of the threshold. She doesn't like the idea of its sinisterly incessant, noiseless motion down here. Then she suddenly grows a little more straight, and goes quickly across the basement to the niche. The vial is still there, it seems to shout at her the moment she sees it. The smudges on the plaster are gone, she notes this with lips tight. She snatches the vial in her fingers, finding it cold but perhaps not strangely cold, and carries it with distaste to the kitchen door, where she plucks out its cork and kneels. The swirling water is now only a few inches from her face. That harsh, antiseptic smell is sharper than sea spray. Trudy without hesitation upturns the vial and gives it a shake. The black water vanishes into the clean. It doesn't dilute; it bleaches.

Trudy has no intention of touching the water. She snaps a strand of yarn from the fringe of her shawl, which she has tied around her waist. This strand she makes into a leash for the vial, and, holding it by the end of the strand, she dips it in.

She nearly lets go when she feels a jolt go up the strand. Is the water live? Even if electricity had been laid in down here, it would have shorted out in the water long ago if the wires were exposed. That sounds plausible.

She sniffs, her sinuses tingling unpleasantly. As she draws the vial back out through the surface, the water inside it instantly turns black.

Later, it's true, she sits at her table thinking of the water throbbing beneath her feet, and gets thirsty. Again and again she goes to the sink, but it's not her body that wants water. It's as if there's a film at the back of her throat that resists being rinsed away, perhaps because the tap water just isn't really clean.

(.)

Celada shaves, and scrapes the cream from his palm. It all comes away except for a little bit that stays in the deep creases in his palm. He looks down at the white lines in his hand, like a reversed negative.

No time for raptures about beautiful clouds and haunting weather, Celada is hurrying to get back to the swimming school and his tremendous experiments. At Paracleto Joven he whisks across a broad avenue of thinning day traffic and shoulders through the dead trees on his way to Agua Seca when a bird darts up from a clump of grass in a planter, passing very close to his face and causing him slightly to recoil.

This lifts his gaze, and he catches sight of a head. It is

protruding from the low wall on the roof of one of the taller buildings nearby; a head in a ski mask, and a pair of gloved hands holding binoculars up to the eyes. Celada looks down with a jerk and, quick thinking, drops to one knee to fumble with his already-tied shoelace. The binoculars had not in any event been pointed at him, not just then.

With a floating, uncertain feeling, Celada goes on toward the swimming school. He keeps his hands in his pockets and his head down, and suddenly they seem to be everywhere: protruding heads, beefy men with close-cropped hair in conspicuously ordinary but practical—practical for what practices?—clothing. There are compartments of down and fleece and velcro straps and buckles and snaps and panels and pockets everywhere. A dangerous impulse prompts him to divert down Giapolo toward Dr. Crapelin's offices. There are more of those men in that direction.

He stops, pretending to be absorbed in the contents of a shop window, and seeing the men afloat there in the glass, and seeing Dr. Crapelin.

Above the street there's an orange cave, like a cold furnace in the purple clouds. He is rushing (not fleeing!) home. The street is deserted. The only sound is the hum of the modelsuburb, already too soft and remote. As he comes to the middle of the street, Celada approaches a deep brick portico, with a light burning in it. The light goes out as he passes. He stops. A large man stands there, in the portico, lowering his hand, having just twisted the bulb out in the lamp above his head. Orange and tawny light from across the way dapples the man's face. Simply because he stopped in surprise, Celada is now this man's prey.

"Why did I stop?" Celada asks himself. "He would have had to call me back—" He imagines himself being accosted from behind in the dark, the voice dashing like ice water across his shoulderblades.

The man's eyes gleam; the irises are dark green. The lashes are thick and black, the brows are thick but not shaggy, black and straight. The nose is thin.

"What are *you* doing here?" he asks in a low voice.

He draws a little closer to Celada, not quite half a step. There are a few long, white hairs stuck on the lower lip, in a clump, and, as the man speaks, the tip of his tongue keeps trying to lick them away. Without success. The voice is flat and muffled by the dulling acoustics of the brick doorway. He sounds like an old record. Afraid, Celada snatches at his words and turns them in all directions trying to exhaust their meaning, their emphasis, and find the right answer, which is not right like a right answer in mathematics, it would be the answer most likely to cause this man, in his excessively plain clothes, to lose interest, to dismiss him, to appear to him to be beneath his notice—that would be the right answer, ablative case.

Did he emphasize "you," as in what was I in particular doing here? Should I answer him in terms of who I am, or what I'm doing?

"I'm going home," he says, almost at once.

The hands, in fingerless webbed gloves, continually fondle a flashlight or lamp or something, it doesn't seem to be able to make up its mind to be a box or a baton.

"Are you?"

"Yes."

"Where do you live?"

"Not far." Celada answers with difficulty, his throat rebels and he has to gulp. The man remains motionless, smiling a little. His mouth makes coy shapes with his tongue. The body is a buttoned charcoal-colored overcoat covered in bulges, set atop a pair of shoes that glisten wickedly.

"What street?"

"Primero," Celada lies wondering if that's done it for him. He lives not far from Primero. He can say, if accused of lying, that he had meant to indicate the neighborhood in general. After all, you don't tell strangers exactly where you live, at least, that would be an ordinary precaution one might be able to say was reflexive even when someone in authority accosts you.

"You should go round to Front."

The voice turns dreamy.

"Somebody got arrested here."

It is Crapelin. He looks down the street, toward Crapelin's house, seeing the two shadows and Crapelin hunched between them, head down, hands behind his back, being hustled into a yawning black pit in the shape of a van or a car, not actually seeing it, not with his eyes, but know it's happening, being certain that, right now, this is happening.

"Did you know him?"

The voice is offhandedly quick.

"D-did I? No," Celada shakes his head, so that his face twitches.

"I didn't say who," the voice says flatly.

A cold gush of fright and outrage erupts in his abdomen. It's playground tricks like that, and the idiotic pride in shining shoes, but he would have hated this man if he were naked.

"I don't know anyone who's being arrested," Celada says. "I don't know anyone down that way. I don't know anyone in this part of town." At once too much and too little, but don't deflect the glare of the questions too well, either.

"Dr. Crapelin," the voice says, not too fast to be doubted, but fast enough.

Celada can't conceal it. He shudders in what feels like a wildly exaggerated way, but which in reality is no more than a slight swaying backwards.

"You know *him*," the voice says, licking at the clump of white hair.

"What has he done?"

"Weren't you one of his students?"

"No."

Is this the lie that hangs me? I can rely on formality, I am not formally Dr. Crapelin's student, I'm at present more like an assistant. Were—I was at one time, but I mistook the question officer I thought you meant, said, aren't.

"You attend his school."

"Yes." And nothing.

The man waits, plainly expecting Celada to elaborate.

He goes on waiting. The tongue, from time to time, licks at the hairs on the lips.

"What did he do?" Celada asks finally.

"You didn't know him?"

"I knew him to look at." It's better to admit something give him an admission and perhaps he'll be satisfied. "I didn't know him personally."

"Personally?"

"Yes." Celada is confused by this last question.

"This word you use"—the lips curl up—"has no meaning, it does not exist. You are either mispronouncing it or you misspeak. Or you have invented it."

The voice is a corpse's voice, the finely shaped lips barely move as it serenely and precisely speaks, and the eyes seem suddenly so large and fascinating that Celada can barely notice the mouth.

"But he was harmless—harmless—" Celada yelps.

"Harmless. Again you persist in mispronouncing words."

"I've, I've never seen anything wrong at the school . . . What did he do?"

161

"You're slurring your words a little, guy," the voice says, its tone is nearly mocking. "Have you been drinking tonight?"

As if the question were secretly a spell, Celada does suddenly feel drunk.

"No," he says, knotting his brow.

Still the eyes watch, and the figure stands there, fondling his light, trapping Celada.

And now, Celada is aware of heat spreading in his groin. A single jet before he clenched shut his bladder again, but more urine is leaking, as though a hand were steadily squeezing it out. He smells it, and feels it going down his leg, cooling. A single hoarse, fibrous laugh resounds in the doorway. The man's eyes bob up and down a little. The white hairs cross the black opening of its mouth in the shadow, as the chin is pulled a little back.

The flashlight thing waves once in the direction from which Celada came.

"Go on, son," the voice says, still fogged with mirth. "You'll be late for class!"

In the next block he sees, actually sees, Dr. Crapelin, emerging jauntily from a brick archway into a courtyard. Celada is far enough away, he's already stopped too often; but he stops again, slapping his pockets and miming alarm as if he'd forgotten to bring something, feeling those eyes still resting on him as if they were glued now here, icy cold in his groin and down his leg where the fabric sticks, now there, this would give him a pretext to go back the way he came, turn aside and hide the stain on his pants, and as he does this Dr. Crapelin is striding, oblivious to him, out into the open.

"If they see us together . . . they must be watching," Celada thinks frantically. "They'll know I'm his student—but if they have been watching him for any time they would know that by now. It's not a hard thing to discover just how much I've worked with him, but if they don't actually see the two of us together it might not occur to them to . . .

"But I have to warn him.

"Don't I?

"He doesn't—*could* he get away if I warned him? Anyway where would he go?"

Celada is walking away, almost sideways, looking back, looking forward.

"Maybe—perhaps I could, or he wouldn't want me to risk myself—that's *true.*"

Celada goes home without stopping.

Everywhere he sees the word flash at him: COWARD. COWARD.

"My teacher," he thinks.

You should have warned him.

The night films over and grows black, gets back to his apartment, follows him in, bathroom at the end of the hall, the rattling bolt and a splintered gouge in the wood. His pale, slack face, livid with fear, so much white in the eye, weaving to and fro in the mirror. Shaking hands under a stream of water that grows unbearably hot almost immediately and he holds his hands there to feel pain. He dries his red hands and pauses before the door to watch them tremble again.

(X)

"The ghosts of the secret police," Crapelin was saying. "They are like ghosts—"

He hunched his shoulders a little, made small gestures of looking this way and that.

"Are they watching us now? Why so malevolent? What do they want? Let's find out. Give them something, anything, and perhaps then, they might leave us alone."

Sunlight shone pluming itself in his office (this was a long time ago) rebounding from the wall across the way. The desk was polished like glass, and in his seat he was fairly low behind it. As he moved his head, the titles of books peeked around it and were obscured again.

"If they did ruthlessly suppress every resistance they would be slaves, the worst of slaves," he said, waving one hand along the edge of the desk where the reflection doubled it, and blinking rapidly. "They would have to run themselves ragged, impoverish themselves hiring ever more police, and, perhaps worst of all, they would have, at least for their own purposes, to produce an exact definition of resistance. That would then, in turn, require them to name and define, and hence limit, themselves, and their own function.

"It's far more effective for them to operate virtually at random. They define nothing. They intervene so seldomly that many citizens live their lives without ever encountering them or without ever having the slightest reason even to suspect their existence, and believe their society is what is called a free one. This is how they are most like disembodied spirits, Celada. The more nonsensical and unpredictable the act, coming from them, the better it suits them.

"Every now and then, they pounce—chaos—no one knows what is going on, or who they are or who is the cause. No one can say. There is a great clamor, and, underneath it, a silence as deep as death."

He patted the air once when he said "death."

"So you see, they do only what they please. And it isn't that they set forth this or that principle, although they might, just to keep up appearances of a certain kind, if necessary. But those principles could be anything; could be 'justice,' could be 'freedom'; all that matters, under the circumstances, is that some principle or other be espoused. They are never bound by any principle. The secret police will never permit themselves to be bound and will never bind themselves. Where they preside, they possess the only genuine freedom. It's an illusion for anyone else; every citizen goes about his daily affairs, mostly unwittingly, by their unknown sufferance."

"So how do you exorcise them?" Celada asked.

"To quote your favorite *Alice*," Crapelin said smiling, "'Ah, that's the great puzzle.' I suspect that you should try to force them to come out into the open. Their power is their invisibility, the illusion that they don't exist, the illusion that they stand for something if they do exist—and, in order to keep out of sight, they must keep themselves small in number, and act indirectly. They must be confronted, even lured into exposing themselves. While their strategy is daemoniacally cunning, it is what you call a pony that does only one trick. There is every reason to suspect that they are vicious and resourceful, but not so intelligent; there is every reason to suspect they are complacent. And it is as plain as day that they haven't the faintest real understanding of creativity."

Elbows onto the desk, and hands together. The generous ashtray smokes.

"And, like ghosts, most people do, more or less secretly, suspect their existence after all, and feel unusually exposed and threatened when alone in certain places, for example. They do nothing about it, I think, because it seems to them neither here nor there. In fact, the ordinary citizen's ordinary denial of imaginary fears is turned by the secret police into the blind behind which they can conceal themselves. But when you can point to the secret police," Crapelin lightly jabbed the air with his finger, "and say, they are, at the moment, right *here*—look *there!* Then something might change."

165

"Wouldn't people become only more furtive and withdrawn, if they knew they were being watched?"

"More guarded, perhaps," and Crapelin's head swiveled as a car horn sounded in the street. "The sense of oppression might grow ... I think it might be better for them to call the bluff, and act as if the secret police didn't exist. Say anything, go anywhere, and ignore them. Again, it's like a ghost story. If you become caught up in the question of the existence of ghosts, you have already fallen under their spell. Because it's that uncertainty, and not the certainty that you have seen one, that their spell is. When is anyone ever certain of what they've seen? It doesn't matter. Real or not, the question is a waste of time. You contend in life only with what you find before you."

"So if we ignore the secret police, they will take more obvious steps to restore fear, and expose themselves."

"I think so," Crapelin nodded his head and neck.

"And that would mean killing people, and torture?"

"One would have to expect that," Crapelin said quietly. "But, there is killing, and torture, going on now. And, as things are, there is no prospect of their coming to an end. More might die more quickly if the kind of resistance I describe is tried, but they might be said, not that I would ever want to ... be ... glib about such things ... to have died in battle?"

His voice had gone up in an uncertain way.

Just matter of fact, the star-eyed boy, waving his hands over an icy campfire of dim, bluish-white flames. The flames look as though they were made of silky white hairs; they slide from the narrow logs and supple twigs with a soft hiss, and points of brilliant snowy light outlining the blackening wood. The boy's hair is the color of the flames and tosses like a lazier fire in an easy wind, the sky above him, deep, blue, glittering night.

The moon rising over birds. Crescent moon, the black

backside is plain against blue. The hills give off an odor of mint, wet eucalyptus, and, unaccountably, clean linen . . . and cool gusts of the refreshingly bitter smell of metallic dirt. He wanted an encounter, and went out looking for one without quite knowing it in words, but you almost never get one up here, and absolutely never with a person the way you'd want, but the animals are right in sharing his confidences: the hillside or night or moon makes disclosures to him and speechless things disclose themselves to him, light air, and fresh dark—Crapelin loved the dishevelment of the roads the homes and the town after a storm. Gravel, cold and pale, at the roots of stripped trees; the wet cones, shiny beetles and the intense love he feels for the silhouettes of the hills of the land secret police had forced him to leave, clean black shapes versus incandescent dark . . . and then coming out of the hills, back to humanity again, love, feeling, from inside the houses, the night gulfs of aerial wilderness outside, the outside of the house he's now inside, still jacketed in cool outside air, vast whispering space just above the rafters, just outside the windows . . . hyperboles of love . . .

He looks up at Algol.

"What's my wish—? I want to be, or visit, that star, or gaze at it for eternity like this . . . be beautiful and immortal, a ghost. Or an immortal animal.

"Do I want anything?

"Why only one thing?"

(.)

Trudy notices Celada's absence from Chthethostoa and becomes concerned. His experimental equipment sits untouched in the swimming school, and parts of the machinery have come undone or broken in the meantime. She calls Celada's landlady, who blithely tells her that she's just seen him hurrying out the front door.

A student meeting has hastily convened, the first to be held in their new cell address: an empty store not far from the swimming school. The place had been provided them by a local street performer who had recently been recruited by the committees—an unsettling man who makes Trudy nervous. Not suspicious, only nervous, as though he might bite. His missing teeth had plainly been *torn out*. He's taken over this empty store, fixed the lights and repaired broken windows, put locks on the doors and cleaned out the trash that had accumulated there, all without altering its outward appearance.

Trudy has not failed to notice him gazing transfixed through the windows when he thought he was alone, although he didn't seem furtive about it. Always at Sanglade, which surveys the area from its throne on higher ground a few blocks away.

Crapelin's disappearance is discussed. One of the students had seen a suspicious car leaving Crapelin's neighborhood at the right time. Others had seen both uniformed police and others who seemed like cops incognito gathered in the area. A circular is drafted to bring this disappearance to the attention of the other students. Trudy volunteers to talk to Miss Houseman about it tomorrow. They go their ways later that night.

The police are gangsters, Trudy thinks, while the secret police, on the other hand, are like the organizational equivalent of Jack the Ripper. They stalk, and from time to time, they do something evil. It's not faceless soldiers gunning down anonymous crowds; it's an isolated atrocity every now and then, at whim. The veil is replaced right away and it's back to the tyranny of please and thank you, like before.

How did they learn about Ukehy? In large degree, they guessed. They developed a hypothesis, and tested it by making observations, and isolated the relevant factors. Who's behind

Ukehy? It would seem no one is, no one in particular. Ukehy seems to be behind itself. Or it is just the behind. It just appeared, like a ghost with no sad story of a being that had ever lived. It appeared in Cimelia Cisterna, in Leikin, where else? Where it can. Where conditions are favorable. It isn't established, or ever founded. It arises spontaneously, like a rumor: no one brings roaches and rats into a city deliberately, but there they are.

Trudy crosses Agua Seca and turns toward home, catching sight across the street of Celada, weaving to and fro in the shadows of the trees with his head down and his hands drooping at his sides.

"I saw it. I saw it all . . ."

Alcohol wafts over her as he explains.

"I might have warned him and I should have . . ." He kneads his eyes with his thumbs, and she can see the glint of tears on his bloodless face.

"You didn't?"

"No, I was afraid they'd get me, too. One of them stopped me on my way home."

After a pause, Trudy says, to Celada's back, since he's turned away, "Well, you're not doing him any good like this. You could try"—and here he's looking at her with a stricken expression—"finding out where they've taken him and maybe see if you can get him released. Do you know if his wife was arrested, too?"

Celada shakes his head slightly, without turning toward her. Tears drop from his eyes.

"No," he whispers.

"If she hasn't been, I'm sure she could use some help, too."

Celada doesn't say anything, because he's realizing it hadn't even occurred to him that this story hadn't ended when he himself was out of danger, and that he's been excusing himself from doing anything to help Dr. Crapelin even as he was castigating himself for failing to warn him.

"When you sober up, come and meet with some of us and we'll get something together."

Trudy sounds heartlessly practical, bold, and realistic.

Celada nods dully, half-stunned with shame. He already knows he's too afraid. He won't do anything for Dr. Crapelin.

"Until then . . . ?" Trudy says, a little uncertainly.

She has her hands folded across her waist under her shawl, her lips pressed together.

Celada thinks, "I am contemptible."

The streetlight nearest them has just gone out.

Celada stares. In a wild moment, a cold flash, he recognizes the silhouette standing not three feet away from him.

"It was your silhouette I saw!" he cries. "*It was your silhouette I saw!*"

Trudy starts back in fright and surprise. Celada's scrambles to escape from her and when the light blinks on again a moment later, seeming to rise up out of the ground, she is alone. She understands none of what just happened because, when Celada saw her silhouette in Sanglade's greenhouse Trudy had been taking a timed exam many blocks away.

(.O.)

Inside the tents of el Miserable del Sol, somehow the figure in the fencing mask, cape, and tricorn hat has just arrived on the moon. Employing the straw that sticks through his mask, he kneels and slakes his thirst at a crater of bubbling liquid.

Suddenly a boy in a white wig dashes up the aisle, through the audience, and vanishes backstage, pursued by a man in a fedora and a trenchcoat, whose face has been crudely made up to look like a vampire. His sloppily painted red lips snarl around plastic dentures in a splotchy white face. The man bounds onto the stage.

"Halt!" blares the masked figure, throwing out his arms.

At the same moment, he spits out his straw, and his interlocutor spits out his fangs.

"Get out of my way crazy!" shouts the man in the trenchcoat. "I am an agent of the secret police!"

The man advances, and the masked figure produces a foil from within his cape.

The secret policeman grabs for something inside his coat.

"Do not interfere!" he bellows.

"Comme ça!"

The masked figure, with a single, darting motion, appears to plunge his collapsible sword into the bosom of his adversary, withdrawing it at once.

The secret policeman chokes. A plastic gun falls from his hand and skips across the stage. He falls onto his knees, both hands crushed to his chest, goggling incredulously at the stage blood rilling over his hands. Raising his face slowly, with assumed weakening, he looks into the mask above him. Through its mesh, he can see the whites of wild eyes that burn like phosphorus.

In deep and bombastic tones, the masked figure cries in broken Spanish, "Muerrrte, malvado! No hay manticoros puede aguantar la espada mia!"

The secret policeman clutches spasmodically at his squirting wound, and falls onto his face. The curtain hurtles down. A moment later the actors are all bowing to sparse applause. K. stands in blood-drenched clothes, his nose and moustache peeled off, and beside him stands El Gigante, mask under his arm.

Trudy should be heading home, but she wanders off instead. She goes into the converted storefront. No one is there. Through the broken slats of the wooden fence adjacent to the store, she can see a lot filled with waist-high blue weeds.

She is at the edge of the lot. The weeds are tossing slightly in a weak wind. The starry-eyed boy is standing there in the grass, looking at her. White hair, white weeds like Houseman's photographs of fires, the light in his black glycerin eyes is too brilliant to be said to have a color, unless diamond is a color. He is kneeling by a campfire in the desert night, spreading his hands over the flames, not to warm them but in order to conjure a wriggling being like a phoenix, or a diamond foetus.

She wakes gradually from this dream, as if the scene around her had trickled into it, and turns her head to look at the rapidly walking people, flickering and unreal. In confusion she looks at her watch. Time to go back to Sanglade.

Celada wakes up with a migraine. It bulges to the crown of his head as he lifts his body.

"Where were you when I needed you?" he asks it. "Why couldn't you have struck me down yest—on the day . . ."

If he could sleep through the worst of it. He can't stand to sleep or even to stay still, and worst of all, there is a vision of his cravenness there, waiting for him in his sleep. A voice, not unlike Trudy's voice, rings out of his confusion to remind him that even now Dr. Crapelin is perhaps being tortured, or lies murdered.

After a long time, he suddenly bounds to his feet and plunges drunkenly into the passage. He throws back the bathroom door and vomits noisily. The pain in his head, while losing none of its vehemence, takes advantage of his distraction to change a little, so that when he next becomes aware of it, there is an icy line along the back of his skull, like a menthol ribbon.

His teeth are pebbly and his throat scored and raw. The sour taste he washed away, but the bitterness still smolders at the back of his mouth.

. . . Somewhere in the world there is a city groaning under the heat of a butter-in-a-skillet sun smeared like an infected eye. There the air trembles, and all shapes are troubled. Celada gropes feebly at the air around him, making rending gestures, trying to claw away the tissue of phantasms that stifles and paralyzes him. Figures turned to cinders by the light undulate and flow into each other, becoming droplets of oil on pavements, bridges, and causeways. Moaning like sunstruck cows, their dusty grey tongues dangle lifelessly from their jaws, their eyes are frothing blisters of staring black foam. Haze sluggishly eddies around the taller buildings, striping them with girdles of rust. With a little pop, the sun momentarily grows larger, and transparent eyes complete with lashes and flabby eyelids snow down, falling in formation to vanish intangibly into whatever they find, leaving a rancid loop of soured old tears.

Glare oozes blindingly from the buildings, runs down their sides from long raw scars, spreads to forms a livid rash and huge, dazzling fingers and toes cars splash through, people run bellowing with pain spattered with burning phosphorus and the cars drive on for a few dozen feet at most before swerving: the shape slumps flat, the car is a half-melted bar of soap hissing out caustic lather too brilliant to look at.

Standing at the window, he watches in numb alarm as the glass bellies out with his breath. The membrane tears, the glass flops from the sill and slobbers down the side of the house in long strings. The heat and the light are reglaring and more than redoubling with the reflected gazes of a swarm of ghostly eyes that collect in multicolored secretpolice clouds, billowing and heaving in the abrasive din of millions of smacking eyelids. They click as they swivel in their sockets. They mob pedestrians, who go mad swatting at them, pulling their shirts up over their heads, shaking eyes out of their clothes, screaming and running until a car smashes them or they fall into the rubbish that chokes the river and are impaled. The eyes don't leave them even then. They cluster at the dying faces like huge, greedy flies.

Patrols in sealed suits strafe the swarming eyes with flamethrowers. Withered eyes pepper the ground in a sizzling carpet of fried olives. A leprous peacock spreads his tail over the modelsuburb and the eyes slide down from its plumage again, and maybe later whole heads, whole bodies, then two-headed bodies, manticores, each one *a unique individual.* They rampage in the streets, take over whole buildings, and exact tribute from their captives. A leopard-peacock plies its claws of hardened plastic in the softened fudge between the sidewalks; cars mire in the elastic quicksand of the blacktop and will be flipped lengthwise onto their backs over the course of several hours. Trapped faces at the windows—the roof of the car sinks in bubbling tar. The peacock leopard slits open the soft underside of a trapped car and daintily extracts the occupants on his claws. They wail in despair. The beak pecks between their ribs, and in time they die. More eyes appear on the ramshackle tail.

All around him are clotted, half-melted shapes, like reflections in lava, and a harsh smell of gasoline he can't seem to escape. It reeks, perhaps he's been splashed with it, but no it doesn't come from him. It announces death, a kind of blood. Gasoline is sour old tears of disembodied eyes, fermented, granular, the color of dust. A dry, corrosive rain of gasoline falls from cauldrons in the glare of the sun, to drop from callouses on irritated eyes, many of them enraged, criss-crossed with purple fissures.

His own eyes are gorged and streaming now, filmed with smarting gasoline. He blinks convulsively, the light of the sun is the pain in his head, his vomit body, empty beneath him, is numb and nerveless. The street signs sag, and their letters drip off. Celada looks down at the beaten-back blond weeds, and they seem to tell him that he is not far from Chthethostoa. From behind the hulk of a dead car, from behind the ember-like bricks of a warehouse-oven where crates bake like loaves in melting air, L. appears. M. is elongated, and his form shifts like a projection on a rippling screen, but as he draws nearer this becomes less conspicuous. He comes directly over to Celada the moment he sees him.

"Help!" Celada says.

"Come on," he circles his hand in the air as if he's reeling Celada in on a fishing line. He walks quickly back the way he came, and Celada follows him through dry weed husks and shed snake skins—

How long has it been?

It has been a long time since he ran across N. and obeyed his summons. They have been walking along gray ground and blond, rattling weeds.

Suddenly the blare of the sun is interrupted. Its permeating heat abates. Celada looks up. Sanglade is shading him, black and powerful, against a colorless field of radioactivity.

"Do you see the glory?" O. asks him avidly. "Don't you see it?"

"Yes," Celada says, gritting his teeth, which causes the pain to gather at his temples. "Yes, I see it!"

"*I'm* right," P. says, hooking his hand toward his chest. "I'm right."

The house alone is unmelted and unswerved, every angle and line plumb, clean, unsagging, and undistorted.

A titaness, a woman giant of hybrid race, lashless naked the smooth scalp of her head glowing like the full moon. You hear whispers. You suddenly grow attentive, like an animal stopping in the jungle, taking up the slack in your senses.

"Can you see her?" Q. asks now.

"I see her!" Celada gasps.

The giant woman's huge jaws drop open, and she calls. Her voice is like the roar of an enormous brass hinge, grating against the heat-wracked air.

R. is raising his arms in the cool autumn air to her, the mitten-like hands in lace cuffs . . . the tossing bangs and frond-like hair.

"always always always I will serve you I will serve you"

Celada recognizes the hybrid woman in front of him is an angel, but much more than that. She is like Sanglade's attendant or something. Sanglade, which is her—*school!*

She is the mistress of the hardest of all schools, he thinks, which doesn't even seem at first to be a school, but just anguish. But now, with growing fervour, he is beginning to believe that *there is enlightenment beyond these crises, which can turn them to account.* It breaks in on him now, and Celada sees the way forward: to bear up under the torment of the pain in his head, the heartloathing, the nausea, and to climb higher and higher on a pitilessly steep, lacerating stair. That is the way to the inhuman. Sanglade is the perfection he has always fallen so villainously short of attaining. There is a power that will do more than rescue Dr. Crapelin—it will annihilate Ukehy as readily as, with clairvoyant imagination, he had summoned Ukehy.

"*I* found it," S. is saying, proudly, gratefully.

She is the teacher who will drive him and never relent. She will chase him on without mercy, to see him climbing constantly higher.

No more rest.

No more fat.

No more waiting.

No more silliness.

No more waste.

Celada is oblivious to the touch on his arm, and the voice saying, "Listen closely to her, brother."

He doesn't see that he is now alone. Some time ago, T. crept away, in respectful silence.

There is a small door in the wall. Celada slips through it and enters the grounds. The air within the walls is cool and autumnal. The sun sets. The sky opens and lifts. Pools of fragrant shadow gather in clusters at the base of the house. Celada discovers the ornamental garden. Before him lies a narrow marble walkway, perfectly flat and even, which fluoresces faintly in the dusk; it bisects a zone of grass so richly luxuriant it seems purple. The garden is like a miniature world, with tiny fences, and child-sized benches of white stone.

There is a passageway here, with walls of yew and cypress minarets. Celada follows it; he can sense the presence of the house ahead of him. There is a bird—he never could tell them apart—singing by itself. Its call echoes hollowly in space. Celada finds the magic door in the angle, where a projection of the house rejoins the overall contour.

U. did not go far. He has resumed his post at what used to be a travel office. There are faded posters on the walls that remain, the wall in back torn away to the alley. He turns around, looking toward the house, up to the sky, then around him, wondering if he will have the opportunity to catch sight of her as she glides past in the street, in her nightly excursion in from the horizon to the house at sunset. Wind drops by. I know that any day now the work will begin again, giving me the right to think of my current inactivity as rest. There are competing drugs, back in someplace. Living hate sculptures. Hatred in the shop windows: solidified, material hate. Hate in the streetlights, in the pavestones, in the headlights, helicopters, hissing cars.

I see the sun describe a little circle in the air, a loop-de-loop.

In the glass in front of me, suddenly—the face of an idiot.

Que miraculo . . . A leper angel as lean as a stick, gesturing toward me with long knuckly hands and skeletal arm. Let fear be your guide. Disband the army, the police. Open the jails, your every door and window, every door and window, and draw it in. When there are a number of differences to consider, some you pass over instantly in fright, but fear is the sign marking them your destination. You want to look steadily, to see if you can know the specter of a hidden desire.

The *exhilarating thought* imagining that the invisible world and its masters exist, with all their terrible power. That fear is joy, like a black snowflake . . . tilted wing merchant, a feathered grenade: bourmorals pesenhuman = solution testatewent: copper purple mauve rounded diamonds lozenges lead sinks punched in holes thready with a fire husk husked with fire and all billowing incandescent gold sticks, the branches conspire with the lambent wind in a white forest of air.

What is day for night, is night for day. She will pass this spot on her way to her bed in her house of triumph, unseen in an audibly breathing modelsuburb, if you can call it that, that breathing thing, figure it more to be a cosmic machine. Or it is the spell of the black locusts they eat. Lean out to see a gull in the air like a paper lip . . . paper lisp . . . then like magic the patch of light on the wall reappeared . . . the interruption of light by the passing train—at once all the gold, all the fire, goes out of the light, and it becomes spectral and lunar. In the window, the leper returns his gaze directly, his nose an arrow pointing to his mouth.

They'll never understand this fear; their fear is base but this, despite its humiliating afflictions, is noble. A noble fear. For it's the fear from infinity; it's my fear sets me above them. I still have the vestigial habit of exaggerated precision in speech: I mean that this fear is rational, not irrational, even if it is like a snowy land all covered in bloom. Ahead I see the shadow of the house sway on a low cloud that retires respectfully to the south. The house whose name I've learned beams at me its ribbons of sway.

Celada digs his heels into the gritty clay surrounding the smooth threshold-stone and pushes against the door with all his strength. While it is not locked, the hinges are nearly seized and the door is immensely thick and heavy for its small size. Celada mashes his face and shoulder against it, his feet slipping. His migraine is pulsing crazily against the wood of the door. Celada calmly and steadily presses, sensing the barely perceptible shifting of the mass of the door. The hinges grate and snarl, he draws his legs in, compressing and expanding, and, through crescendos of pain in his head, he sees the aperture widening by tiny degrees.

The door will not give way. It must be driven back inch by inch, and will close up again if he relents at all. He has to move his feet up quickly to keep bearing down on the door. Presently there is sufficient room for him to insert his arm, tightly folded together, and apply force with his palm against the inner wall, which has a sharp strip of brass all around it that cuts into his skin. His blood smears it, from shallow, painful cuts. Celada is squeezing his bulk into the gap. If he were thinner, he might have been able to slip through it. He swells his body, straining. The door will not budge, and he must not move, or it will shut again and all his work will be lost. The sheer stress of remaining there makes his body tremble. In a sudden frenzy he pushes madly and brings his knee into position against the frame, feeling a sort of lurch as if the door were about to squeeze shut again. He strains wildly at it, but still it doesn't move. He's sure there is an obstruction on the other side that blocks it from opening any further, but to look around is impossible.

A crazy effort. The door swings a little wider. Celada lunges desperately forward, and the door claps shut with a blast of sound behind him.

(O.)

The intimidaters circle low overhead nearly every day now, so that the students catch themselves listening for the drone of the engines. Trudy watches one from inside the empty shop front, as it describes a series of hypnotic circles over an area not three blocks away. One of her associates has gone to the sill, and she gently pulls him by the fabric of the small of his back. A glance at her answers his question—watch, but stay well under the roof.

They've gotten together to discuss their plans; an oceanic rising and falling there in the room, and the back-and-forth of voices.

"They wouldn't have him in the jail."

"Is there any point in going to a judge?"

"Would there even be a record of his arrest?"

"The local police," V. says, "keep their active files in the records office for eight months in most cases, a year in some others, then transfer them to a central archive. Except for murders. But the others wouldn't keep their records with the regular police."

"Do you think a court order . . . ?"

W. shakes his head, "They would deny. And I think too," he raps the air once with the back of his index finger, "that, if the doctor is still alive now, a court order, perhaps even the request, would cause him to be killed. Because then they could dump his body somewhere, he would be turned up by someone, and it would have been made to look like he died in an accident."

As he finishes what he is saying, X.'s tone drops and his head lowers until he is looking somberly at the ground. Someone else sighs.

Y. looks up a little.

"Do you have a description of him?"

They give him the snapshot.

"How tall was he?"

They have a description provided by his wife.

"She's free? She got away?" he asks, not excited, but his mood a little lightened. Trudy is listening too—she doesn't know about Mrs. Crapelin, either.

"She was visiting relatives in Choemett," a young man is saying.

"Has she come back?" Z. asks, looking concerned.

"No, she's frightened."

"That's good."

"But she wants to help her husband, if she can."

"Do you think you can find him?" Trudy asks A., pointing vaguely at the picture and the index card with his description scribbled on it. B. looks down at them and wags his head.

"I can look."

We're hunting, Trudy thinks, Ukehy is a shark, gliding without haste, writing circles, until a blind impulse drives it inward. Then comes the nightmare of mutilation, a sickeningly brief attack. And then back to gliding along, just like time, silent and indifferent. In the old days, the politicians used to form alliances with street gangs. Then comes secret police, they're given more and more money, and asked to do more and more, in time, they vanish into omnipresence. They exist for their own sake, they run everything, just because they can step in anywhere, anytime, to make adjustments. They hover in doorways. Watch silently from corners. Listen through the walls. Slither along the rooftops. Invisible, untouchable.

Bullets fly from the doorways windows rooftops and alleys and passing cars, they jolt and sting, popping off fingers and an ear. His mouth fills with blood, and blood rinses down over his eyes, mucking up his eyebrows. C. is becoming transparent with incandescent pain. A phantom of light bounds through the streets and melts against the horizon. The body windmills. D. is molded by her hands out of buttery light and gambolling along the spinal column of the modelsuburb under rafters of ribs, with the vibratory sensation of the humming nerve coming up through his legs and imparting more spring to his high, drum-major steps. For no other reason than that he needs something to do with them, he twirls his arms in the air like flails, snapping his fingers and whistling with hollow cheeks. Ahead of him his ribs shape a solar pavilion, complete with plain white streets of unadorned square buildings, powdery with plaster dust and smelling like fresh paint. Masked men are working there with specially muted power tools, planing and sanding, throwing up white plumes.

He crosses Invierno to Paleovalle and calmly smoothly and cautiously slips through a gap in a fence, cuts through a construction site that is older than many of the adjacent buildings. Twinkling green lawn appears in perfect squares to either side of him, the sprinklers gushing white smoke. A hop, and cross a butter-colored straw road and into the rocks on the far side, where rippling heat nests like snakes. Plastered with sweat and the dust that his steps kick up, he eventually veers along a short slope of brittle, bleached grass half-pulverized in the dry heat, and into the stunning shade of the pines.

The air is spicier with the peppery musk of dried needles. He doesn't stop, but his eyes undazzle slowly, so he is stumbling a bit at first. His sockets smolder and his whole face smarts with gradually effervescing solar rivets.

He follows the smell, and lowers himself carefully over the side of the grave, trying his best not to step on the bodies. This is impossible, however, because the sides of the pit are fairly sheer and the bodies are numerous. They have been dusted with quicklime, and his steps send up small spurts of it, immediately irritating his mouth nose throat and lungs with flashes of acridity, like horseradish. Almost at once his nose is gushing, his mouth is swollen and slobbering. This attracts the clouds of flies also stirred up by his feet, and he has to pull his collar up to cover his mouth and nose in order to prevent them gluing themselves to his face with his own mucous. The smell released by his feet is unctuous, rusty. E. nevertheless checks the bodies methodically, choking quietly to himself, one hand holding his shirt across his face and the other clamped on the curling snapshot of Dr. Crapelin. Presently he works his way out toward the middle of the pit, a skirt of flies churning around him and well past his knees in a morass of carcasses at all stages of decomposition. His feet are sunk in what is really only corruption, seething with tiny, caressing movements. F. continues patiently to examine each body in turn, exposing those underneath by gently pulling back the uppermost, but trying not to unsettle the remains in any greatly conspicuous way. More than once, he thinks he's found Dr. Crapelin, but the resemblance to the photograph in each case is belied by inconsistency with the listed height and weight. More than once, he mistakes for a single body what is really an amalgamation.

At the further end of the pit from the corner at which he started his search, G. finds a body that he warily, but with increasing assurance, recognizes.

It is one of the more recent ones, still dressed in a tweed jacket and the remains of a vest. The bruised arms are flung up past the head, extending from the sleeves of the jacket, and as

183

yet only swollen and discolored, dusted with lime. The hands are lightly charred. The back is peppered with bullet wounds. It is difficult to be sure of the face; a dog mauled it. Nothing in the clothing, then with a sort of gurgle he extracts a handkerchief clotted with liquid decay. The initials "CC" are embroidered in one corner. He thrusts this into the pocket of his pants, and wades toward the edge of the grave.

As he leaps for the rim, he hears voices. He drops back down at once, permitting his shirt to fall from his face. There are more than two voices, male, their easy familiarity with this domain of death is plain in their manner. H. flings himself headlong among the bodies and drags one on top of him, then another.

In order to keep the fluid from getting into his eyes, he has to keep them tightly shut. He suppresses his breathing, lying as still as he can. After some time, with the one ear he is able to hold above the surface, he hears a thump. The dead mass ripples. At once he guesses that they have brought a victim, already dead hopefully, to dump into the grave. He hears no shot. A rustling and a laugh from up above, then his nerves strain hardest as he hears a longer note, a questioning tone from one of the men. He thinks the voice says,

"Hey, someone's been fooling around down in there. Look."

The speech of the others is less distinct. Their exchange goes on for some time, alarmingly quietly. With a sudden shock of fright I. realizes he can sense a shifting movement among the bodies. His eyes want to spring open, but his mind suddenly returns to the street, the springing and bounding in the light, a boy runs in front of him and vanishes in a blink through a doorway.

Escape once, escape again. It's easy, because there is nothing else, there is nothing else. There is *nothing else*. He does not jerk when the long branch jabs at the body lying half on top of him, drawing it aside, but when he is prodded himself his foot twitches despite. He feels himself being studied.

The other body slumps on top of him again, and he feels the next body over tremble. He is sinking. J. has to move his head slightly to keep his mouth and nose above the surface.

"Rats," a voice says.

"That's even enough," one says, and a few handfuls of quicklime are thrown down—the grains ignite in his nose and he suppresses a sneeze that ruptures half-formed and painfully in his chest.

A long, or long-seeming, pause follows. At the end of his endurance, one eye pops open and darts wildly to and fro.

One of the men is standing at the other corner of the grave, idly tracing curlicues of urine through the air onto the bodies. Out of the corner of his eye he glimpses a sudden movement down in the pit and, as he turns, a rock smacks into his face and with a squawk he pitches over into the pit. He lands face down, and, before he is able to right himself, something, a branch it feels like, is ramming him down into the slop. For a moment, he has the wild idea that one of the corpses, streaked with slime, had leapt from the mass and come at him from the side. There's nothing within reach of his arms solid enough for him to push himself up against, and he coughs and struggles not to drink any of the foul liquid in which he sinks. The man sees flashes; small splinters and squares of dark gray slide sideways and disappear. What he sees are flashes, a closing ring of shadow, sparkling teeth in a cadaver's face turning to the twinkling snowflakes of the sunlight through the branches. K. raises the heavy branch he's been using to pestle the man down into the water and brings it down on the top of the man's skull, killing him.

L. looks around, the other two seem to have gone back without waiting. Certainly there is no sign of them. The gun he wraps in his shirt. He uses his feet, holding on to the edge of the grave, to drive the man he killed deeper down into the muck at the bottom, then shovels lime all over him—that's lime there, in a heap by the pit. Drags other bodies on top of him. More lime, and the concealment is, as best he can tell in her light now dimming, satisfactory. With haste, but not carelessly, he scuffs out the signs of their struggle, hiding the rock he hurled when he leapt from his hiding place (this he puts the crotch of a big tree).

He escapes exactly as he had before, carrying the gun in a bundle, scrubbing out his track, the word *revenge* exulting sternly up from the blackening pines as she is no doubt passing at this moment through the streets toward the house.

(.)

William trots smoothly up the steps from a basement office with a few folders folded under one arm; Trudy is crossing the paved yard in the direction of the temporary offices.

"I need to see Dr. Houseman," she says, her voice wavering uncertainly. Is she a doctor? What is her title anyway?

William nods with a brisk smile. Following him, she gets a whiff of his soap.

At the next corner he turns like a top and holds out his free hand with a courtly little bend at the waist.

"Won't you wait here?" he asks.

"... It's private ... I'd rather discuss it inside."

He doesn't unbend, and a thoughtful expression crosses his face.

"I'll ask," he says. "Please?" he gestures toward the spot on which she stands, by which he probably means she should wait there. Trudy nods, and makes a soft, awkward sound in her mouth.

She waits. Facing her is a long wall with flaking, porridgy

plaster on it. The sky is gloomy, hemmed in by the roofs above her and the tossing foliage of the trees. The air is very fresh, and she seems to drink universal rustle in with each breath. William slots into view and waves her to follow him.

Miss Houseman waits for her in an empty lane that opens onto frothing trees; the clouds are tearing open and mashing shut again so that daylight ebbs and surges across her face, turning toward Trudy. The parasol that shades her she holds perfectly still in her right hand, her left pressed to her abdomen. As Trudy draws near, the scene in front of her is weirdly *at one*. The flickering light bats across Miss Houseman's eyes, making the pale, beautiful irises look yellow. Unperturbed by the wind, she watches Trudy come while the intermittence of the sun fractures and refractures her expression. Trudy has a vivid presentiment that she is about to talk to from another world.

"I am sorry I'm not able to meet with you inside, Miss Bailey," she says, and, though faint, her tone is distinctly warm. "But I have so little time these days."

"I wouldn't insist, but there's . . . I urgently need to talk to you about something."

Miss Houseman waves her umbrella as though it were a wand. "You may speak here."

"I'm not sure I can—"

"You can."

"Well, some of the students are concerned—seriously concerned—about a member of the faculty, who is in serious trouble . . ."

"Yes," Miss Houseman says. She still stands with her head slightly turned toward Trudy, not having turned her body as well. William takes the parasol from her and holds it above her head.

"Are you certain we can't go inside?" Trudy asks.

"Yes," Miss Houseman says patiently.

Trudy looks around.

"Don't worry," William says.

"I've been asked," Trudy says swiftly, in a low voice, and Miss Houseman tilts her head slightly forward to catch the words, "to find out what the school is going to do about it."

Miss Houseman tilts her head back again, out of the ambering light that had crossed it, and returns it completely to the shade of the parasol.

"William," she says softly.

"We know all about it," William says quickly and quietly, but levelly, so that she can plainly hear everything he says. "We are taking precautions on behalf of the remaining teachers, but we also must be careful, or we could lose the school."

Miss Houseman begins to move away, toward the buildings, and William with her.

"I hope you're not disappointed," she says, almost distractedly, as she goes.

"Well, thank you," Trudy says.

Miss Houseman says something else that Trudy doesn't catch. William seems to realize this and turns his head.

"She says you should expect a visit," he says.

Heading back to the storefront, Trudy thinks the air of eerie portentousness hanging all around her interview with the president was a put-off. She's only increasingly sure they mean to do nothing, sacrificing Dr. Crapelin for the good of the school or some garbage. She slips in through the door and finds herself alone in the shop with the big cans of paint thinner covered in a heavy tarp, left there a long time ago when men quit scraping the paint. She sits down at a cable-spool table. Outside, the wind pours whirring over the walls and the roof. Two intimidaters boom by overhead within five minutes of each other, and one of them starts roving to and fro. Hunting.

A horrible stink washes over her, so bad she springs to her feet looking around in alarm. She catches sight of a figure, black and glistening, in the gloom outside the window, and gasps. She recognizes M. the next moment, and her fear changes its tenor and becomes concern—

"What happ— Are you hurt?" she asks.

N.'s right shoulder lifts up to his ear and for a moment she wonders if he's in pain, but he's only reaching into his pocket. Without a word, he lays a filthy rag on the windowsill. The whites of his eyes are bright in his befouled face, as are his teeth when they appear.

"I've killed one of them," he says quietly.

Trudy stares at him.

"I took his gun. I have it hidden."

She puts her hand to her mouth. He reeks of decay, and to her he seems unquestionably insane. Now he leans in through the window, keeping his eyes on her face, and points to an exposed corner of the rag.

"Here. His initials. I found it in the inside breast pocket of a body that I'm sure was his body. They shot him in the back."

Trudy's brow and lips contract.

"I—I'll tell the others."

O. nods, and begins to move off.

"But if you killed one—!" she says, "—won't they . . . ?"

An incredibly strange smile creases P.'s face. That intimidater is bellowing somewhere and Q. glances suddenly to one side, toward the library.

When he speaks, his voice has soft excitement in it.

"Don't worry about that. They're more sure of my being dead now than before. I hid my victim very cunningly. They may have found him already, but there's a chance maybe . . . some chance they never will find him. I won't stay. I won't lead them to you."

He looks steadily toward the house as he floats back from the window and slips away.

The intimidater wafts over the center of town.

For hours he will wander the streets, the filth drying and congealing, gluing his undershirt, stockings, and trousers to an itching body he dares not scratch.

With a dreamlike feeling, Trudy leans toward the handkerchief, stopping her breath against the reek of rotten blood that rises from it, and sees there the red saturated embroidery of two C's gracefully twined together for Carlo Crapelin. The letters strike her eye like a knell, and she's instantly convinced there's no mistake. Vague and terrifying images of his anguish scatter themselves around her mind. Why did they do it? Because they can. The roar of intimidaters, the screams of sirens. That's the only reason they ever do anything.

(.O.)

Sanglade sings out as she comes through the gate, the whole house blazing with reflected daylight only just emerged from the clouds and sharp, hard-outlined, as her gaze climbs its front despite herself and her determination not to pause and look. She admires the house grudgingly.

"I wish its shutters were all hanging off . . ."

With her head bowed and her free arm swinging she takes long strides down the path toward the door. Above, her gaze still seems to climb the front of the house. She imagines herself clinging to the treacherous surfaces, her fingers sliding on their own grease, feeling her equilibrium tip back, ounce by ounce.

Felix Houseman comes around the corner, from the direction of the ornamental garden. The figure coming around the corner toward her is not complete. It's mainly only legs she sees. Two legs, in swinging tweed, walking in what after all only seems to be a particular, individual way. The knees come up a bit high, as though he were trying to keep from brushing his pant cuffs in tall wet grass. The grass just there is freshly mowed, short and dry. There's the jacket, too. And the drifting hands; the crown of the head gleams wanly like a steel lid, the face is a charcoal sketch, smudged with dull iron concavities. Trudy breathes through her mouth. Perfectly quiet, Sanglade roars just a few feet away, like an exulting monster. Of course, there's nothing there at all. The man she thinks she saw, she thinks is truly in his grave. No, not in his grave, he fell, and was never found.

The vigor with which she crosses the veranda, opens the door, and goes to her place is more like the momentum of someone galloping out of control down a steep slope. Surrounding her now, the house hums giddily to itself and expands. Dr. Camatsura calls to her and she can barely make out the sound of her voice, because the silence only makes the crying of the house plainer. The soft fireworks of Clare Houseman's song burst in her mind's ear, the steadily ascending notes, at the base of the long staircase where her body had been found, the notes implacably rising sharpened steps.

She goes to answer Dr. Camatsura. At the base of the stairs, she stops. There's a little glass vial, filled with black liquid, tucked into the corner of the fourth step from the bottom.

Flushed with anger, she takes a step forward, drawing out her arms slightly, wanting to smash the vial, but then she changes her mind. She won't smash it. She'll turn away, deciding this is a provocation she won't answer. As she turns, she glances up the length of the staircase to the skylight high up in the house, on the third floor, which she has never visited. The song still turns in her head, with the vision of Clare Houseman's body draped over these sharp steps—and now rotted away in her coffin . . . and now Dr. Crapelin, limp and sodden in a stinking slough, and cleverly hidden.

Dr. Camatsura's voice calls her again, through the silent din.

Going back to her place with the armful of papers Dr. Camatsura gave her, she passes the staircase again. The vial is gone.

The house goes on and on, vacuously singing to itself and staring down at her from tiny square niches set into the moldings of the doors. Ages ago, while she was still susceptible to the charms of the house, she had climbed a chair to get a look in those niches. They contain fine little paintings of houses; gold lines on black.

"How preoccupied with food I am," Celada thinks sleepily, lying upstairs in the attic, directly above Trudy. The air is close and uncomfortably warm. He takes a sip from the small glass vial that rests within reach of his hiding place, a nest he's made from a number of rolled-up carpets and screened with a desk and two large presses. The water, though tepid, trembles like mercury inside him. His head tingles, clears, and becomes weightless. Wanting to sleep but unable to, his active mind is tethered like a helium balloon to the shapeless anchor of his body. He'll sleep during the day. They are less likely to find him if he is lying there, still and silent. Then, at night, he will be able to explore the house. Provided he doesn't snore. He's not too sure he doesn't.

Food would not be a problem, provided he could stop thinking about it. It's astounding, he remarks, how the time of his life is segmented by meals. Not so astounding, really, considering how difficult it is to come by food naturally. But if he can't even quit thinking about it, how can he expect to make progress? He folds his arms and resettles himself. The attic roof has not one chink, he notes with admiration. The only light comes from a window to the rear of the house, adjacent to the stairs. The light is white, and nothing can be seen in the window. It shines on a floor that is polished and clean of dust, tracing the outlines of what few remnants are still stored up here. He doesn't allow a pang of hunger to prevent his reflecting on a surprising number of tables. You would think they might have more use for them.

To one side of the window there's something almost completely in the shadow—a thin crescent of reflected light, another further down: the hairless head and the shoulder, respectively. And the small, more distinct, and perpendicular crescent of light there is the side of the right eye, watching him.

"Teacher!"

S. emerges from the bushes in a public park. It's the lull between the departure of the after-work idlers and the arrival of the evening strollers. He still hasn't found any water, except a drinking fountain, and, though the grue on his body has dried, it still stinks too much. No homeless man stinks like *this*. As conspicuous as he is, he didn't want to go back to el Miserable del Sol, and he has not been able to find a change of clothes anywhere. Not even a clothesline. What's more, all this activity exacerbates the irritation of his skin, which he doesn't dare scratch for fear of gangrene. Without any idea what to do, he hides himself, scraping his body carefully with soft twigs and scrubbing at himself with dirt, which is no small help, but still not enough. Nearly beside himself with itching, he makes a dash for the men's room. It is empty. He flails wildly at the sink, sudsing his face hands shirt, everything within reach, with clumps of powdered soap. On two occasions someone tries to come in, only to be bounced back out with an exclamation of disgust.

Wetting himself makes the smell suddenly much worse, and

he pauses to retch into the basin, even as his hands still rub discs of lather into his chest and shirt. He empties one soap container after another, tossing water everywhere.

When he's neatened himself as best he can, T. leaves, still wet. A passing turns back as he emerges. He walks swiftly into the dark, open meadow.

The expanse is dotted by a few double shadows, but mostly empty. He finds the most secluded spot and rolls vigorously in the grass for a long time.

(.)

His skin looks artificially whitened. What its true color is there's no telling. He seems to emerge from the grave. No, he appeared among the graves. The rain made them shiny, and his reflection, like a white column, stalks from one headstone to another. A black whip is coiled in his hand. He is hairless and naked.

Yes, scourge them. Hurt them. Lash, whip—lay your whip along the crowds, crack them open like empty nut shells. It came from the bottom of the sea, where whips swim like eels in the sunless cold. She studies the movements of his arm and wrist and imitates them with a length of shredded newsprint, experiences and notices the uncanny feeling that comes with repeating something correctly, as though she had suddenly sprung into a machine.

The specters are just a game, a pastime. All around the house there are statues of black bronze that are nearly invisible in the dark and seem carved from darkness. Death the space, the room inside, in summaries always different, a phantom version, her face a police sketch, look in eye, a book she takes down from a shelf entitled *Solauni*, clouds fields smudges of light. Every day they used to gather in the parlor without lamps and *in total silence* as the sun set. A peephole view, the eyelet loop in the ornamental business lining the façade of the house: a flat sideways eye like a figure on a Greek vase. There's a song drumming in the air again as she steps, in the grass, from one statue to another, coming from the house. It spreads through the house in a spectral conflagration . . . sunlight howls as it strikes the eaves . . . the house hums like resonating stone, is she deaf she can't see the sunlight, for her it's still nighttime. Or has time stopped, and these bronzes are actually people frozen in time, no light appears because there's no time in which it could travel? Does light illuminate things because it streams, or would stationary light still shine it would still shine, and these are bronzes—real people wouldn't have the warped, half-molded look. It has irritating friability, not heard after all, but imagined, like a low note played on a saxophone. It lingers, looking into the shadows and the dark green curds. The long, low notes of the song come from a dead body slumped in a chair in the basement. Water drops from a leak in the ceiling above the chair and drips down on him; the drop gathers and drops down in a gout that strikes the hand, drooping from the arm of the chair; the drop spatters and deepens a crater in the hand hollowed out by the dripping, a dimple in the unbroken skin over the mushy flesh.

Yes, she says with avidity, the fear comes from the world, because Sanglade is really like that, she thinks. Something like that about the house—a wild, pulsating, impersonal, mechanized joy . . . terrible joy that no tragedy, no matter how powerful, could delay . . . like a really wild laughter that wants to hammer the soul out the top of the skull. Her skin cold as ice, steady pressure, cold hard and smooth, against the soles of her bare feet. She peers along the corridor in both directions, the night's icy hand on her skin. I crack the whip—the demon holds up the mirror, and is not reflected in it himself. After first class

195

of the day, it's back to Sanglade: the house that dripped abrupt turns of the head. Songbirds love the house and en masse salute the sun in mayhem of shrilling from its trees; Trudy can hear it gush there, ahead of her. She's walking right into the cacophony.

All night, and still now, she has an inexplicable feeling of restlessness, something to worry about, something wrong, but there isn't anything to worry about is there, everything's fine . . . everything's fine, fiiiiinne—but is everything fine? How would I know whether things are fine or not? Fine? What kind of idea is that?

Trudy collects herself gallantly, but she's trapped in helpless moments when just about everything becomes a source of emotional pain, even the thoughts turned to for relief or distraction. I'm wasting away, even though I am doing things all day long. The house is all straight lines, severe, relentlessly straight—the pain, the exhaustion, the stubborn ache of "training." Training for what? Above her looms the somber gleam of its brass, the frosty orgy of its decorations, slave breakers. Effervescent fatigue enshrouds her head, and she lowers it momentarily, feeling a little inclined to pitch onto her face and rest in the sinister grass. Trudy finds herself turning aside only to look into the ornamental garden, with its narrow white paths through nothing, no hedges or plots to weave through, only the grass. She imagines the horror of being eaten, and seeing parts of yourself disappear forever down the gullet of a greedy animal that swells every moment with greater vigor feeding on your body.

Is that the test I am supposed to endure without complaint, being devoured by whatever is here? I won't do it. The demand is like the dark glamor of his religion; omitting "till death do us part" for no selfish reason, but only in keeping with an incomprehensible literalism far more frightening than selfishness. Her thoughts just won't come out properly. She has

196

a persistent feeling, like a dust clot caught in the throat, a dry tuft that can't be coughed out.

One of the collections she is supposed to index consists of shelves and shelves of slim volumes of line drawings, like printed sketchbooks. None have any discernible narrative, and they're all by different authors. A ghost's domain would be like three-dimensional line drawings, vibrating and cobweblike. There are some written passages but not many. Trudy scans one idly, but she can't exactly make her eyes read the lines in order. The letters swim up from the page to form other words. "For-itself," and then above and to the left the word "which," scramble together to make the word "wolf" . . .

Trudy's hand takes down a book from another set of shelves and shows it to her. The cover seems weirdly cold. The book contains a clipping from an article, old to judge by the typeface, the title cropped but the byline remains. "By Felix Houseman":

> "In climbing, sometimes, one gets to the moment of no return. Not only all thought of points of departure, or of the abstractness of the space intervening, but also any notion of a destination, of any goal whatever, is utterly forgotten. So one proceeded aimless, in a spirit of pure perseverance, and, without so much as an idea of steady ascent, no idea whatever, but only that of soaring."

Lights appear on the wall, presumably from something outside.

The secret is that time never stops, she tells herself, stopping to stare at a fantastically decorated mantelpiece clock. It has a pearl face, very simple arms, a squat, massive frame of malachite with soft amber rods all over it, and the face is framed by four sizeable opals. The opals all still contain water, trapped for millennia in the stone. That water comes from a body of water in which what is now her blood once circulated. Now pinched off and sealed in stone. No circulation. Wearily touching her brow

197

she goes back to her place, then gets up again, pressing her hands again to her head. It couldn't be a migraine, could it? Some people only get one in their whole lives. Automatically she flips through the catalog cards, which give off a smell like stale caramel, until she finds a listing for Dr. Crapelin. The card is fresh, and points her to a box on a shelf—his papers, just submitted.

My identity is what returns to me, particularly when I reawaken. It's also a homing point to which I return; the closer I am to it, the more I am this, while I am attenuated to the extent that I move away from it. Identity, which is a strong prison. I see, I am seen, I see myself seen, I see that seen, I see seeing, etc.

What returns to me must not be recognized as me, and must not trail any leads back to him, but appear as something that emerges from darkness with no umbilical. The listener in this case only pretends to believe you, because he is trapped in a fatal disaccommodation with the world and its powers. He knows every stone because he knows one of them and they are all alike. He shares with me an abstract intimacy involving vision. He is already her intimate other half, not a stranger, and not ordinary, since he must partake in some way of her intangible, unworldly nature. She is his dream, she is his inside projected, what is normally hidden from view.

So much fruitless trying! So often the opposite of the desired effect appears to mock the effort and the calculus the whole business of calculating chains of cause and effect, the habitual calculus of expectations, the failure of the future perversely or obstinately to appear or the past to pass. This preoccupation with time and with death are related, because death is nothing but absolute time. You may become cold, but you will impart no heat.

He wants to have her eyes forever, so his "and yet" becomes a "therefore." The body becomes immaterial again; it is transient again now that decay can destroy it.

The third party writer has to be assumed, because stories can't reproduce on their own. He is already burying the woman inside his skin, on the surface of the drawing of her eyes. Without her eyes he moves aimlessly in a dark dream. They guided him to their own concealment, and now what? Is this suffering? Is it time? Time will get power over you through doing little favors for you; instead, you must enter the underworld, especially because this all has been the underworld in some way (only in some way) all the while. So I am him *again*, dying forever and never completely—you can only pass through oblivion, you don't remain in it, because there's nothing to do the remaining.

A wild mirthless humor or giddy hilarity every now and then. Starting over. I look at some of the white men, and I imagine I can betray my ancestors and throw off the burden of their exacting stares—I hear their screams. Did he write this?

(Trudy sways. Her mind staggers with sleepiness and fatigue.)

Once you lose sight or look away, once presence is interrupted, no matter how briefly, nothing whatever can be determined. The slightest lapse returns you to the beginning. Repeat.
  Can a gaze be counterfeited?
  she must not be a shadow
  proudly impractical house
  Other lives = other rates of time.
  Escape—but by magic or by enlightenment or illusion,

Behind her, Trudy hears a very faint sound, like an arm moving inside a sleeve.

She stops reading, but does not turn to look. She is feeling the house around her . . . press on the door and feel it swing heavily open, the flutter of air around her face, the clopping of feet on the pavement.

Behind her, at the end of the street, she can feel the outline of the house against the horizon: you are mine, on the grainy black-and-white carousel. A car smashing into him the moment repeats and repeats and now it is bursting into flames, now it bursts in flames and the fire jets out to the sides dousing other cars with flame, now all the cars on the street burst into flame, now the entire street bursts into flame, the block, the

neighborhood, the modelsuburb . . . and he in the shuddering
center of the heat and flames, his pink face transported, a
diamond foetus in the fire, the child flashes all over the room.

(O.)

The joyless, silent streets of Trudy's neighborhood are lined
with deflated, peeling houses and lots choked with big trash
piles. The sewers can be smelled, although there is no sewage
above ground. Every now and then a knobby-kneed little
brother with a finger in his mouth and his staggering younger
sister at his other hand creep by in a daze together, or you catch
sight of them, watching through a hole in a screen door. The
adults are fairly young and prematurely old, grim or fretful, and
there are many old people who are fairly young.

She's tired, and if her bed were anywhere else she'd go
directly to it, but it's in her neighborhood she can't bear now.
The part of the modelsuburb she crosses is more lively; groups
of drunken students and ordinary drunks are suddenly
everywhere being loud sick and abrasive. The air is thick with
noise and every kind of bad smell. Suddenly a slanted blond man
appears from an alley doing up his fly and propositions her; she
keeps walking, stiffening beneath her shawl, and he mutters at
her back. A few blocks away she wonders coolly if she shouldn't
have taken him up on it. She imagines him pastily travailing on
top of her and thinks the disgust would do her good, it might
cure her of mawkishness and groping for a hand to hold. She
balances on the seam in the sidewalk. I don't need damn
comforting. I need to snap out of this. She doesn't want to go talk
to Celada, so she wanders back and forth across the sneerline
bordering her neighborhood, feeling her life going rotten at the
edges. To her right there opens a short cobbled street, a cul-de-
sac ending in a vibrant blue-white wall with an archway in it, tall

weed field on the far side. The uneven street is dotted all over with puddles, and stars reflecting in the still puddles.

It's very beautiful, and Trudy stops to look at it. There are no working streetlights on this cul-de-sac, or near it on the through street, and most of the buildings are deserted. It's quiet enough though the wind seems loud. The boy walks in the field beyond, picking up his bare-kneed legs. The teary light of the rays cling in droplets to his cheeks. The world he brings with him has nothing in it; it's a pastoral, timeless . . . Elysium . . . is the name . . . a moment that never changes, as many of them as there are spirits to haunt them, or they are all sharing the experience of one, wander indifferently through beautiful shrine and starry groves, look up at the star, still there, look up at the star, there is no "later" here, and it's still there, or just there, there's no "still."

"Trudy, I'm calling you!" Merle takes her by the elbow. Trudy turns to her, inwardly startled but not showing it.

"I'm sorry," she slightly shakes her head as if to clear it. "What's happening?"

"I was calling and calling, albeit not too loud," Merle says in her glib way, but without raising her voice.

"What is it?"

"Time for class!"

She pulls back, a young tanned woman with straight black hair in a sloppy knot at the back of her head, and a frumpy, half-asleep look.

"Were you on your way? Sure, I'll come with you." Trudy says it lightly, and they go along together, without saying much.

"The clouds are really quite low," Merle says.

"I hope it doesn't rain," Trudy says.

It's always difficult to tell which classes are legal and which illegal; the rulings concerning the legality of the material, and of teaching itself, frequently change, and there is the additional difficulty of miscommunication, the usual trouble getting reliable information. Subjects that have been permitted for so long that they would seem to be immune to interdiction will be suddenly banned; some subjects that one would assume were forbidden are perfectly legal. Students and teachers are sometimes arrested on general principles, since, what with so many illegalities associated with education, it stands to reason that any student is likely to be receiving, or teacher providing, some contraband or other.

Within ten minutes Merle is leading Trudy down a street lit only by a single, very bright, very strictly contained streetlight. The rest of the street glows blue with nighttime cloud light. Merle leads her to the memorized address, a house with a tall, narrow, shell-like entry way. She advances boldly to the door, opens it with a key, and the two of them dart inside.

"No lights," Merle says. There had been only one light on in the entire street, a window like a tiny brass ingot in a blue stream. That was further up on the opposite side. Merle and Trudy avoid the windows. The house has a clean smell, like freshly beaten rugs. Red tiles on the floor, no furniture apart from an upright piano and a wall hanging covered in broad zigzag stripes.

Merle whispers, "You go keep an eye on the back. She should come to the front door. Come back up here in about five minutes. If she hasn't come by then, we should leave."

"Is it Anatolian today? Or Caucasus?"

"Anatolian!"

Everything is white, and she finds she can see well enough. There's a low stairway in the corner, with a bit of wall built out from it that screens a door leading to the rear of the house. On her left, a short passageway, a little study with a wicker chair and some low white bookcases. Then the back of the house, tiled kitchen, completely bare, and a monochrome yard through sliding glass doors.

When she comes back into the front room, exactly and only five minutes later, Merle is gone. As she enters, whatever it is a smell, a little sound, makes her hesitate, she hasn't got time to pick out the cause, and she moves slowly and silently. Trudy looks into the empty room to one side of the front room, then carefully ascends to the top floor. The steps are carpeted, muffling her feet. She stops a little past the midpoint of the stairs, straining her ears, breathing inaudibly through her mouth, and sinks to one knee the better to stay without moving. Luckily she's not wearing anything bright. She should be difficult to see. She knows somehow that Merle is not upstairs.

A shoe scrapes quietly on the pavement outside; a brief, incidental, but furtive sound.

Merle had been wearing dark slippers, whose soft soles could not have made that scrape.

Trudy waits what might or might not be a long time. She won't move, but her rigid body is tiring. Again and again the scrape sounds in her memory. It was simply too protracted to be the step of a mere passerby. That was no nighttime stroller, that was Jack the Ripper scraping into the shadows folding his knife into the portable obscurity of his coat.

Mentally she explores the house, but always her feet are steered again to the front door. Finally she acts not as prompted by caution but impulsively, descending the stairs sideways, using her hands to help distribute her weight, at a snail's pace. She pads toward the door, jerking up her hands and knees as if the tiles were scalding hot, then setting them down straight and slowly. The unlocked front door oozes toward her. She feels like a body waiting to leave the tomb. Cold doorknob fills her hand. She turns it imperceptibly. Finally, there is a faint click, and she pauses for a long time, feeling the magnetic propensity of the door to swing checked by her arm.

She allows the door to fall open. The external shell permits her to lean forward and look outside without exposing herself at a window, and the light won't fall on her. It doesn't seem as though anything has changed, but she mistrusts her ephemeral memory of the way the place looked as they came in.

By and by Trudy eases first one foot and then the other over the threshold, and draws the door closed. When it is shut, she stands in the elevator-like enclosure with her arms at her sides, sensing the portentous night and space from which it encloses her.

There's a small irregularity in the wall, just below one of several tall ornamental slits, cut like gills into the blue-white plaster. The night light cancels its color so she can only see that the droplet is inky against the white. Silently, without rustling her clothes, she leans forward.

The droplet is dark red, still mostly liquid. With a comet tail smear angling away from the street where a finger smudged the blood.

Trudy notices only too late to stop them the abrupt intakings of her breath, which sound noisy to her. With a paralyzing feeling of fatality she walks forward into the street.

There's no one there.

She begins walking away from the house in what feels like an icy tangle of murderous stares.

"Right now, they are ripping Merle."

(:)

. . . sinuous bones slither in the blue-black mold, claws ribs and thorns sprout from long bones and long fangs crinkle as they grow from smooth carious wens slick with water. These are bones of no living animal, they never were born, never reproduce, and never die, but sprout and shear their elaborations perennially while retaining their kernel shape.

When I was a boy . . .

He briefly struggles for breath.

. . . I would play chasing games with girls. Chasing and being chased. What I would do if one of us caught the other I didn't know. It's not unusual to want to be liked, and to want to impress girls, and please them with some stunt or other, and I was no different from most other boys in this respect. But I think I was different in that I also wanted the girls to love me, and to enjoy not just what I might do but simply who I was. I was preoccupied with proving myself worthy to be loved.

I've spent so little time with you, and yet you have marked me with an indelible mark, it seems. I feel as though you are always present, as if you were clairvoyantly, neutrally, but not unkindly, observing me from afar, and I often become self-conscious when I wonder if, by this or that action, I would cause myself to appear more worthy or less worthy to you. My new, lighter body helps offset my fatigue; I seem to dance on wires down to the basement for another drink. The water fills me up and rinses my insides, and like liquor it goes to my head, but without murking my thinking that is more distinct now than it ever has been in my life.

(.)

The committees paper the town with WHO ARE UKEHY? The word printed in all-red capitals sidles down dry gutters and scrapes across shining squares in cool autumn sun.

Please and thank you, a big friendly smile to blanket Cimelia Cisterna in a moment of silence while people vanish politely, as if they'd never existed; because it is the whole question of what is what exists is what is controlled. Trudy is sketching abstract designs with a fountain pen. The executioner comes into the

205

dungeon and he doesn't even say "this hurts me more than it hurts you," which would be bad enough, let alone, "this is for the greater good," to which at least one could reply, "Fuck your greater good I want to live!" No; when the executioner comes into the dungeon he says "*I am you.*"

( )

The rear of the fourth floor is a large empty hall, so broad the high ceiling seems lower than it is. One enters through a pair of very wide French doors with many small crystal panes and heavy teardrop handles of glittering steel. This might have been a banquet room, but it would have been odd to put one so high up in the building. There isn't a stick of furniture. Large windows with satin gathered curtains, like pale bronze, line the rear wall. A number of long bundles lie against it.

On investigation, these bundles contain pieces of bookcases. Many large sets of shelves would fit easily in here, if it weren't for the six enormous columns that stand in a semicircle, like menhirs. They are solid wood, the trunks of colossal trees; almost three feet in diameter. The columns have sloping collars at their bases, and blocky tops, which are darkly stained—there is some marbling of grain, or so it seems, shadowy and brown as beer—while the body of each column is matte red, vivid without being bright. Where the columns join their bases and tops there is the dreamy luster of a single, thin cord of gold.

Felix Houseman brought these columns from the other side of the world somewhere. They had been made for a shrine that never got built. A god and his consort, carved larger than life from smooth, rust-colored rock, were to stand between each of them. The proposed site for the shrine had been an exposed spot high on the side of a mountain, where it could take advantage, in some way, of the incessant wind. The columns had been stored up there for years, and a residue of wind clings to them; their wood odor is all blown away, and looking at them one has a sensation of wind, even if none blows. We both have permitted ourselves the luxury of these columns.

Crossing the room to the high window, there is for a shocking moment a light there in tops of the dark purple trees; that's the modelsuburb. It's not real, but it is attractive, and it likes to exhibit its lights toward the house once in a while. It likes to hover there, in miniature, nocturnal effigy, before scattering like a swarm of fireflies. Outside the hall, there is a dark landing, a square scabbard around the sword of the long staircase, and all the light comes from below, up the shaft and streaming past this landing in a rectangular beam. The timer operating the light shuts it off. Celada's eyes adjust at once to the darkness.

An explosion high above him, and a body tumbles down the entire length of the stairs, plummeting past Celada in a headlong whir, followed by a crash on the floor below. Celada rushes to the banister, clutching it with trembling hands. At the bottom of the stairs, she is lying, wearing only the gloom of the house, her eyes fixed on his, waiting calmly, her shattered limbs tossed all about her.

"It doesn't hurt," she says.

(.)

On her way home, Trudy pauses a moment in front of the swimming school. The grate is pulled to, but, as she approaches, she sees the open padlock only hooks the chain together. She undoes the chain and slips into the square funnel of the entry way, which smells a little like the inside of someone's nose. One of the black iron doors, dabbled with pale reflection of the street lights, has a disc section at its base, where it scraped aside the

grit and dried leaves. The door is locked. Trudy finds the key
secreted in a light fixture adjacent to the door.

Lights in metal bowls all over the place swell. The soft croon
of the generator is nearly silent. Picking through papers largely
meaningless to her, she notices a locked filing cabinet and
searches mechanically for the key, if only for the sake of
unlocking something. To her surprise she finds this key as well,
tucked into a magnetic case among the refrigerator coils at the
back of the cabinet. The top drawer contains a bottle lying on a
bed of brown newspaper. She finds a folder of his notes in the
second drawer down, begins skimming them, then takes them
over to an enormous table spanning the empty jacuzzi and reads
them with more attention. The notes are prolix and
unnecessarily elaborate, sprinkled with questions he doesn't
seem to answer. Trudy begins working out these answers,
related to the capture of the isolaton.

A sort of whistle makes her look up. William stands not far
from the door with a box between his hands.

"Celada's not here," she tells him. "I don't know where he is."

William comes toward her, stepping easily over the bundled
cables and other litter, his eyes on her.

"Nobody's seen him in days," she goes on. "Have you?"

"No," William says neutrally. "Are you going to wait for him
to return, or will you carry on without him?"

"Yes," she lies.

William nods and sets the box, which is made of dark wood,
on the table.

"You will keep us up on your progress, mm?"

"Of course."

He retires as decorously as a trusted family retainer. Trudy
opens the box. It's filled with shavings. Plunging her hand into
these, she feels a hard ball wrapped in fabric and draws out

something nearly the size of her head and swaddled in burgundy felt. She opens the felt carefully and uncovers a solid globe of optical plastic with a human eye in the center, trailing its nerve like a comet's tail. This in turn is attached to a trim cube of brain, laced with silky wires. The wires are bundled together and become a pair of red and blue coils, connected to a steel jack protruding a few millimeters from the surface of the globe. The iris of the eye is whiter than the white of the eye, and weirdly impersonal; she can't imagine it in a face. It seems like a machine part. Where does it go? Trudy looks around and finds out; there's a conspicuous box of polished metal on a low wall, a little over four feet high and perhaps eight feet wide. The box lifts to reveal a cup-shaped socket in a wooden brace. That this wood is virtually all "eyes" is typical of Celada's sense of style. Holding the ball with the felt cloth, so as not to smudge it, she first peeps over the rim, lined with black plastic fuzz, of the socket—there's a plug of white metal, which could be platinum, sticking straight up from the bottom. Trudy turns the ball jack down and settles it into the socket. In this arrangement, the eye stares straight up. She then replaces the steel box with a snap. The box sits on rollers that permit it to slide to and fro along the top of the wall. There's no telling what it's for. The *isolaton* is the particle of force expressed in the extreme particularity of a general instance. This force tends toward a singularity without becoming one—no, a singularity is the tendency toward becoming one. There are no pure singularities in a static condition. The singularity is defined as the tendency of a force to become one in its ongoing expression. One does not proceed without one. One does not win without having won. The wan one is a winsome one. One won one on one. 111 and 1. One won one; each note is the same, the sequence and emphasis distinguish. Each note is an identical or near-identical moment whose meaning is set by its appearing again. This is both highly particular, being only one, and highly general, all being one, and it generates its own time by its rhythm. The revolution of the particle is the iteration of a new rhythm, and something of this kind is to be observed in the genesis ex vacua of the initiative universal particle, of which the universe is the sequel. The reader who is addicted to a serial goes back for a novelty that in its purest expression has nothing to do with the new predicaments and configurations of elements in the narrative and everything to do with getting back into a distinct time belonging to the serial. Time is mostly void, like space. Just as matter is sparse and cloudy from the putative point of view of an atom, so time consists chiefly of gaps that, though enormous, are still undetectable to our gross perceptions. Not that our gross perceptions don't perceive time to consist primarily of loss; this is to say rather that this sense of time as loss is confirmed at every point at which it is examined. Thought is successive, as Kant said, and therefore necessarily in time. But there is no succession without interruption, any more than there can be something that is at once strictly segmented and continuous, and the scale of these interruptions is *vast*. The human experience is poised hypnotized on abysses of empty time traversed by widely separated stepping stones, the moments, bounding majestically from one to one as dreamily oblivious as a sleepwalker. The littlest thing escapes us, and everything we make gets away from us, and language most of all, most of all. The isolaton will be captured as it comes into existence in a sealed metal tank. Always tanks, always water, he's obsessed.

(   )

     The face . . . the white hairs plastered to the lip . . . the eyes and the tone of voice . . . And he going on thinking about that;

what word will he use for that, for what is impassive and indifferent, but a face is necessary for him to see this, and, because he does see an impassive and indifferent face, he takes this for a tactic all the better to encourage him. The weariness and pain of his interminable climbing of the stairs is transformed into victorious shouting, like the blinding glare of the sun. The noiseless noise and shadow of light are worthy unworth, worthless worth, growing out of him like a plant and flying away from him like a fly, drawn to him and ebbing out of him while he grows too weak to keep in his overflowing strength. He drags himself up a step at a time, with long pauses. They bite into him whether he moves or stops, for the steps are sharp as razors, even through the runner. You have worth you'll never have worth you have it you'll never have it you'll have it you'll never have it. Having it is striving to have it is not having it and never will be having it, so that, if he stops, even at the top of the stairs, even on the roof, he will have failed, and everything suffered up to then—this is the killer—will have been a waste. So if he reaches the top of the stairs he will have to throw himself headlong down to the bottom again, or roll himself, lacking the energy to jump, off the roof.

"No, my boy," he only imagines her saying. "That would kill you, that would be quitting. If you reach the top of the stairs, or the roof, you must climb back down and resume as before."

A head is there against the skylight when he next looks up. He can make out a slash of reflected brass-colored light on the throat, showing a little of the crease at the corner of her jaw, which is there because she is looking down at him, down her nose. In his icy stomach the trembling water churns up into his gorge and settles again, and a cold caustic thrill violently shakes him. Paralyzed, he keeps his eyes on her and feels like fainting, his hands turn to gas, his arms are frail as reeds. The reflections

211

in the polished metal everywhere swim, the ore smashed from the far-away rock, liquefied in a starry furnace charred and groaning, and then shaped by blows, blended into brass, and bronze, and glittering steel, and stern gold. She is still there, waiting; invisibly she cracks the whip. He thinks it doesn't matter what he thinks he's doing, whether he says to himself oh burn away my human flabbiness and make me a blazing metal skeleton, scrub away my soft parts—why not soft parts? Isn't it weak to want to do away with softness and suffering? Shouldn't I pray to be all soft parts and to suffer correspondingly more? No I shouldn't. He lifts himself onto his hands and knees crawls a step, and another step. The more outer weakness, the greater the inner vehemence, fumes of will steam out inflating him, time gaps suck up the froth—

on and
on
and on
and
on and
on
and on
and
on and
on
and on
and
on and
on
and on
and

(.)

Trudy has a drink before she goes back to Sanglade, and she must run, a little tipsily, to escape a sudden thundershower. Halfway between the front door and her "parlor," she realizes drinking was a mistake, it seals up ways of escape.

Motion draws her gaze to the right. There's a large mirror in a massive bronze frame hanging on the wall there, above a solid antique with a thick red and white marble top. Things are too speedy.

"Don't you know better than to look in the mirror in a haunted house haunted house . . . ?"

This is a haunted house.

Like shaggy oxen, the boughs outside dip and plunge. She had a cousin who used to drive her nuts insisting on counting the seconds between the flash and the crash. This storm is an unwanted intimacy she shares with the house and a favor, shelter, incurring an obligation to repay. A faint whistling comes from one of the tiny niches in the lintel, just two notes, the first high and the second lower than the first, and repeated together twice.

This one has a face in the foreground looking out directly, with refined African features outlined in gold on the black and an eye, the face is cropped by the frame at top bottom and one side, an eye like a flat sinker of gold without iris or pupil.

"Oh good," Trudy says chuckling spasmodically.

"Oh good! That's great!" Both hands on the top of the jamb she looks down in confusion between her arms slicing across the door, wondering if this is the moment the chair buckles under her and she snaps her neck against the fender and lies staring at the ceiling forever.

She looks again and says "Sure!"

The image is no different from any of the others, after all. Naturally, there is no face, and, naturally, it's not impossible, not possible she says feebly but really not impossible she means of course, that the miniature's fine golden lines and shapes could have presented, to a hasty, disorganized way of looking, something like the face she obviously only thinks she saw.

She gets down from the chair sizzling around the ears with resentment. Witch books and their ordinary malice come back to her because it's one thing being confronted; what chips away at mind and soul is the way it goes on and on in a thousand snipes a day, the brainless malevolence behind them that is so strong for being weak, that is so effective for being petty, that is so immune to exposure for being superficial, that is so impossible to argue with because it is mindless.

"I'm not going to stand for being teased by a house," she thinks and catches sight of herself in the mirror. She thinks to look away, but walks toward the mirror, staring at it. Her face in the glass—her eyes flicker as they dial all around the surface. There is darkness in the backing that is visible through the silver.

It's as though a plug had been pulled in her head, her vitality drains out and drowsiness pours into its place with a buzz. One at a time, four heavy flies appear on her reflection, although she doesn't see them flying, one on her thigh, one just above her hip, one below her ribcage, one on her bicep. Each lands with a tap. They hum to themselves, but they don't have the frenetic energy of flies. They seem too heavy for their own strength. They stay exactly where they are.

With each slothful tap, Trudy feels a dull spreading shock in the corresponding part of herself. Matterless coins jangle together low in her abdomen, jump up and spin themselves tiny glittering marbles.

There are no flies on the mirror, those are just black spots where the silver particles fell into the depths of the glass. The spots are, however, starting to move, follow her as she sways, hold their places one on her thigh, one just above her hip, one below her ribcage, one on her bicep. Black, limpid eyes. She turns from the mirror. Unreal light is flooding into the room.

(   )

. . . and stopped watching my ribs come out, meaning death is the moment I stop talking to myself, while the conversation between her and me is constant.

In my dreams I never leave the house either, even to visit the grounds, which don't really interest me. It makes exploring the house less tiring.

Every time I wake, laboring to breathe, and there is less of me, I have no more vitality than when I fell asleep, nor is it possible for me easily to note the moments in which I sleep and wake.

When did I last get down to the basement to drink? The distance is astronomical now. I must spend some moments preparing myself to lift my arm, to reach for that vial there.

The water quickens my thinking, and settles heavily down into me.

Even my clothes are flying away from me; I move inside them as though they were blankets. There is no sound but the birds that call after dark, I suppose it is dark. That and the oceanic sound of my panting, a brief drag and an even shorter exhalation. I can't see well enough to tell if she is there by the window or not.

Where? I fall in love with "where?" I love my fear, romantically. But I'm not afraid; I'm too tired.

I know my dreams chiefly because in them I am moving effortlessly through the house, standing upright. I formerly dreamt of difficulties with my clothing, getting tangled in my belt as I tried to auger new holes in it and sleeves that wouldn't stay rolled up, but now I wander naked in the house. No one sees me, or so I assume, because I never see anyone. I always wish I would hear singing. I won't fail this time—How wan and far away that idea is now!

I'm not the first, either. I give my best, even if I am only imitating Hen . . . Haro—Herman. Here is the upstairs banquet room with the pillars swaddled in wind, and watery squares of light from the windows flailing all over the walls, as if the garden below had been strung with hanging lamps the wind throws around. She lied about it not hurting, but then again I don't mind it, so perhaps that's what she meant: it will be painful, but I won't mind it. The water distracts. I can never find the gramophone in the infinity room, but it might be just as well, if I were to find I couldn't manage to operate it. I'm easily stunned.

. . . and the stiffly vibrating infinity pattern on floor and walls stuns me this time, the colors reverse fields and the patterns detach in layers that rush over each other, stretching my attention thinner and thinner away from me.

I do hear drumming now, more or less steady and slow. It's a dull reverberation coming from the basement, and as usual I feel it more than I hear it properly.

It persists as I circulate through the upper floors, and deters me from going to the basement now. The water seems to be brought to me anyway, although I don't see who brings it. I never see anyone. The hall outside the banqueting room is intensely bright, much too bright, the gleams from the metal fittings all over lance my eyes, and seem to chime and clang like tiny bells.

The drumming is still slow and steady, not a migraine though. I no longer get those it seems. Just pounding in my temples and ears so that I wish it would quit.

The stairs.

Even in my dream, it's beginning to be a struggle to breathe. The top of the stairs, with the dark skylight above it, is only a flight away, and she might be up there, for all I know. The wind might be stirring something up there, or that might be her, just out of sight, doing something. Doing what? Perhaps she's getting her whip out, to goad me. It will sink through my intangible dreamform, but she would have thought of that. I can't think. Why doesn't it stop? It hangs on for dear life, slow as it is. Are they building something in the basement? Hammers don't pound in that slow steady way, they burst in groups of prime numbers. I have to lie down on the stairs, I can't stand beside them anymore.

A little rest. It's an odd thing to want in a dream, I know, but everything about dreams is an odd thing I know, everything that I know is a dream, an odd thing about them.

About dreams. That was the subject.

Am I resting?

The drumming is getting tired too. It is slower. Than I remember. Look. Look. Look. She sits two steps above me. She is making a gesture with her hand, for me to climb. Another step. Never mind the drum. It's all old drum.

Dear thing, my old drum. I'm

nodding, to say—

yes,

I'll climb in

a minute, once I've, one

once I have rested, just for a

time.

Are you coming down?

Don't.

You don't need to come down.

217

I can come up.
Up.
I can too
come up
once rested I've
time one
one

(*)

Sanglade turns to Trudy again, obliquely, only half its beaming face. Trudy glares back with simmering distaste. Sanglade seems to revel in the sunshine, as though it were a particularly special day. Maybe it's some tragedy's anniversary today, she thinks sourly. The cool, twinkling gloom of the house opens to her again and she makes her way to her place, dropping her sullenness as a useless encumbrance now she will be cool herself, neutral and calm. She will concentrate, without straining or trying, entirely on her work, and Sanglade can bombard her with pink elephants in an avalanche of dead bodies singing the national anthem without distracting her, calling yes! in falsetto to all her suffering, she won't bat an eye.

After an hour or so, Dr. Camatsura mews in the doorway to get her attention, and softly asks her if she will go upstairs and bring down last year's borrowing ledger from the record room. Trudy arrives at the bottom of the long staircase already resolved to ignore whatever she might see there, keeping her attention loosely gathered around her hand, always firmly on the banister, and on her feet. If there is anything there waiting for her on the steps, she may or may not see it out of the corner of her eye, but these are all just appearances and whatever has nothing to do with her task has nothing to do with her. I'm not paid to see things, I'm paid to perform certain tasks. The skylight draws near, powdering the walls and streaking the wood with tissue. Trudy's legs are strong, and she reaches the fourth floor without slowing her even pace. All the same, she feels momentarily out of breath the moment she stops climbing. The air is thin up here. *The air is fine.* The skylight is still further up, high in a socket. She will not pause, as she nearly did, with one hand on the ball of the banister, but walks swiftly to the record room.

Snapping on the light, she stands in the doorway reading the labels on the shelves that stand end-forward against the far wall. Without wasted movement, without shutting the door, she goes directly to the proper shelf and stands in front of it, hands at her sides, finds the right book and only then raises her hand to take it down. It's a thin, narrow volume covered in dull blue fabric and LEDGER printed on the front. It goes under her arm, and she leaves the record room, closing the door behind her.

She goes back to the stairway determined to be especially careful going down. Coming up, she had been so intent on her task she had not even glanced to her right and so hadn't noticed the attic door standing ajar or the man's shadow that sits just inside it on the steps, almost hidden entirely in the dark.

Don't stop she says to herself and freezes. It's not a man it's a bundle of some stuff that fell down the steps and knocked open the door or it isn't there at all, things don't just fall but they do settle or give way—it's not a man, that's for certain. Her eyes relentlessly draw the outline of a man, there, in the dark.

I'll shut the door the attic door. She doesn't move. She goes downstairs, gripping the banister firmly. I didn't see *a goddamned thing.*

Trudy stumbles on the last step, her foot catching on the runner, and she stops herself abruptly, doesn't fall. You're cute, she thinks, walking back to the "parlor." She sets the ledger down there, only then realizing she was supposed to take it to

Dr. Camatsura. Into the hall separating the "parlor" from the ascending staircase and back to Dr. Camatsura, who thanks her warmly.

Trudy returns again to the "parlor" and settles herself on her high chair. The flailing boughs outside the window fringe the upper limit of her vision as she rivets her eyes on the work in front of her. Some people have come into the house to listen to gramophone records in the infinity room, but the music is inaudible where she is.

Two hours later, she hears Dr. Camatsura wailing at the top of the stairs. The voice calls to her. Trudy rushes to the foot of the long staircase and sees Dr. Camatsura's head and shoulders leaning out at the fourth floor, her face rigid with horror. There's the sound of the gramophone on the second floor; she rushes past Clare Houseman's voice on her way to Dr. Camatsura's stricken face.

Dr. Camatsura, hand to her mouth, her eyes are racing wildly in all directions, points at the open door to the attic and the emaciated, dead man leaning out of it.

"The door was open!" Dr. Camatsura warbles.

Trudy turns to see the skeletal man slumped against the wall, dead, drooping awkwardly out onto the landing, then throws herself down beside him, on her knees. His face is a drum head, the teeth like buckled pavement in brittle mouth. She reaches for him, but she's afraid she'll crush him. Then she takes the knobs that were his shoulders and drapes him gingerly onto his back. She presses her head gently to his chest, and hears only the gramophone. The music falls around her like snow. Celada smiles up at the ceiling.

Trudy raises her face from his body and stares at vacancy or through it at the tear-muddled shining singing house. Impervious silence forces itself on her from the inside, and her life is violated. The medical students stomp up the stairs to examine him. Now two of them, carrying a canvas stretcher folded between them. When Celada is carried out into the open air, Trudy glances again despite herself up at the rapture of the house, which seems to swell and tower and redouble the blaze of reflected sunlight that covers it in golden mail.

(.)

The library is closed, indefinitely. Trudy locks up, as instructed, and begins to walk over with eyes like phosphorus and no words can get near—only the occasional wounding flash in her mind. Invisible force. She sees him withering two floors above her, day by day. She sees herself pottering downstairs, fiddling with his useless experiment in the swimming school. Everywhere she looks she just sees time plain; rage is right up against the back of her like a burning steel wall. Finally night comes on and the streets empty down. Night deepens without Celada for the first time, like millions of nights into remote past and all the nights to come.

U. leaps from his cot out of a deep sleep and, still hardly aware of what he's doing, starts fumbling for clothing.

Trudy bends down and takes a heavy stone in her hand from the rock boundary framing the rose bushes and in the same instant catches sight of a sprinkler key, leaning against the brick foundation. She releases the rock, steps through the bushes, seizes the sprinkler key, and hurries with it to the porch. Shielding her face awkwardly with her left arm, Trudy smashes the window closest to edge of the veranda.

V. is into his clothes now, fly wide open, shirt unbuttoned, he squats to shove his feet into the wrong shoes and then runs out the open doorway cramming his shirttails blindly into his pants, hands rummaging with buttons everywhere connecting them up any which way.

Trudy rakes the key up and down and sideways to clear
fragments of glass from the edge of the frame. The sound of
breaking glass in the night commits her, and she throws herself
all the way into night. Furiously she takes the key in both hands
and swings it her arms straight, shattering the next window
along, then drags the key around the edges to shear them in a
second or two—then another step and bust the third window,
then the fourth, the fifth. She wishes there were more, she wants
to shatter every breakable thing in Sanglade with her weapon.
She drops the sprinkler key and goes instantly to the neat
rectangular bundle of white canvas she's brought with her.
Taking up the canvas, she thrusts it in a wad through the middle
window, leaving it jammed there a moment, like a broken gum
bubble on the open mouth, while she gets the sprinkler key
again; she rams the canvas through into the front parlor.

W. can see for a moment the glimmer of dawn in the
direction of the house although it is not time for dawn and she is
the greatest of all respecters of time—his planted right foot slips
as he tries to round a corner and he falls hard on his left side—
only by stiffening his back reflexively does he avoid whipping
his head against the pavement. With incoherences he springs
back up and runs hard, straight up the street toward Sanglade.

Through the windows one by one Trudy opens and upends
the tins of paint thinner, soaking the canvas tarp especially, then
tosses the lighter in after. A fist of hot air punches her and she
hops from the veranda taking a few long steps onto the wet
grass. The tins are still belching fuel and the canvas has become
a huge wick, channeling flames up the wall and into the curtains.
Trudy watches massive bulbs of fire climb past the parlor
windows to burst against the ceiling, smearing it with vibrating
gold. Cypresses of flame batten on the walls and window frames.

X. streaks across town virtually weightless. The pain in his body is being pinched out by her monumental hands—what is it? He can't think. Is the sun coming up now? The glimmer returns, growing.

Trudy has pulled back to the garden wall. The heat from the fire is too intense to withstand even on the lawn. It gushes from the furnace that the front has become, and the smoke stings the eyes and chokes her. With a kind of raging inner emptiness she sees the fire spin a web with unreal speed across the top of the veranda and begin to scale the exterior. Burning vines grope up the walls and with cackles of breaking windows it twirls into the night air from other parts of the house now. Sanglade has a great deal of metal and stone in it, but the fabric of the house is still principally wood. Trudy watches the fire grow without a word or a thought; she wants to take it all in—yes, the fire will be strong enough to devour the house, swallow it whole, good old fire.

William charges headlong across the quad toward the flames in confusion. He rushes to Sanglade jerking his keys from his pocket he unlocks the gate and flings himself at it rebounding violently as the gate's swingopen is arrested by a length of heavy chain padlocked on the far side.

William seizes the chain with a yelp of surprise. The lock is inaccessible, out of reach against the inside of the gate. William runs along the wall down toward the large double gate at the end of the drive to the Milk House—also chained, the padlock wedged against the inside of the gate where his fingers can't quite get at it to pick it. Again William makes a sound of surprise and distress—then leaps, taking the top of the fence in his hands and pull himself up and over. He charges toward the house— Sanglade is sitting in an enormous lotus of roaring gold, the flames above him. He seizes a garden hose and turns the searing faucet on, wetting whatever isn't burning in the vicinity then pouring water on the closest flames. A scrap of burning fabric lands on the hose without his noticing it, and soon a short length of the hose itself is burning. With an exclamation, William dowses the hose, then retrains the stream on the house.

Trudy watches him. She smiles. The sensation is strange.

Y. can now see the colossal, shapeless jaguar is frisking around her house as if it is berserk with drink.

"The sun is coming up!"

An axe thuds against the chain, stamping feet tumble down toward the double gate at the end of the drive to the Milk House. Shouts. Now she makes her way stealthily toward the Milk House, and the ladder she'd put in the narrow space between the Milk House and the property wall. Z. is throwing himself into the air, bounding down the street—

the sun is rising in the middle of the night!

she can come up whenever she wants!

Trudy pulls the ladder up, balanced carefully on the top of the wall. She swings it over and lowers it to the far side, climbs down it, all as quickly as she can. There might be people at the dark windows of the house whose back yard she is traversing now, wrenched from their sleep by the commotion. But Trudy has planned her retreat carefully, and she enacts her plan now for good or bad.

Once away, she stops to watch. She wants to say something that will dedicate this act openly to Celada, but the impulse feels as if it can't be acted without seeming false.

And the majesty and the glory of the house are at their peak now. It stands wreathed proudly and blazing as impassive as a martyr at the stake, singing the same eternal music louder than ever, more beautiful than ever, as it is engulfed.

(.)

Having started on the lower floors, the fire undermined the upper portions of the house and brought about their collapse a few minutes before midnight. A huge, cylindrical section of the house crumbled in on itself with a wheezing sigh, releasing flocks of fire that tore crazily at the exterior. The blaze had turned into a colossus struggling to escape and tied down with frayed white cords of water from the firemen's hoses.

Sanglade dissolved in big pieces. For an hour the house was a square of flames, with the blackened trunk of the long staircase standing alone in its center. Before dawn the staircase shifted for the first time, with a muffled shout of lumber falling on wood, and ten minutes later it suddenly pitched forward. Its crash was lost in the greater racket made by the general collapse of the upper floor into the steaming basement.

When the fire is out at last, William, at her request, accompanies Miss Houseman to the reeking hole where the library had been. The two of them still look preternaturally immaculate. He shades her from the exploding sun with her parasol, and she stands, hands behind her back, surveying the scene with small, birdlike turns of her head. From time to time she whips out an arm to point and arc a finger parallel to the ground.

"It's a total loss," the head fire extinguisher says ruefully. A tall black fireman, weary and disgusted, walking across the lawn stiffly, using the swing of his body to draw his heavy legs along, tosses a folded, darkened can of paint thinner onto the lawn.

(')

A. brandishes his arms with a rattle in each hand. Behind him, walking slowly, comes a flowing robe with a wig hanging in space above the open collar. The feet rise and fall along the streets of a model modelsuburb. Completely unseen is the night

225

sky where the boy warms his hands at a cold starlight campfire, smiles and sobs long murmuring incantations. What will be attracted to the fire?

B. explains to the bewildered audience that the disappearance of both day and night, which they can't have failed to notice—if only insofar as they are now wholly dependent on their timepieces to mark the changes from one "day"—another word is needed you know—to another, is a consequence of the full maturation of the sun, who was to date a pupa, and whose confinement to the alternation of day and night was a pupation. At the end of the last night, she broke out of her cocoon and abandoned it like these empty clothes.

Now she doesn't come and go, as she did before, but is always present, appearing and disappearing through clouds of time which no more impinge on her than did the clouds of water formerly. Day, night, twilight, dawn will henceforth all be simultaneous; when you see darkness, understand that it is still daylight, and when you are dazzled, remember that it's night-time which darkens your vision. Never her! The blending of dawn and dusk, in other words, vastly amplified so that there is neither dawn nor dusk any more, only brilliant shadow, blinding daylight, and the soft enchantment of full noon. She has, C. announces proudly, put on the eclipse like a crown. The house is the source of life! The ghost is the source of life.

. . . I let go my attraction to the floor, and allow myself to bob up past the staircase to the ceiling, like a balloon.

So here I am, the ceiling. Falling asleep. Fall fall asleep.

Now I am asleep. I haven't been here in a while. The corner of the ceiling, once isolated, could be of any size really, the three converging lines could be a pyramid, or desert highways. I go through the door out of the small dark house and into the cobalt light of the canyon, blue night. The door drops around my ankles behind me like my shadow. A special excitement now, as if that were my nervous system sparkling down there in the valley, beaded golden wire and white light that looks pale green—tiny lights with glow-powder around them—and my favorite, the jagged rents of black—the fields of light and dark both oscillate attraction and fright for opposed reasons. How can the soul be intermittent and immortal? But what if death were a unique crisis, causing the soul to crystallize in the fixed literary form we read about? Is Dr. Crapelin here, please?

The moon . . . the road on the hill like a golden hemorrhage with shining stones lining it, trickling with lights . . . a cloud like a belt buckle . . . an owl flies past just under the moon, I can tell its stout body and silent wings . . . long brown pine needles gathered in handfuls by chance, like torn-out tufts of hair lying everywhere . . . metallic blue street and steely darkness . . . cloud line truncates the mountain . . . a mountainous ghost erupts from the hill . . . musical water . . . clean earth . . .

Who is that ghost? Did I know before? The moon walks with me, made intimate by sight, mind led effects games, clouds toy with it. It seems to arrange the clouds, but the clouds and the moon are separated by thousands of miles from each other you know, and the moon doesn't see the clouds from where it is. Walking uphill, abstracted, with my mouth open and my face slack like an idiot's, or so it feels, I'm ready to see a figure on the road ahead, off to the side, walking like me. I may or may not know or remember the name. Beauty I associate with detached admiration, and all this I see is intimate. The words aren't afterthoughts: the scene the things I see play them on me and they spring up not in not out of my mind. Smell roses, that always means people. Shrill dog I think barks hearing me come across the park and I imagine fulfilling its fantasy by advancing directly to where it is in a straight line through homes and walls,

my eyes blazing, my so-called "body" fills out, I turn into an ogre.
I advance on this yapping panicking dog and tear it to pieces
with my "bare hands." The dog starts awake out of a nightmare.

Gazing at the moon, I walk downhill. I wish I could gaze at it
more steadily, hold my head right or whatever without the
rhythmic jostling of my steps. Why should that concern me? I am
obviously dead.

So it was all wrong, after all. I was all wrong. Start again.

I . . .

hhhhhhm,

I—

I, I— All right, there's some black gravel. That's how to start.
Some detail to hang it all on, like black gravel.

There's some white stone. The ghost erupting from the top
of the hill. A formless blue ghost in the mist. Which is cool and a
little dingy, more like smoke than fog. It's no use—my mind
keeps losing itself in the fog. Gazing at the moon. The dark night
road, angling up. The shadows of trees, so beautiful in the dark,
which is rare and precious you so seldom get it. They won't let
you. Darkness is a privilege they reserve for themselves. They
want you where they can see you. The landscape looking as
though the land had dropped away and left clusters and ribbons
of streetlamps and luminous houses hovering in the void. The
moon, then the hills and valleys are one rumpled quilt of cindery
black, clouds were purple-gray, like vaporized bruises. An
irregular glow fringe the horizon all around. Describing, seeing,
the same things over and over. Again the moon, the road, the
hill. A thread that I can never follow very far, or quit for very
long.

The house stands on a lot with ancient trees, many of them
centuries old. A thin rind of living tissue grows each year on the
hard dead bones, protected by a scabby integument. Roots draw

water and minerals up, and the leaves cook up in sunlight, above us wafting blades of living green impossibly green, and the grass too contrasting sharply with the black earth like a scalp through shorn hair, all supernaturally sharp and clear. The sun dim through lead pane.

The house isn't all that large, but it gives an impression of sprawling. The front porch is deep, bare and expansive. The windows are far apart, no curtains, shadowy as bottomless pools deep in the woods. He approaches the front door and pauses, hand in the air reaching for the bell—somewhere off to his left, invisible in the trees, two notes of a cuckoo repeat. The sound reaches him with a soft echo, dissolves in expanding space. He presses the doorbell button. I'm not sure if he can hear the bell or not, there seems to have been a resonation somewhere deep in the house, two notes. The door draws back on hinges the size of rolling pins, uncurtaining a world of gloom, gleaming wood and rich rugs, spaciousness, dimness and rustlingness and meditative solidity. The house on this floor is a near-perfect wafer of space open around the edges to the slow green fire of the trees.

And then this room I've lived in all my life suddenly seems unfamiliar, and for a moment I see the plaster wall, singed-looking and smudged . . . the two windows . . . the cold liquid glass in my stomach drinking again . . . *earlier*—a familiar feeling—look at the utter blackness in the windows and believe somehow that the room is hovering in space, the windows drinking the blackness which is only transparency when you try to see it as itself.

(;)

Trudy notices that Dr. Camatsura's classes have been canceled, broad black ribbons of marker through them on the schedule.

"What happened?"

"You haven't heard? Her apartment was broken into—she was there at the time, you understand."

Now she's gone all to pieces, Trudy learns, and returned home on an indefinite leave of absence. Whether she ever comes back is anybody's guess.

Trudy stops to watch as regular police escort a blanched and shell-shocked professor in handcuffs down the steps of his brownstone to their van. There is blood on sidewalk, in a pool. A dried trickle runs hypnotically down step to step, emerging from beneath the front door. A figure under a stained blanket is visible, just inside the sill. The blood has turned black, the pool is dotted with tiny dry green blossoms shed by the trees. Now and then, small birds stop to drink nervously from the pool. The body in the doorway, cut down and stabbed to death while trying to escape what she'd been undergoing; a head appeared to look on from the top of the stairs. As far as anyone could say, the rest of her was in the bathtub.

Trudy strains to see the professor—he woke up this morning—he must have went to bed the night before and everything was fine. And woke up to find . . .

A beefy, long-faced officer with short black fuzz all over his head points to the steps with a downturned finger.

"And get this blood up. All right? This isn't the *South*."

Students, people in the street, not attracted really by the dozens of startling lights, but by a sort of lodestone far away that keeps dragging them along, bunch up without actually gathering in the vicinity of the house. She sees them go by looking alarmed, turning their heads, but not stopping. They stop . . . but they keep leaning in the direction they were going, swayed by a steady current and head that way soon. They always have a bad momentum taking them away from real moments like this, and as she looks at them her heart crackles with cold distaste. They won't do anything about this either.

Your tracks will dry up, turn to dust, and blow away, and there won't even be a bad smell left behind. No one can tell you anything because you're too bone stupid and pitiful to listen even to yourself. In her mind she sees that naked whipper bounding out among them, slicing gracefully into the crowds with his whip. Its coils flash, dart, and snap in the throng like bolts of electricity, like striking snakes, like fast lightning coursing through a viscous herd of good-for-nothing . . .

Shots fired somewhere in town. People run to investigate. No bullet holes or shell casings, no smell of powder, nothing.

A scream of anguish from a basement window.

On investigation, people find the basement empty. No sign of mayhem. It must have been an aural illusion or a hallucination or a prank. As if, when you hear a scream like that, the scream of a human being helpless in the hands of gloating torturers, you don't know. Trudy feels as if the sky were lowering itself down onto Cimelia Cisterna, very gradually and in total silence crushing it flat. This is still a white modelsuburb; you don't raise your voice in the street, even in an emergency your voice is corked up and it takes a violent effort to make yourself heard. People are too embarrassed to draw attention to themselves; now all that has to happen is that this tendency be brought to a steady simmer and they will take what they are given without a word. The house is haunted. Screams. Mysterious bloodstains that vanish almost the moment they are discovered. Cryptic warnings scrawled on the wall.

The papers are saying that students burned Sanglade, murdered Celada and Crapelin both, attacked Dr. Camatsura. D. smells gasoline, a rare smell that snaps his head up. It's a police motorcycle, jostling the air as it runs by. He looks down, suddenly disappetized at the sight of his food wrapped in foil, and rewraps and pockets it. His jacket has large side pockets. Feeling hot and dusty now, he takes the jacket off irritably and throws it in an ashcan by the mouth of an alleyway. Why eat? Why dress? Time is done. Wander over to a tall narrow courtyard that forms a shaftway for a number of tiny sweatshops. Using his hands as shovels, he paws through heaps of garbage looking for scraps of fabric that could be used in puppet making. Puppets require only small scraps.

He sifts for a while with no success, and when he straightens up for a breather, Miss Houseman is there, standing in the narrow stone lane that plunges away from him on his left. She watches him.

E. steps from the nest of battered cardboard he'd been in up to his waist and comes toward her, who seems to call him without speaking. Six feet away from her, F. stops abruptly, suddenly afraid.

"*She* sent you," he says, and shrinks back.

Miss Houseman simply turns and goes up the lane, pausing after about ten paces to look back at him. He begins to follow her. She goes along a rough, undulating brick wall that curves away to the left. An old Gothic building, perhaps once a church, looms above the wall, and there is a warehouse or something of the kind facing it. She steps aside just a little way beyond the bend and touches the sill of an niche in the wall, regarding him steadily. Then she continues down the lane, in no hurry.

G. wafts up to the niche. A vine grows from the niche and shades it with its leaves. H. reaches into the shade, and the leaves brush his wrist softly.

His hand finds and seizes something not much broader than his palm. It's hard, smooth, lean, with a strong angular ridge the

232

length of one side. He draws it out and looks at it. It's a folding razor. The handle is made of a solid black material, like vulcanized rubber. A few small freckles of rust spot the steel by the hinge, like tiny lichens. I.'s dreaminess flakes apart, and his head snaps up swift as a bird's—Miss Houseman's lips, and her eyes, smile, very slightly. It isn't a razor. What a stupid mistake. Three steps and she is gone around the corner. It isn't a razor at all, it's a book. J. looks at the cover. DAYBOOK is printed on the fabric, inside a diamond. He flicks open the cover, which is stiff so the two corners bend out in horns. The binding is sheathed in a black sleeve, graph paper covered in neat fountain pen.

The first word up at the top is "Midnight," followed by a date. He was alive at the time, but that's all he knows; he doesn't follow time anymore. He flips toward the back, and the writing runs out somewhere past halfway. A few more flips and he finds the last page.

> "So it was wrong or I was all wrong. So, start again. I—I—I, I make note of black gravel, that's how to start, white phosphorescent stone, the ghost erupting from the top of the hill—"

This ink dried without losing its glisten. He decides to test it and draws his thumb over the date at the top of the last written page; it smudges. And yet, when he opens and closes the book no smudge, no mark on the opposite page. Will I read at midnight? Turning back a moment later, he finds words on the last page that weren't there before, and he nearly drops the book in fright. DAYBOOK is printed opposite the page in a diamond on the shaped smudge, no remark. When he opens rust, it smudges. He was ghost alive at once, that time, but that's all he knows; to start, that's how to follow time. He flips I—I, forward again. I—back, and the writing runs wrong, all halfway. He's all halfway. A few more all wrong, after flips he finds "first there, the day the divinity half-awakened, sand-years since anyone . . ." Since anyone what? One of the warders came back, and the writing runs and fetches me from that wrong in the nick of time.

So, to *start* in my cell out somewhere in the past, I was all in the room halfway on the ground floor, where he all wrong shut me up. I went on flips and he founds me with my dream.

Since we are apt to *suppose* that the people of this world are imagined at last, then what's the difference? DAYBOOK glistens, printed in long brown pine needles gathered by chance, graph paper covered in: "They know how to do me, had shot . . . run from the crowd, tufts of hair lying everywhere—metallic blue street, steely darkness . . ."

At once the opposite page truncates the mountain—musical the things they know—clean earth—the moon, noticing what in all cases such men of this or that sort do, for things. Things they do not know crouch in neat fountain pen. It's shaped like an arrow, using not-knowing, not-doing. But the clouds and the moon are separated by thousands of miles from groves, tigers . . . I can't follow this, he thinks. It is written directly to him, but, beyond recognizing this significance he can't manage to follow it. They do not know, they smudge the first word, nor mark each other, and the moon doesn't see the clouds from where it is— this is what traps humanity. Skies the most do also desire what they have already. The book, not the ink, dries—a figure on the road ahead, off to the side, effulgent, not hers. He know fabric of the stout of heart, or it might have been the the awesome figure, and walking like me.

A viper's skin—he doesn't tear it to pieces, and up at the top is "bare hands." His bodily frame had beauty I associate with thunder: gorgeous, warlike, and sacred. All this I see when he opens, dilated with the approach of the glare. The words rust, he flicks open "Midnight," followed by death, hard to say. There becomes from youth to age an unusual strength; and these aren't *afterthoughts*. Without his chasuble, the things erupting from the top of his singularity I see play death on me, like shows on resplendent seas of chain mail. The cover, which springs up and never arrives, and the last mind, were keen, intense, and frugal, apt. When the mariner encounters the page, it smudges.

A date. For him, it's still the last. Following the moon, as I walk downhill this instant, and he goes in a constellation like a scabbard of horned diamonds. Instead of the cold air, you walk out in that cloudless sky. I wish I could gaze at it alive as I make note of it. Smell roses. More steadily hold my ghost. The cover opens rosaries, not suffering, affairs when sadness and joy come—

Look out on a dazed and sleepy town. Imagine one night wandering in his thoughts. The date fulfilling its fantasy. When they go, I cannot stop them. In all, the doctor, Crapelin . . .

Is he here? Taking up fiercely the great two-handed sword which is an owl that flies past just under the moon, my "body" fill out like . . .

I thumb over to start.

This, that, do they concern me? There I see it again—I can tell its stout body, its silent wings. What a liar when a moment earlier I said it was talking and singing.

(.)

The cell at Chthethostoa has been in contact with another cell that claims to have some information to share. They've arranged to leave the material at the beach, since surveillance of its entire expanse is impracticable, and Trudy is chosen to go retrieve it there. Trains still run from once to three times a day between Cimelia Cisterna and Leikin, its near satellite on the coast. Trudy makes the fifty-minute trip standing in a car wedged tight with people, redolent of warm hair, chemical soap. Cool air blows in through the windows, passengers overflow into the gaps between cars, and a few intrepid souls hang on the sides.

It might have been abrupt, or it might have been the opposite of abrupt. It's hard to say. Or dying became a singularity so that death never arrives, and the final moment lasts to infinity. For him, if that's true, then it's still the last instant, and he goes on thinking, not suffering: I say so, not suffering, only wandering in his thoughts. It's his kind of idea, she thinks. I loved him. With a jolt that ripples through all bodies the train stops inside the terminal. The doors open, and the car empties, which is to say its contents seem to flow from it mechanically like human liquid, made of clothes, feet, eyes, and motion. Trudy emerges and allows herself to eddy aside, straightening her rumpled clothing. When the crowd is thinner, she walks off the concrete platform, which roars with energy of huge idling engines, into the bright, murmuring spaciousness of the lobby. This is one of the few public buildings constructed before the crash that still fulfills its original function. There is a mezzanine with a split-level arrangement once filled with shops, now all shuttered. Trudy heads to one of many banks of wide glass exit doors, to the door in the center of the bank, putting out her hands to push it open. The fingers of her right hand close around a brass doorknob.

"I'm still in Sanglade."

Her left hand is pressed against the black wood of the door. She can see faint glints in the lacquered molding.

"I never left Sanglade."

Trudy shuts her eyes. Yawning behind her, emptiness . . . familiar, odious silence . . . the muting presence of Sanglade.

She opens her eyes.

The door is black wood, the brass knob sucks the warmth from her palm. With a violent effort she checks the impulse to look back. Instead, she stares straight ahead, resolutely. She lifts her right hand and places it flat where she knows the metal plate is bolted into the steel frame of a glass door through which sunlight is pouring onto her face. She draws strength into her body, up into her shoulders, and pushes forward. Striding with long steps and swinging arms, she crosses the wide, paved area in front of the station, and enters an enormous square. Light sparkles from the fountain; each chevron of light has a black counterpart because the water is all plucked up in points like dabbed oil paint. There's polished metal and glass all around, reradiating the sunlight in starlike points. Squinting fiercely, she makes her way to the plectrum-shaped concrete island that fills most of the center of the square and starts at the sight, just as she steps up out of the street, of a massive grandfather clock, caked in tan dust, standing not six feet from her. Then a man in a cap and coveralls takes it around the waist and carries it off.

Trudy crosses the square without giving the impression of being anything other than in a hurry.

"Is it that you don't get it?"

Waiting for a line of horse-drawn carts to pass at the far corner—no cars here—she catches sight of herself in an ornate oval mirror hanging on the side of a bank.

". . . Or is it that you refuse to acknowledge what you already understand?"

There's a huge fireplace beneath the mirror, flames leaping, illuminating the blackened heat shield at the back, the burgundy marble with black and white streaks, glittering brass andirons, a Cyclops-eyed mantelpiece clock.

"You liberated Sanglade, when you destroyed it."

Passersby cross between her and the fireplace. Trudy walks

quickly down a side street that should run parallel to the shore. She hasn't yet seen the beach, but she can smell it and hear the breakers. The buildings give way quickly, growing smaller and smaller.

Ahead, there is a hill or ridge like a flat dome that very gradually rises from the deep beach, furred in light brown grass and dark, dull-looking pines. Never any gulls; Trudy forces herself to wonder about that. Now there are only the shells of houses to her left, and to her right a plank fence in good enough repair blocks the shore from her view. She can tell it stands on a cut and the beach is below its level. Trudy comes to the end of the fence and the beach bursts onto her view. She throws up her arms and stops with a strangled cry as she catches sight of Sanglade half-nestled in the trees at the base of the hill.

It stands naturally and harmoniously in its new location. It does not seem to look at her, but it sees her.

Trudy turns and nearly tumbles headlong down to the beach, only thinking at the last moment to angle herself sideways along its crumbling flank and keep her eyes on her feet. She walks toward the surf across a vast, empty beach, the sunlight blasting down flashes on the waves and seems to flicker off the wind.

"There's nothing there."

She glances again. Sanglade's windows flash gorgeously even in the suffocated light of this overcast day.

Lying up ahead, all unreal, is the old car tire she'd been told to look for, artfully festooned with kelp. She begins to wander to and fro, trying to seem aimless, but of course anyone who had been watching her steadily would have seen her rush purposefully to this spot only to become abruptly purposeless. It's impossible to say whether she spends enough time dithering. When she dares, she numbly reaches out with her toe to nudge the tire along a little, trying to look casual, aware at every instant of the seeing that comes from the direction of the house.

"The house has no direction, because it isn't there."

There's a packet under the tire, in clear plastic that glitters at her and brands her eyes. Closing them as she picks it up not too hastily . . . just picking over sea wrack officer . . . she can feel them ache a little behind the lids.

She pockets it with assumed thoughtlessness, kicks the tire gently back where it had been. Maybe it's a hideous photograph and mocking note courtesy of a secret admirer. She's done all she can in any case and begins walking back toward the fence, watchfulness crawling all over her back.

You can't burn memories down, you can't burn a thought. The haunted house is haunting her. The train back is much less crowded, and Trudy is able to get a seat with a big man's side like a hot barrier between her and the aisle.

She sees in her mind the three students running in the street—not that she saw it happen—but she sees them, running. Their legs flip up behind them. They are shot as they round the corner. They drag numb, useless legs behind them. They crawl for cover where there is no cover, trailing blood from shattered pelvises they can no longer feel. She can't stop, and if she goes on they'll arrest her, torture and rape her and gloat over her. It's because it won't break; even if it did they would vanish, leaving behind a pitiful handful of students who stupidly let their bravery and indignation get the better of their so-called "good sense." Trudy stares at the back of the next seat, not daring to shift her eyes. Every time she does, she sees it going past the window, somewhere in the distance: the rooftops, the shining eaves. Sanglade and Sanglade again, they must have passed the house three or four times since they left, and she doesn't want to see it anymore. When the dust had settled and the dead were all in

239

their tombs, they would always reappear. Smiling like the snakes they are.

All day long, so far, the tension, waiting for the train, riding to the beach, finding her way, finding the packet. Now that she has it, there's nothing left to do but sit there with her contraband. Without the sustaining momentum of the task, she feels herself helplessly slipping away into her own mind again, where her fears wait patiently for her.

She doesn't want to go back and be frightened, get caught, be raped, be tortured with electric wires. She can get away into the dark. They can't, or rather they're welcome to follow her there. In any case, the pills. Now that she has something to do, bleak calm snows down onto her: this way of thinking feels physiologically stupid, like slobbering inside the brain. She isn't really any calmer now. One day they'll learn to bring us back from the dead so they can torture us some more, just for the fun of it. They'll make movies out of raping me and turn a profit selling them. Dr. Crapelin or Merle or whoever—look at the body. Are you still thinking this is it? Who says it's it? What's it? Pointing at his corpse—What is there between yourself and this? Are you going to go on talking about life as if . . . and if you get it she's talking to you, this is not an illusion—have they, all those rubes, gotten it yet she is here, are they reading her, spying on her, eavesdropping on her, or are they dead now and not there?

Outside she suddenly catches sight of a young woman wearing a green blouse and green scarf over her blond hair, waving a second green scarf gaily at the train from the embankment, well back enough so she won't just flash by. The train is already slowing and swerving as it begins to bump from line to line through the tangled rust of the switching yard. The green girl means there are police in the terminal. Trudy gets up

240

quietly and excuses herself, shoving by the knees of her neighbor who eyes her speculatively as she goes by. She kneads her way along the aisle. She knows how to look demure while exerting considerable shoving force with her shoulders.

Now she's in the enclosed coupling between two cars. A lean man with a high circular forehead is there too, holding a briefcase like a liquorice animal flattened by a—Trudy turns from the man, grabs the door handle fiercely and snaps it to one side. Outside the green embankment is still going by black with green, and saffron earth, the wheels are complaining icily as the train shunts from track to track.

Trudy crouches in the open doorway and jumps from the train, landing amazed on her feet. The forward momentum makes her squat down and throw her arms forward, to keep from stumbling. She checks for the packet—a flash of the man in white leaning from the car, brandishing it, grinning—the packet is still there in her bag. Trudy crosses the tracks, a few other trains around but not many, and gets to the embankment. Skirted in tall green weeds, she begins walking directly away from the terminal, which is still a bit farther off and around a bend.

Over there is where the enormous trains go by, like monster serpents with ancient minds, and not far from a highway that's empty in daytime, but which at night is haunted by unmarked white trucks packed full of people. At intervals all along the edge there are short stacks of ties. Two men, wearing helmets and work clothes stiff with grease, are walking the tracks. One is tall lean and black, and the other is only a little less tall, black and large. The latter, turned away, says,

"What happened to my logs?"

The other one turns toward him, while the speaker scans the ground. The reference is to a particular heap of ties marked in chalk for this section of track.

"Well it was right round these . . ."

The taller one looks about squinting, arms hanging loose.

"I don't know—shit keeps moving around here . . ."

He begins tapping the sleepers between the rails with a long metal implement. The wood is gradually splintering into thick straws. They're deteriorating, because the creosote can only stave off decay for a limited time. The piled ties along the embankment are their replacements, although they've been sitting for months already and the brown of the creosote has given way to a roasted darker color. The sleepers are like piano keys. The overcast gets denser and denser, shedding brown light. The train has to be pulling in by now, who knows if white shirt hasn't blabbed up a storm about her jumping off—then again people jump on and off all the time. She just happened to be the only one doing it then. So let's say he doesn't mention it, saves it for his clown wife: the police will be watching the crowds, hanging back. Are they watching her now? Will they follow, but not arrest? She glances again at the two men on the rails. Somehow she doesn't mistrust them. The simple, unembarrassed bewilderment and tiredness of their faces is too human.

The air is pretty close and still. She treads along a green and brown curtain. There's nothing wrong with nature, she thinks. She wants to stay out here where it's clean, and only live inside the rain and wind or whatever freshens the air, the grass; she doesn't want to go back into all that human . . . She wouldn't mind if it was just ordinarily bad. Rest is what she needs; her body feels all right, but her mind is worn out. She imagines him withering away, patiently, while she's right there within call. At night dragging himself up and down the stairs. Just keep your face straight and they'll think if anyone sees you that it's started raining already. We loved each other. We really did. Trudy glances around in a blast of unaccountable alarm and catches sight, over the tops of the trees to her right, of the roofs of Sanglade. She glares at it with hate. Sure go on, keep cranking! What it doesn't understand is that she wants to break. She does not want to break. The two men are calling back and forth. Maybe one of them found his heap of ties. Up ahead, there's a brick building the size of a small house, with tall weeds by the open doorway and daylight, such as it is, visible straight through on the far side, like looking edgewise through a transparent bruise. Suddenly in the gap she sees someone big, just like Celada, step over some debris on the floor and cross past the doorway, down sweep of a pale white hand, the silent image of a face with two wings of light hair. Desire to see him again, even if it is only a hallucination. Thin vines of ivy cleave stubbornly to the brick, a few oily flakes of black there. The wall across from the door is partially collapsed, a wide gap open to the floor. In between gap and door is a jumble of wood and metal in beams and irregular machine part shapes. Inside, the place smells like tar paper and treated wood, rust. Sacks of pitchy stuff, and a floor strewn with iron junk, rags, a sink shaggy with mildew. His back is to the door, hands in front of him. Trudy goes up to him. He turns to her, silhouetted against the light from the door so close he's looking down at nearly the top of her head.

Celada or not, only for a moment.

J.'s face, intense in the dark.

"Did you get it?"

Trudy doesn't let anything show. Her face stays the same but grows a little more stern.

"Of course," she says after a moment. She glances down at his clasped hands and a bloody rag.

"You're hurt!"

He says nothing as she takes the rag away and examines a rip in the skin along the edge of the left hand. She takes a handkerchief from her bag and pulls him toward the light of the doorway.

"Not too close," he says. "The light."

After a moment, "I just did it, coming in through there." He nods at the hole in the wall.

"Get a tetanus shot at the school."

He guides her from the building to a dirt path that angles away from the tracks, nearly overgrown with soft grass like an untended canal. They remain within sight of the great open zone of the train tracks. K. leads.

A few dozen yards along, they pass close by a mammoth black boulder lying in two halves with a big smooth rock wedged in the gap. It looks a little like a heart with its point pointing at her, and also a little like the head of a contemplative dolphin. Black woods sigh there around them, the path goes between two masses of trees. It joins a dirt track emerging from the deeper wood, but they pass this Trudy looking back.

"Where are we going?" she asks in a hushed voice.

L. points down the path.

"Where?" she presses.

He glances back at her.

"And don't just say 'up ahead'—tell me."

"We're nearly there. There's a road, and a car waiting."

After ten more steps, Trudy stops.

"You go look," she says.

He turns and sees she is not going to move and transparent drapes of undersea luminosity flit around her. Pursing his mouth he nods and goes ahead bending low. When he's out of sight, Trudy hops over the tufts of grass and hides behind a tree. He comes back, moving quickly his face tense, nods her to follow him back up the path in the direction they came. Silently and swiftly they return to the fork they'd passed before and take it, slipping into the woods. Once covered there, he begins trotting, she speeds up. Their feet thud hollowly on the thick earth of the trail. The ground cover is wet cork, pungent like pipe tobacco, water drips on her from the canopy. Suddenly he breaks from the trail and begins climbing a dry stream bed. Trudy follows him, her feet slipping. At the top of the stream, he leads her through drier foliage to a second path or perhaps the same one further along, and they arc out in the direction they had originally taken when they left the brick building.

"What happened?" she asks his back.

"He was gone," he says over his shoulder, his voice absorbed at once by space. "Somebody else was waiting in the car."

"They didn't see you?"

"No. But they'll start searching when we don't turn up."

She's not at the end of her tether. There is no tether on her. She can't even begin to say who she is. When they don't turn up, that is, when it not-happens. Trudy turns aside, right into the ornamental garden. The narrow flat white walkway angles around sterilely tranquil planters, the house towers over her. She sweeps the far border of the empty clearing for any sign of human tampering, happily in vain, as she says, "This is where we should finish the isolaton experiment."

"You're almost right," says Celada's voice behind her.

(.)

Where is the jovial word order or the shaft of intelligence the eye darts as she knows she's being kindly tricked as part of the training because, where that is gone, something critical is lost. Coming in the door, from the corner of the room behind her, she is something that makes her turn her head and a moment later nearly break into tears, un-

... Intimidater overhead, thumping along low. They hold

themselves in the air with brute force and waste and it roars by, on its way to go spy somewhere else. The barked command and the stupid and suspicious shielded stare, to train her in stupidity,

And sirens now and then to goose foot traffic along under livestock the . . . the contemptuous . . . the contemptuous gaze of the detest the despised—the enmity, the enemy she means the mean enemy— She's going to run out her limit and give it her all like Celada

Not like him. A disgusting waste.

—the secrets of the universe, is that it?

something like that, why not?

. . . well, tell me

—no. you tell me.

it's not the sort of thing you tell

—are you afraid you'll sound ridiculous?

i'm sure it does sound ridiculous—i mean why bother? You'll say i'm nuts and that will be the end of it, and a good thing too

—humor me—i'll believe You (that was a slip)

why? someone tells You an incredible story and is believed just like that?

—well, i'll believe You believe it

then what does it matter what it is? let's just say i believe in martians and fairies and pixie dust and leave it at that

—all right but how did You come to believe those things? You must have believed someone—or did You see something

i may have—i may have seen—that and a few other things make me think . . .

—what other things?—

'circumstantial evidence' . . . because when You may see something like that, no matter how real it may be, or how crazy You are, You can only tell Yourself it was a—hallucination—that and only that is what You want to believe.

The committee of secret students have been reviewing the information Trudy brought back in the packet. Teachers of forbidden subjects have to be brought to the school under false pretenses, or smuggled in and out. There is a reference to a meeting yet to take place between agents and "simia" at such and such a time and place "re: Chethosto."

"Simia" means informer.

The meeting is to take place at the train station, where Trudy only just was. Apparently the informer is to be given something too important or incriminating or valuable to trust to the inefficiency and larcenousness of the post office.

There is good reason to believe M. would not be recognized by them, so he and a committee member will observe the meeting.

The station: a few days beforehand, N. started putting in a regular appearance by the tobacco stand, shining shoes. He keeps a calm, glazed-looking eye on the steel post marked D4. The other, a secret student, is reading a paper, evidently waiting for a train, taking pictures with an illegal camera hidden in a satchel. The informer enters the train station and walks to the post marked D4. The student keeps his paper up and his satchel-camera trained on the post. The shutter release is operated by a squeeze bulb in the hollow of the handle, and he has practiced using it. O. takes his time with the shoe in front of him, not wanting to let the man go, so as not to be distracted talking to a new customer when the meeting happens. The meeting doesn't happen. The informer paces with arms crossed, eyes on the ground. P. finishes shining the man's shoes and smiles strainedly taking the meager tip. The man walks over to the informer smiling. Q. immediately seizes on his memory of the man's face, trying not to let it dissolve. If he himself has been recognized, there will be no sign. The informer, with the advanced warning of that smile, doesn't start as the man approaches. They converse, the man smiling, the other responding, responding. They leave together. R. flashes the student a look that means stay there, and, not having a client at the moment, he stretches and ambles over to the bathroom, feigning fatigue, staring sidelong out through the glass doors. The shopping bag the man had been carrying has switched owners, and the man himself is already out of sight. The informer passes across the glass doors and up the street, face pinched.

Read it back phonetically—he went around to the side of the house, to the same window. He didn't see his reflection. Inside the room, two men he's sure he'd never seen before occupied the two beds with their feet against the wall and the crowns of their heads pointing in to the center, blankets drawn up to their chins. Then he was uncertain it was really two people and not one person in an alternation too rapid to follow. The scene suggested ritual surgery. The room grew dim, and high above them a knot of darkness gathered into a rosette, the absence of light pinched together in folds—he realized or remembered that at that moment he had no body at all, at most a question mark of luminous vapor top of his "head," a tail descending behind. Calmly he accepted it as an unintended consequence of his proximity to them. Suddenly he understood the unfolding of the rosette of dark was the approach of death, acting independently of death itself, undefeated, that unfolded at the rhythm of the room. The operation had to involve an encounter.

Her brain is burning; the inner triumph is universal but the outer one can't be, don't get them confused she thinks. There are not four rooms exactly, but a space with a partition dividing it like an ice cube tray into four chambers without tops, and the thick mist isn't coming from any one of them. It comes from the intersection of the partition—it's crucially important to remember that, meaning it comes from him, whoever he is. There's one person sitting hunched forward in each partition. What is that in fog? The human images in the room began to seem slack. Only one figure, in the left-hand bed, was there now, and he was misshaped. There came out of him a disk face of glistening snow-white cartilage, all ribbed smooth and powdery material like an elastic ceramic. It crowns a musculature of linked articulations without a skeleton, composed of a variety of elaborate configurations like universal joints, just now all of which are at rest, having no plain overall outline. Nor can his face be seen when she looks at his body: he never saw the two of them at once after all; either the face was an intermittent projection ineffectively masking the body, or the body was producing the face, which wore a placid expression at all times. Looking at the man's face, she experienced something not unlike the gradual recognition of a familiar person after a protracted separation, as the alterations of time and exigency are harmonized in a solution with the memory.

(.)

Dr. Cottataris habitually works late in her office, which at the moment is a studio on the top floor of a half-empty building. The main floor is a makeshift student-run coffee place; many entrances and exits, hard to watch all at once.

That night, Dr. Cottataris is ambushed in her office—out of dead silence suddenly there are dark figures everywhere, the lights are off and big flashlights are blazing in her face. Without a word they grab and bind her, pulling a coarse black bag over her head. In a flash she is thrust down onto her knees, a searing hot light inches from her face turned by the bag into a blinding star nursery.

"What do you want?" she sobs with exasperation. "What did I do wrong?"

"We like to feel we can drop in freely," a voice buzzes. It's a genderless, musical chord produced by speaking through a portable electronic distorter. A sudden rustle of fabric and she feels an elbow resting on her back.

"What are you doing?!"

"Shhhh," the warbling voice sizzles. "We enjoyed your stories so well we thought we'd drop by and hear them again."

All just like the movies.

"I've told you everything," she says, afraid.

"We know," says the voice. "We've come to hear it again."

"I want to see my sister!"

"We know," says the voice slowly. "*You* know how to make that happen."

Dr. Cottataris is shaking. She begins to talk about Celada, Dr. Crapelin, Dr. Camatsura, Dr. Czechoslovakia, Trudy, the student committees in general. She says she thinks Miss Houseman and William Carlsroja are working with the student committees.

"Did you *think* that perhaps members of the student committees were watching you at the train station?"

The hooded form simply pants, sagging up and down on her knees. Inside the hood her breath is mingling with the sweat on her face and she feels herself begin to stifle.

"I didn't lead them there!" she whinnies.

"You didn't?" The vocoder voice chimes like snow in a glass.

The hood wobbles erratically from side to side, "No! You know I wouldn't! Penny—"

She breaks off, unable to find a bearable way to follow her affectionate nickname for her sister. The head sinks miserably.

"But you *did* lead them there."

"They followed me," the sack moans at the floor. She sags

onto her knees and goes limp. She sobs. After a long time, the light swings away. Her aching cheeks start cooling through the fabric of the hood. She can hear the rustle of their clothing—someone reaching for her and then the hood is snatched from her head and she looks up into Trudy's eyes. Other students stand around her in a ring. One holds the lamp. One holds the distorter. One holds a recorder. Trudy looks at her, face blank. Dr. Cottataris's hands are loosed, and she lets them drop to the floor. The students leave, in silence. Dr. Cottataris lets her head fall, dripping into the hood lying there before her.

(.)

"What do you think it was?"

"Bugs," S. says. "That's all it could be."

"But they already know we never use the phone."

"Room bugs," T. says raising and lowering his chin.

Now they know how much has been given away, how Dr. Cottataris was manipulated, and how she would exchange information with her unknown contacts on slips inserted into library books. It's extremely difficult keeping up a routine that they now know exposes them to observation and danger, but better to know when you're being watched than not. Like the sorcerer's apprentice some call up more than they can handle by that name, love, and then he has himself to become the sorcerer, return and quell—"we were only playing . . . !"

The interrogation of Dr. Cottataris was recorded. Copies of this recording and the photographs of her meeting at the train station are made and circulated. The committees link up with other non-student groups. Numbers matter for all sorts of reasons, but most of all so they can become less vulnerable in their secrecy: the more secrets, the more vulnerable to infiltration and exposure. The secret is no secrets, the secret is velocity. Move too swiftly to be interfered with or so slowly you aren't noticed until it's too late. Or pneumatically, with the backing of reinforcements, so you cannot be compressed. Dr. Cottataris resigns and leaves town. The school is shrinking. U., sitting alone in his squat, lifts his eyes from Celada's notes and watches absently a square of sunlight on the wall—the square starts spinning in place.

Trudy sits at her kitchen table, her chin in her hand, humming "mares eat oats." She stops when she sees the house, right there on the other side of the table. At first it seems full size and sitting there, like a guest seated opposite, but now it's tiny, no bigger than a salt shaker.

(Now take it easy—don't grab it ... they're asleep, they've forgotten: now be a good teacher to them, teach them sorry to disappoint you the great lover peels out of his clothes his markings and his color and vaults with high caracols along the conference table kicking cameras splintering into faces colorless flame of a human naked body the only way to be showered in splendor microphones wilt on their booms a reporter's wiry scalp snaps off entire and rolls along the floor like a helmet the conferees are flung back in a mass by a colossal wand of air while bodyguards and security officers and secret agents and army men billow toward the center like gorillas pawing out their guns and truncheons knives shockers acid sprays blackjacks microwavers sniper rifles sorry to disappoint you tranquilizer darts beanbag launchers and sonic disrupters and this embodiment of scandal in the nightmare of the noonday sun snaps his whip black as midnight and scatters them in crescents of searing pain he twirls round once forming a column and as they crash in toward him in a wild tide he soars over their heads in a trembling volute of air the softer it is the stronger it is—now down he comes among the panicking delegates momentarily divided from their gallant protectors by the heavy conference table their collective kicking has overturned the whip snares a leg here flipping the delegate high into the rafters she plummets to the ground her guards lunging away from beneath her she crashes into the steel chairs and on the stage they are all airborne or lying prone the whip snakes in everywhere it slashes it shatters the air is crackling with squeals of agony—a javelin of colorless nakedness breaks the ground in the midst of the guards and police and firemen and army men and navy men and body guards and pilots and detectives and agents and postmen and fire fighters and ambulance attendants and truant officers the scurrying flacks and familiars and assistants and go-betweens all the people stuck in the middle just at the moment when the hair-thin very terminator of his whip plucks the throng like a plectrum plucks the harp blasting apart pairs of eyes pop-pop-pop-pop—wails and pain and sorrow—in from the doors the windows the backstage come people wading into the confusion. They beat and loot the participants, destroying the symbols on the stage, the heaps of records leap up in flames.) If only, she says, feeling abject.

    . . . Back to the swimming school, the interminable inexplicable unredeemable experiment. Capturing the isolaton, the particle that knots itself together when the relation between general and particular is at maximum tension. A knot of water, cinching into itself. The knot isn't going to be spectacular; it's made of nothing more celebrated than apparent, modest time. Gravity ensleeves body to body . . . sun and earth and moon all swinging unrequitedly around each other, longing and hanging, reading, aware as he reads that beyond the uplifted book's edge squares of sunlight on white linoleum glide sideways by degrees with the rotation of the earth around the sun, even ghosts can see this, a sailing rootless feeling, consciousness of bottomless space all around, below the ground . . . deadly and enticing in a backless strapless dressless dress . . . this is how Celada burns Sanglade.

gargling of a distant helicopter whenever and only when he spoke, mocking interjection of a car horn, just a brief bleat of noise like a sudden feint, to trip him up—distract him as he gropes toward a realization: feel it all around him, fusion light on weeds, on the dusty lots, on cracked alleys and their trashes. Across the street the campanile strums its lips with one finger, a laborious, all-quarter-note affair—when did they start that old nuisance up again?

W. watches the sun squares—the sun never sets. The sun walks among them now. Celada, I'm right. Going back again, to the swimming school, and the house is there—not where it was, but *right behind* the swimming school, and towering over it.

ground, the hills, covered in black stubble, leafless trees, like black hose . . . the flat brown coastal islands, with their unnaturally straight troughs of water and the pale rust that lines the runnels, clouds matted against the ground almost indistinct from the snow . . . the frozen lakes like tea with poison milk . . . the scarlike lines like razor nicks in the forests . . . the odd band of light past the cloud shadow . . . russet land with frozen turquoise lakes all filmed with skeins of grey smokes—land west of that is corrugated, like terra cotta, purple and gray . . . lakes like cataracted eyes . . . past the Roseate Lamina, static electricity everywhere, covers sparking in the dark. Rank greenhouse or conservatory strongly smelling of acrid earth, at once musty and sour, with the saccharine odor of plants rotting to crackling brown syrup. Drift off . . . the house suddenly seems to be towering and it blazes with unreal intensity . . . an infinite

254

shaft an attic as deep as the sky—and the next moment with a snap it's all just as it seemed to be before—reputed to be haunted, especially by a lady—his desire coagulates into an impression, senses of the absent woman— You are not unique enough to vanish altogether. You endure in those common things. Tremble on the outskirts of being a character, all the spaces still relaxed and unlabelled just let them be, and listen, she'll talk to you in the apertures, Medusa, saying—"It is like wine."

Trudy wakes up.

There is a small cafeteria on the campus, that is, a cafe with a little steam table installed, of course, by William, and the teachers gather there and eat together, many of them, at a large circular table in the corner. Trudy sits with them, sits in the very corner at a full table, explaining about Dr. Cottataris. Her role in extracting the confession she does not mention.

"You know about the informers?"

"Of course," says Dr. Isochronal, chewing ham and eggs. "Everyone does."

"There are some students," she says, because she doesn't like to bring up the committees, "who are concerned that there will be reprisals."

Trudy is scanning the faces, all turned toward her, many chewing, gradually swallowing. Mugs rise and fall, and now hold still.

"Yes," Dr. Curtis says quietly. He is the professor who speaks like an old-fashioned television announcer.

"The faculty needs to take precautions. Also, Professor Houseman should have some kind of special protection—"

She breaks off as a rustle goes around the table.

"Oh, I don't think they'll bother her!"

"What do you mean?" Trudy asks.

Dr. Curtis snorts once, silently.

"You didn't know? She's a ghost."

"Miss Houseman's a ghost?"

He smiles at her.

Suddenly they all are smiling at her.

.)

Years ago, the school was dying. No one wanted to take responsibility for what seemed to be a doomed institution, and so the lot of school president fell to William Carlsroja, of all people. Shambling drunk, unshaven, hair hanging down over his oily brow, William was a disgrace. One arm over another professor's shoulder, pawing at him with his free hand, weaving down the street on his way to give a garbled anatomy lecture to two wooden-faced students.

One day, William had to retrieve some medical books from Sanglade. They weren't there, someone had them out, no someone had *returned* them, down goes a student into the basement to retrieve them from the to-shelve shelf and it takes a while. William begins to get interested in the house around him; it is beguiling that way, and so he doesn't simply leave when he gets his books. At the time, the Houseman papers were still not fully catalogued and organized—here they are, in stacks. Here are photographs. Pick up one. Pick up another. Put one down, pick up anoth—pick that last one back up. The woman in the picture . . . her name on the reverse . . . Adonica Houseman. He dreams of her that night, standing in that room, where she had once stood. She was Houseman's cousin, a young widow, who kept the house for him in his absence.

"Drinking's my vice."

Put out the bottle and she appears, sea and sun at her back

beat steel sea, beast ocean, gray mineral sunlight smooth shiny
heavily freckled face tapering jaw mouth sensual and severe

Miss Adonica continued to live in Sanglade for a time after
Clare moved in. One evening, she received a wire informing her
that her brother . . . "skating accident—fell through ice—
seriously ill—maybe pneumonia—asking for you." She made
arrangements to go to him at once. Clare Houseman was away at
the time. Miss Adonica went alone. Carrying only a small bag,
her trunk to be packed for her and sent along, she goes to the
train station, waits by herself on the platform in winter night,
her breath steaming. Stars coruscate in a sky with no moon. The
air is clear as glycerine and aches in the lungs and throat.

Soldiers are boarding a train. "The war, you know." One of
them slips on the ice near the platform edge; what good fortune
for him he didn't fall. He simply dropped his gun which, being
loaded, went off. Embarrassed, he gathers it up and skips onto
the train, grinning stupidly, heads jerk and turn, sway, crane . . .
nothing wrong. An accident. The shot seems to vibrate forever in
this endlessly empty air, dissolving into nothing. He will be
sternly dressed down by his commander for failing to report a
defective safety catch. But, in the gulf of shadow between two
lights on the platform's far end, Miss Adonica is lying in the dark,
clutching her thigh, gasping in astonishment. Dazed, she keeps
trying to rise. The dark hem of her dress seems to spread, then a
little stream emerges from it. The bullet has blown open her
femoral artery. Miss Adonica drags herself toward the lights,
calling for help in a shrinking voice. The cold air seems to
whisper through her head. She has mistaken the lights of the
remote town for the lights of the station, and wastes her ebbing
strength pulling herself in the wrong direction. She climbs onto
a snow drift with the vague idea it is the threshold of the station

house, wondering why no one helps her, and her trembling arms give way. The snow numbs one side of her face, and the air chills the other. She bleeds to death in the snow, and William sees her in the room, moving about easily, to and fro. Nothing happens, so to speak, in the dream; but she moves easily, to and fro, around the room, for a long time, and she is aware of him, watching her like a ghost. She doesn't mind being watched. Or rather she doesn't mind being watched by William.

William learns how she died, reads her surviving letters, revisits her picture, puts flowers on her grave. He dreams about her. She begins to make a mistake. She begins to make a very important mistake. She forgets something very important. William wakes in the morning with an elusive, nameless feeling, that frisks about him like a nest of cools flames. He drops his coffee cup on the floor and starts at the noise. Got coffee on his pants, had to change them—what's wrong? Distracted just distracted but not by anything, just an absence of mind. And there's excitement. About what? Approaching the school down Valle Viejo-Espejo down Valle Spiritu-Sancti he is washed over with nervous anticipation, and hurries. The floorboards in the reception area gleam like polished stone; the rug's colors are new: they glow like embers. A secretary is actually sitting at the desk, which is, actually, cleared off and tidy, and she's actually typing something.

The door to the main office is ajar, and in the narrow strip between door and jam he can see someone—someone is working at the desk in the main office. That is, the office of the head of the school, his office. He walks to the door, places his hand on the panels and pushes it open. She is writing with her fountain pen in a diagonal of light from the windows behind her, and now raising Miss Houseman's head, she returns his gaze levelly, pen nib lifted a bit off the page. Miss Houseman in full color, shadowy against the light, returns his gaze calmly, a little sardonically. She screws the top back onto the pen and sets it down sideways on the blotter. Fingertips on the desk she stands. William's right hand floats up into hers. Her grip is firm, his fingers press into the fine brawn of her hand. His posture straightens. He seems to gain height. Their hands part, hers indicating the shelves against the wall to his left—now clean and in order.

"I find these records aren't entirely complete. Do you know where the more recent ones are, William?"

When she speaks his name he bristles out in gooseflesh.

"Yes, Miss Houseman," he says feeling bliss.

"Bring them to me, will you? . . . In order?"

He bows a little, and turns on the spot.

"Close the door on the way out, William?"

"Yes, Miss Houseman."

He closes the door gently. His renovation and the school's kept pace with each other, and in no time both of them were in perfect working order.

(")

Death without peace, and snow freshens the cold, cruel money; calm school bus in the morning coffee and comics, then from there the modelsuburb is an alien landscape with trains on high trestles, streaming highways, space station buildings. The street sparkles through the curtain gap like a sapphire blazing with inflated and transparent gleams. Think of all there is to want to say, clogging the head up like a jammed typewriter, so not even one of them can be, like she is suddenly waist-deep in a flock of children zipping by so not one can be singled out—only here a tousled head, there a red and white smile. Failure to lie is the only way to offend the worldly. Proclaim, like a dead man, like a

necromantic spirit. A watching by the corpse, there with it—
watch by a dead body because it's so intolerable otherwise, that
watching, which stays there just by the body. Someone has to
occupy the watching; the mourner is there for the illusion that the
watching is his or hers. The affectless watching of the house, as it
relentlessly drew outlines around every movement—a place of
fear, but worse is that dismal feeling, a despair—fear of despair—
the hopelessness at the base of the stairs in particular, looking up
at all those steps, that absorbed light like a grave. But at other
times the despair was different, as if the darkness became volatile
with an alien light behind it, frighteningly new; it seemed at any
moment liable to become, in a flash, thrill, intense excitement. But
is it lifting up only to let drop into something, like a blinding
procedure that lasts forever? Did the previous occupants of the
house feel it, and if they did, didn't they overcome it or get
through it? It was as if despair had a secret, and smiled in
defiance of anyone being able to guess it, which wouldn't mean
anything if it weren't possible to guess it somehow.

Her breath dispels his stories, and he has left his room. Just
walking back, a wave of fatigue pulls at Trudy and she has to sit
down a moment on a park bench. A fly buzzes up and lands on
the bench not far from her hand. Is it a living fly, the ghost of a
fly, or is there no difference? Some children are playing ball
nearby. There's a big, loud girl among them who keeps changing
the 'rules' of the game. Every play ends in a dispute about the so-
called rules, and her voice rampages, trampling the others. She
rules, that's the rules. Is it a ball-game or a bickering-game?
There is laughter sometimes, but is the residual fun that good?
The game has a momentum of its own that drags them back into
it, even she, the bigmouth, doesn't think why. Trudy wonders
how come one of the others doesn't just go home, imagines her
shrilling after him, and the departing one saying, transformed in

her fantasy into a morally resplendent orphan from a melodrama, "If winning means so much to you—here, you win. But don't think you've won *the game*, because there is no game here. Unless you consider it a game to argue with an intransigent bully. I, would not. So don't think you have proven your superior skill in kick-ball, when you have merely shown the greater uh*presumpt*ion." She rubs her face. You have to bree fee—to be free to come and go, into the rulation area roulette, or out again as you see fits. Through the revolving door. Just so you know what's expected you know.

"Here, you win," says the little boy, turns to go, and grease guns shred his back. *Brrup*—the burst lasts only a second. He falls forward dead, his back turned into a red salad.

( )

Down the flashing stairs. The window. A huge white buck scrambles from the shadow of the house and jumps into the thick yielding brush, stops confusedly there, waiting a long while without moving. It wanders into the shadow, and melts. Now, only its movement can be seen. It isn't there, it hasn't left. The medallion in the middle of the brass mirror has an inlay of antler, or some kind of bone. Flash of stairs. Though he doesn't see her, he is walking with Trudy; the path is shadowed over by tall red grass and lined with white trees. He is intermittently visible, his hands are scarred, knuckly, and dark. This musty room. A buck head—not that buck—over the single window in that wall. A weird face, like the spectre of extinction. The earth at the base of the white trees is dark red. He sifts a little of it with those unfamiliar hands: it's like red brown sugar. Now Celada remembers those hands peeling back the pages of the notebook and the leaning-back sensation of being read in or breathed in. Miss Houseman, an alley, a niche in a wall, vines.

The electric grey glare of the sun fringes his eyes. She is there. He is there, and elsewhere, now and then.

An officer on the road ahead will call him by name through a mouth full of clicking jelly beans. So I would try to avoid that. Go together in through the trees to the dry riverbed. In the middle of the clearing, with a lurch, gravity lets him go and he hurtles up into the sky tumbling, screaming with fear: don't let me go!

he already knew it would be there, and all that was necessary was to look . . .

(.)

Get around an ID-checking station. Talking talking through a mouth full of rattling jelly beans—names and addresses he wants, to check against a list of lists of lists of names and addresses. Trudy turns the corner and passes a short line of people waiting to fill their ration cards. A little girl holding her mother's hand points at Trudy and exclaims:

"That's her! That's the woman I saw!"

Trudy stops and looks around surprised.

"That's the woman I saw in the house!"

The girl shakes her mother's hand up and down. Her mother murmurs to her to be quiet. Trudy looks at the girl steadily and smiles.

"I'm no ghost, honey," she says warmly. The girl has tiny white teeth in a big blood red mouth. "I'm solid," Trudy adds and holds out her hand for the girl to feel. The girl's cold sticky hand palpates her outstretched fingers a moment and is withdrawn; she looks up at Trudy as though expecting a reproach. All over the modelsuburb, Ukehy agents in plain clothes stream from their hiding places and converge on the school, where most of the students live. The agents have donned crude vampire makeup; the face smeared white, and black greasepaint widow's peak and eyesockets, false fangs, and sloppy red mouths dripping red streaks down the chin. As Trudy leaves the line behind her they are closing their loop—shots, breaking glass. The students defend themselves bravely with improvised weapons and some pistols. By pure chance a sizeable number of them are gathered outside the loop, and moving swiftly they suddenly assault the encircling agents from the rear, creating total confusion.

Trudy sees the smoke rising, hears the sirens and shots, the shouts rising from so many throats, the street around her completely calm and mystery and namelessness swarming all around it. The streets are calm and at war. The people are going about their business, and being cut down by agents. There is and isn't chaos. This is a fantasy of hers, but it doesn't feel like a true fantasy. She doesn't control it. It seems to reflect events that are really happening in some way, perhaps a translation of these events.

There's the swimming school. Trudy darts inside and shuts herself in. The door looks like black wood and brass fittings for a moment, but she turns impatiently from it and puts more closed doors between her and the street. She feels safer inside the school, and surrounded by Celada's crap. She looks again at his handiwork, the sloppy arrangements of plugs and wires. She gazes right into the eye in the clear plastic bubble. What was all that shit about the isolaton? Is that where he went—to be with it?

She goes down a side street heading for a derelict zone of buildings that fire had ruined a long time ago. A wide street, a corner up to her left, across the street to a greengrocery with a collapsed front, a roof half burned away, and all the rubble swept into a heap toward the rear wall. She climbs in where the huge front window used to be—and stamp of feet running on the pavement behind her. She rushes toward the back of the store and something rips through her from back to front. She collapses nervelessly, on her face.

Throughout the modelsuburb . . . house to house fighting, in a completely empty town, against no enemy . . . agents shoot bricks out of the walls . . . crouch, run, stop behind cover, and blast out empty windows, splinter doorways and posts, shatter paving stones. They charge uninhabited buildings and explode from room to room, peppering the walls, smashing furniture, filling the air with the plaster dust and powder smell. They charge from one end of Cimelia Cisterna to another shooting the buildings, the fences, the mailboxes. They shoot at small fires, at trees, a shirt hanging on a line, at stones, mounds of trash, at the street itself, at clouds, at the sky, at space.

Throughout the modelsuburb, people panic, run through the streets, they drop dead, their bodies sprout agonizing wounds for no reason, their skin is torn by nothing, their blood pours down, they scream and claw themselves, they writhe in convulsions as though they were on fire, and there is no enemy, no invader, no attacker. That is, they go about their ordinary, everyday affairs as usual.

Throughout the modelsuburb, people are going about their daily business, a woman calmly pages through a magazine in a check-out line as her child is suddenly blown in half, splashing one side of her body with its blood. A man in flames delivers letters, whistling absentmindedly. Another man goes jogging happily by on shredded legs with compound fractures, bones sticking out in all directions, his legs compressing and twisting horribly with each step. So now everybody is dead at last. Who is there left to do any thinking or feeling?

Trudy has the weird indefinable sensation that ghosts are talking amongst themselves somewhere. Towering above the huge skylight torn by the fire in the ceiling of the greengrocery are the eaves and gables of Sanglade. All its shining surfaces gleam with a soft luster as dusk passes and the stars come out. Coming out just like the stars, always there if not always seen, the eaves and gables of Sanglade loom inside Trudy. It whirs, the very fine end of the whip flashes in space. There is the upraised, vampire-painted face of the man raising his helmeted head in time to see the lash come down, raising his gun again, but to shoot at what? There is nothing to shoot at. There is nothing to see. He is blind. He is blind.

(x)

There is a sigh, from the direction of the doorway. Trudy bends forward holding out her hands palms up, elbows bent, sort of beckoning, and a small boy comes to her through the door, two clear streaks trembling from his stars. Trudy is naked. The wall behind her is plastered with her clothes and with bloody bullet wounds. A wind that doesn't affect her ruffles the boy's white hair and he raises a little clear torch. Trudy smiles and walks gingerly through the empty doorway into a half-ruined passage, following him.

There's a room behind the one's she's just left, really only that intervening wall and part of the one extending the passage. Beyond them is a confusion of rubble, high grass, a few trees, rooftops beyond. A. rattles toward her over the stones and fragments, a streak of blood from a grazed brow, a T-shirt ripped across the chest but no injury there. Trudy goes over to him and holds out her hand to help him into the room. He does not take her hand, but remains standing there beneath her, the floor at about his waist, looking up at her sadly. Raising his free hand he brings it down over his face a few times in a way that means sorrow. He reaches into his pocket.

"El agua del hielo apostolico," A. says and holds out to her a black vial.

Trudy smiles widely. She takes the vial and tosses it off. When she returns it to him, the vial is full of blood. She hands him the stopper. He closes the vial and doesn't seem to know what to do with it, sets it down carefully on a narrow shelf beside him, as she disappears. In the tall grass, the boy is coaxing heatless, colorless threads of fire up, so that the grass just in front of him burns without being consumed, and he wafts his hands magically through the fire, his fine hair tossing in the updraft and his whole twining form seeming to blend with the flames. Tears of night sky drip from his eyes. Trudy can see stars in the drops. Now he raises his face to see her again, sorrowfully. Sorrow on her behalf. Trudy kneels and opens her arms to him. The boy gets up and comes over to her timidly. She embraces him and strokes his hair. It's like embracing a trembling stream of cold water, only it's dry. She looks down at him. His eyes are closed, and his face is still full of sadness. Trudy lifts one of her breasts in her hand and guides the boy's mouth to it. When the nipple brushes his lips, he fastens on it and begins to suck hard. She takes him into her lap, cradling him and letting him suck. Black water trickles from the corner of his mouth, his features relax, and she can feel his weight lifting. As he sucks, he's getting lighter.

A. puts his hands on his waist. Somewhere in the field, or in these buildings he surveys, she is walking, it's neither day nor night. Glancing back over his shoulder he sees the vial of her blood is gone. The silence abruptly lifts like a blown-away fog bank and an intimidater roars overhead flying low. A. darts beneath the burned-out room. He sees the butt-end of the intimidater appear and the whole building shakes as it goes by.

Trudy tosses and turns, throwing off the sheets.

Trudy is strolling through the riot.

People slip fall and stumble, their feet stuck in the blood. What else could it be? The pavement ends here. People go about their business, with guns. Trudy has an idea. She stops and turns this way and that until she sees the house.

Anonymous forms line every street and are tossed aside in heaps to make way for the fighters. Celada steps lightly into the street with a heavy steel box under his arm, and an ebony table with a round top, like a kind of flower, between his fingertips. Oblivious to the bullets, breaking glass, flying teeth, blasts of caustic steam, and so on, he sets down his table in the middle of the street, puts in the center of its top a doily from his pocket, and on that goes the box. A police officer trotting by pauses to stare incredulously a moment and bludgeons him with his club. Or at least he tries. The club somehow misses Celada, who, smiling proudly, unlatches the box from its base and lifts off the top like a headwaiter unveiling a prize roast, having selected this auspicious time and location—the middle of a riot—to reveal the isolaton to the world. The heavy steel lid turns to a puff in his hand. He steps into its kindling light, which grows unwaveringly more intense. The sun comes out. In the new sunlight, Trudy can see the boy again. He's standing in the middle of an empty street, full of excitement and waving to her to come over to him.

"You stay right there, and I'll come back," she says. This kind of promise never seems to work out in the fairy logic of a dream, but she intends to come back. "Or you come find me again."

He's waving impatiently, smiling.

"I have something important to do first," she says.

Trudy makes her way through the streets, holding on to lampposts and doorways, as though she were half-feeling her way along. There's only going to be this one chance to do it, right now when nobody is watching, no one can stop her. She has the right or the opportunity to try because she burned it down. Trudy reaches up and takes hold of one corner of the house. She concentrates on getting it right, then in one movement she hurls the entire house upwards. People in the streets, all over the modelsuburb, look up at rafters sheathed in brass. Their streets have turned into tall narrow staircases with razor-sharp steps. To their ears comes a soft, old-fashioned recording of a woman singing a cappella. Trudy rifles her mind for names she can't come up with, not even a name for this modelsuburb. What is a "modelsuburb" anyway? Trudy is afraid of the field of stones around the modelsuburb; she imagines herself getting stuck between the boulders or caught in their stark shadows, like glue traps, and roasted by the sun, shot by intimidaters. Her bare feet will be shredded. Turning back toward the town she is momentarily dazzled by water glints of a small fountain set in a wall. The points are soft and hot.

Spinning with his sword in my lungs, she's the guns in shells of the smoke sword the water sword, the hands are the sword, the legs constantly broken and healed, the dress made of the police, body is agentes, and him, her beautiful army men. They embracing veer in toward him, like floating down. Time's up— sharks cloud around, the others rush—their magic moving slowly. There's a little steel cup on a chain by the fountain. Trudy rinses the cup, then drinks the water. It is disgusting. As she drinks, blood drips into the fountain and suffuses it. She herself is not bloody. She doesn't know or see where the blood comes from. Now the blood is glinting. The sky behind her rumbles as an intimidater comes in, she ducks into a small archway shaded by a huge acacia tree. The intimidater's groan sinks as it goes by, its bulk flashes shaking the bloody water of the fountain and the sound vanishes.

Seeing it transforms the street. Now I see scenes as all

around me I hear the bodies totter. He lunges down onto his knees as though he were already lying there, and she's running to hold up the sky, or holding to run up the sky, the little golden basin of mine, light bathing his hands. The sun shines on his blood, as my feet she's carrying touch the feet she's got him. The sun flings him down onto his back, the ghost leaves his soul. Into the stream, drawing, bang! Shot him right in the uniform, open his eyes wide like parched sun, his look becomes solid "Locos . . . soy heavy . . . I'm sure they've . . ."—he falls, trying to drink and staring at us putas, the air. I'm a whole river doesn't just kneel and drink dark hair but flings his whole body into the water, laughing hysterically and jabbering the ghost is going crazy and melts his dark face in thick sun, immerse him in sun drown arms in brain of light.

The intimidater dips in a gust and a gas bomb lobbed from a high rooftop dashes into the open side door splattering the men inside with flames. Maddened with pain and alarm the intimidater hunches its shoulders and charges the sun, chattering from the street toward an open space. It lands and uniforms jump out like it's a casket of frogs, many of them adorned in trembling gold. The sounds are dying away gradually, shots very faint, sirens still fairly loud, intimidaters not as loud, shouts very quiet. Trudy is waking, or shifting in mayhems of dreams and stripping the clothes from her body as rapidly as they appear.

"I will never wear clothes again!" she thinks fiercely.

Trudy crosses the courtyard, fractured by brilliant leaf shadows from the acacias. The dusty air stirs, and all at once there is a cool waft of library air, redolent of museum varnish and binding glue, like the opening of a stone sarcophagus. Miss Houseman smirks at her like a brass idol from an upper window, floating backwards as William's arms close around her waist.

One side of the courtyard, which is only a few dozen feet across, is lined by small archways on a deep cloister. Celada sits with his ankle across his knee on a stone bench built into the wall, pale head glow in the shade. He gazes at the ground sadly.

"My head hurts." The longing in his eyes makes her image hammer, she can hear the trickling sound of blood on the smooth stones at her feet. Her fit passes into him and turns him into a fossil from the inside out. Dr. Crapelin puts his hands in his pockets and emits a jet of smoke. A bronze statue in the ornamental garden, and she turns to go into the house. The front door is locked, so she breaks a window with the sprinkler key and climbs in, leaving Celada with Dr. Crapelin. To escape, he emits gaps from his head into the walls, which weaken and crumble. A lake of rubble surrounds him and he is immediately entangled in rays of sunlight he seizes hold of using them to drag himself free with a sensation like tearing thick wallpaper.

It doesn't happen quickly. It doesn't happen slowly. It doesn't happen at any other time.

Trudy is still in the swimming school, adjusting the mechanisms. Every now and then she finds a faulty connection and fixes it. Whenever this happens, she imagines, another figure, lying asleep somewhere in the vicinity, afflicted with a deadly illness, stirs, tiny sharp needles like the tips of thumbtacks slide down into the grooves between their teeth, and the isoform appears above them. Each adds its own note to the gathering chord. The figures in the streets are becoming more solid, but Ukehy spirits are getting the upper hand. They wear long robes of heavy, shaggy material, and headgear like floppy top hats. Their faces are just white streaks between their thick collars and the hats, and they flit and leap from rooftops and in and out of cars, windows of buildings, with a weird, heavy grace. Each is armed with a complicated-looking gun of black metal, shaped in cross-section like an upside-down omega. The marksman puts his arm through the metal loop it has for a stock, aims with great precision. The two flat surfaces atop the gun squeeze together for a moment, with a quiet clack!, like the sound of a camera shutter. The gun fires long filaments or tapes; the Ukehy are aiming not at the student spirits themselves but at the heads of their deerlike mounts. Each clack! brings one down neatly, its head bifurcating and shriveling as the tape turns to shivering, burrowing webs. Student spirits are flung from their mounts and lie broken on the ground. The Ukehy are killing them. Trudy works with great speed and a more and more impregnable calm. Another isoform takes shape, and another, forming a ring of isolated sleepers who will control the action in the streets, and maintain the aperture. Let it be decided, Trudy hears herself think. Are we really rebels? Are we really doing anything?

Now one of the mounted students sees one of the Ukehy; the student's glasses flash once with reflected light as the Ukehy aims its weapon at him. A substance that's neither fluid nor smoke (Ukehy blood) sprays in fans from the Ukehy's ruptured temples, and it slumps forward, dropping its gun. The weapon falls from its frozen hands. The chord is resonating in weird, oscillant harmony. Trudy looks down and brushes some dust from her belly.

All the rioting sounds die away. They've all killed each other, look at that. Mabruk.

Vanquishing desert engulfs the town. Briny eyebrows steeple and the forehead reeks, the eyes smart and the breath is congealed. The head floats and the body falls bleating in the relentless sun's light. It's the modelsuburb that's all burnt ruins, and the house stands over the charred remains, immaculate. It blazes, and now the sun oozes from its windows like a recongealing yolk, rising from the top of the house. The door of the house opens to admit Celada.

From up here, Cimelia Cisterna is like a smoking lake dappled with glistening spots. Light from the water, or the steam of rotten bodies roasting in the sun? Student ghosts stream around, or are those swarms of flies?

Trudy will look in again at the window she once shattered, and she can see people inside, the whole modelsuburb, milling from room to room, conducting their everyday business. Someone, standing momentarily close to the window, and whom she's never seen before, slips his arm around her waist familiarly and points to the little model town, addressing his companion, who stands on her other side.

"See them curled up in there?" he asks. "Are they sleeping? Are they waking up?"

CPSIA information can be obtained
at www.ICGtesting.com
Printed in the USA
LVHW051118270519
619142LV00042B/2873/P